The P… of Desperate Situations

a novel

by

[handwritten inscription and signature]

John Harrigan

Bridge Books Press
St. Paul, Minnesota

Many people have my thanks for help on this novel in one way or another. I especially want to note those who read excerpts and lent me their insights. Colleen Angelar, Carrington Ashton, Dick Axelson, Irena Axelson, Tom Boylan, Maria Cristiana Casella, Mike Carroll, Russ Christensen, Kevin Durgin, Monica Durgin, Mary Gardner, Reed Grano, Sandy Harrigan, Thomas J. Kelley, Jennifer Manion, Tom Montgomery, and Katy O'Brien.

Publisher's Cataloging-in-Publication
(Provided by Quality Books, Inc.)

Harrigan, John J.
        The patron saint of desperate situations: a novel/ by John
Harrigan   p. cm.
        1. Wellstone, Paul David–Death and burial–Fiction.
2. Death–Fiction. 3. Legislators–United States–Fiction. 4. United States–Politics and government–2001–Fiction. 5. Minnesota–Fiction. 6. Historical fiction, American. 7. Detective and mystery stories, American. I. Title.
PS 3608.A7815P38 2006   813'.6   QB106-600337
ISBN 0 964 2568 1 9

Printed in The United States of America
10 9 8 7 6 5 4 3 2 1
This book can be ordered from
Bridge Books Press
1769 Lexington Ave. #181
St. Paul, MN 55113
www.bridgebookspress.com

For Sandy

OCTOBER 25, 2002

U. S. Senator Paul Wellstone, his wife, daughter, and three campaign aides boarded a charter flight in suburban Minneapolis headed for a friend's funeral in northern Minnesota. Neither the senator nor his wife liked flying, especially in small planes to remote locations. But rites like this for close disciples could not be skipped. The flight was uneventful until the end, when low visibility forced the pilots to make an instrument landing. They flicked a switch to turn on the runway lights and activate a radio beacon that would guide the plane to land.

The radio beacon was not calibrated properly, and that may or may not have contributed to what happened next. The plane came in at a bad angle as it slipped out of the clouds, and its air speed dropped below the stall point. When it failed to touch down as expected, the airport sent out a pilot to scout around. He spotted the plane blazing in the snow a few miles from the runway, a big crater where it had struck ground, pieces of wreckage strewn about, and no signs of life.

I

Until I met Sonia, I never questioned the plane crash that killed Paul Wellstone.

I first saw her at the president's banquet kicking off the school year for Northland College of Arts and Science. She was sitting to the left of the place reserved for me, her hands on the white table cloth, a glass of red wine at her fingertips, and a pensive look on her face. I plucked a cola from the tray of a passing waiter, slid into my chair, put out my hand, and said, "Jake Morgan."

She turned to me, giving a swish of her black, velvet gown.

"I am Sonia Lindquist." She smiled as she clasped my hand in a warm, soft grip. She had a trace of perfume and her black hair shined in the lights of the room. "I teach Art History at the college."

I groped for something to say next, because I never know how to start conversations with a woman. I couldn't just say, "You are the most dazzling person I've seen in weeks." Certainly not to a college woman. At least not until I found out if she was one of those with that touchy instinct for taking such compliments as insults. So I said something a little stupid.

"You don't look like a Lindquist."

She furrowed her eyebrows into a frown and let go of my hand. I needed to recover fast. "You see, people named Lindquist tend to be blond and blue-eyed and reserved, and Norwegian. But you're brown-eyed, warm, and . . ." I ran out of words.

"Brazilian." She smiled. "My ex-husband is a Lindquist."

"I've never met a Brazilian before," I quipped.

"In that case, it is my duty to make a good impression," she joked, tilting her head downward with a coy grin, looking up from the corners of her eyes, and locking her eyes onto mine. "I hope you're not disappointed."

Disappointed? To be flirting with a classy young woman? But she was better at the flirting game than I was, and I was floundering. She threw me a lifeline.

"I haven't seen you before. Are you a trustee?"

"No," I said. "I'm a financial advisor for your colleague Lars Johanson," nodding my head toward his place card by the plate on the other side of me. "I brought some papers for him to sign." I lifted a thin, leather folder off my lap for her to see. "And he was going to introduce me to the guest of honor. But he seems to be delayed."

"How lucky for me." She had a husky voice that sounded like the singer Diana Krall's, and her smile was so broad that it spread from ear-to-ear and showed off a set of perfect teeth. Her father must be a dentist. Or maybe a plastic surgeon with a storeroom of botox, since her dark complexion also was flawless. Not a mole or a scar or even a zit. "If Lars is going to be late," she added, "maybe I should take you over to meet Mr. Radezewell now before he gets mobbed."

"You know him?" I nodded over to the guest of honor sitting at the head table, under a blue and yellow banner, Northland College – The Stanford on the Mississippi.

"I met him through Lars. He wanted me to help Mr. Radeze-well build an art collection."

"Did it work out?"

"No. All he wanted was a deal on some Thomas Kincaid paintings."

That didn't sound like a big endorsement of Kincaid's art, so I decided not to mention the piece hanging on my living room wall.

"But he didn't need me for that. I gave the information to the Kincaid shop at the Mall of America. And do you know what?" Her face went back to that coy grin.

"What?"

"Three weeks later, he sent me a thousand-dollar check as a finder's fee. Can you believe that? For finding a Kincaid shop!"

"That's a nice finder's fee."

"Yes. Too bad I couldn't keep it."

"You gave it back?"

She gave a shrug of her shoulders and lifted her hands. "What else could I do? Accepting that kind of money would have put me in a bad position, no matter what his intentions were."

I could only imagine what his intentions had been.

"So I gave it back, and we stayed on good terms."

She grabbed my hand, jumped out of her chair, and tugged for me to get up. "Let's get over there before the program starts." She pulled me to the head table where Radezewell and the president were talking. Some other people crowded around us, awaiting their chance also to meet the great man. He was the picture of power and wealth, with the wide shoulders of a football player and gold jewelry that gleamed in the room's bright lighting. He continued talking to the president, looking pleased to be drawing this audience of people straining to hear his bits of wisdom.

"If you tighten your belts here at the college," he advised the president, "things will start looking up. Just like they are around the country." He leaned forward and stared the president in the eye. "Of course, they really started looking up once we got that little, tree hugging, chicken shit Wellstone out of the Senate."

A gasp went through the crowd around us, followed by the

scraping of shoes on the floor and the clearing of throats as people strained to think up responses. And jumping into the gap was my new Brazilian friend who stepped toward the two men. The words exploded from her mouth.

"Little chicken shit? You got *rid* of Paul Wellstone? What are you saying? You got *rid* of him? Little chicken shit? Sir, he was a giant. You are the chicken shit, you old lecher!"

There she was in that elegant, black gown cursing the man who had tried to give her a thousand-dollar finder's fee, her chin thrust forward and her index finger jabbing at his face as she spoke.

With one last curse, she stepped back and bumped into me. Radezewell's face turned red with anger. When you're loaded with millions of dollars to create a Stanford on the Mississippi, you're probably not used to being called an old lecher. The president wedged himself in front of Sonia and motioned for me to get her out of there. I took her by the elbow and steered her back to our table, where she grabbed a clutch purse she had left by her dinner plate and strode toward the exit. I set my leather folder on the table and headed after her.

Astounding! First Radezewell's boorish statement. Not that he was the only person to have ever called Wellstone a chicken shit. After all, the first president Bush did it one time at a White House reception. Then Sonia's wild outburst. Even to me, a transplanted New Yorker accustomed to people insulting each other in public, her reaction was shrill. To the staid president who ran the college, it must have been over the top, and I didn't envy her prospects there over the next few months.

When I caught up with her outside the front door, her face was twisted as though she was bouncing back and forth between wanting to assault the man for what he'd said and wanting to weep over the trouble she had just brought to herself. What did Wellstone mean to her that she would do that?

She was still steamed, and she gave me a piercing look. "Did you hear what he said? He got *rid* of Wellstone!"

We stood facing each other outside the atrium of the Minnesota History Center where this banquet was taking place, her slender body in that black velvet gown framed by the floodlit dome of the Minnesota Capitol in one direction, the St. Paul sky line in the other, and the valley of the Mississippi River winding past the downtown. I didn't know what to say, and she must have perceived that as regret over what had happened. She added, "Oh, Mr. Morgan, I didn't mean to ruin your chance to get him as a client."

"Call me Jake. And don't worry about it. He wouldn't have worked out anyway."

That was the truth. Not that I turn down clients because of their political views. But I have a sixth sense for spotting difficult people. And Radezewell had all my antennae twitching, given his contempt for the Wellstone enthusiasts within hearing distance and Sonia's story about his attempt to buy her affections. "That guy's a loose cannon."

She still looked a little shell shocked, and thinking she could use a friendly ear, I asked, "Would you like to get a coffee somewhere to talk about this?"

"No," she said, a note of dejection in her voice. "I must relieve my babysitter. However, I have a late class tomorrow. I think I could meet you for breakfast." Think came out as theenk. With that husky voice of hers, it was the most exotic sound I'd ever heard. We parted, and as she walked to her car, her long, black, hair bobbed back and forth with each step, and her hips swayed gently.

I was hooked.

II

Lars never showed up, so I phoned to leave a message. When he also didn't answer his phone the next morning, I left another message, this time a mild complaint about having been stood up.

But I had more pleasant things to think about. Wanting to look casual for my breakfast date with Sonia, I put on a pair of chino slacks and a light blue, cashmere sweater over an off-white shirt. I phoned my office to say that I would arrive late. Then I got into my brand new, silver BMW and headed toward the Day by Day Café on West Seventh Street where Sonia and I had agreed to meet.

Nancy, the waitress with the ring through her nose led me to a booth by the back window overlooking the patio, and I asked her to keep an eye out for Sonia. "If you see a slim, black-haired woman in her thirties, would you bring her over here?"

"Any slim, black-haired woman, Jake? Or do you want to hold out for Halle Berry?"

"Everyone's a comedian," I quipped with a chuckle. "Just get her back here when she arrives." Which she did a moment later, pursing her lips and dipping her head in a nod of approval just before she filled our coffee cups and gave us our menus. Sonia wore a white sweater and a loose skirt that swirled about her as she slid into the booth and sat across from me with the perfect posture of a TV anchor. Perched on top of her head was a pair of designer sun glasses. She wore no makeup, not even a trace of eye shadow or lipstick. She didn't need it, what with that flawless complexion. I decided that her father was definitely a plastic sur geon. Or, given that straight backed, perfect posture, maybe he was a general.

We looked at each other in a moment of awkward silence until I said, "Sonia, there is something I want to ask you about last night. It's none of my business, so if I'm out of line, just tell me. But why is Wellstone so important to you?"

Her eyes flashed, letting me know that it really was none of my business, and I braced myself for her to explode as she had the night before. But she took a second before responding, and her voice was soft. "He was a great man, don't you think?"

The truth be told, even though Wellstone had been far from the worst politician in Washington, I agreed with a local newspaper pundit who had once called him Senator Blowhard. But I wasn't going to say anything that blunt to this captivating, olive-skinned woman across from me.

"He was a little hard to work for, I've been told."

"What's that got to do with anything? Lots of great people are hard to work for."

"Sonia, I'm not trying to start a fight over this. You asked me what I thought, and I'm just saying that he was a mixed bag. His stridency and his style were turnoffs. But his work for veterans' benefits and mental health was first rate. So I contributed to his campaign and even planned to vote for him." I paused and softened my voice. "I'm just trying to understand why he was so important to you that you would challenge that man the way you did last night."

"Oh, dear." She put her hands over her face, looking embarrassed. "You must have thought I was a nut case."

"Nut case is too strong," I joked. "But you were, maybe, just a teeny, little bit of a spectacle." I lifted my palms and smiled in an attempt to be playful.

She raised her head, a cold look of defiance in her eyes. "You can think what you want. But that pehDAHsso gee bosta deserved to be put in his place."

"PehDAHsso gee bosta?" I mouthed the words, trying to repeat them exactly as she had said them, having no idea what she meant.

"Never mind. He said he killed Wellstone."

"No, he said he was glad that Wellstone was gone from the Senate. There's a big difference."

"Well, somebody killed him."

"We don't know that. The feds said it was just pilot error. They came in at a bad angle and let their air speed drop too slow."

"How," she challenged, "could two experienced pilots make such a fundamental mistake as that? And why wasn't that plane not equipped with one of those famous black boxes to record what happened?"

"I don't know," I said. "But even if somebody did bring down the plane, why do you think it was Moneybags who did it?"

"Moneybags?"

"Radezewell, the guy you sent into a fit last night." I smiled as I recalled his beet red face. "Lars calls him Moneybags, and I got into the habit. Why do you think it was him?"

"He said so. He said he got rid of him."

"No. He said he was happy that Wellstone died. That's pretty bad. But it's not the same thing as saying he killed him."

She flashed me a glare, then looked down at the table without responding, like she was regretting having met me for breakfast in the first place. She was forced to look up, however, when Nancy the waitress came by to take our orders.

But the act of ordering our food didn't break the impasse between us, and as we sat in silence, my gaze went out the window to a duck paddling in the pond on the patio. My mind wandered to an image of Wellstone's plane burning in the wilderness and all of those "Wellstone Lives!" signs that sprouted up right after his death and were now disappearing.

Then I heard her say "Jake." That was the first time she had said my name and it came out as "Zhaak."

"Jake, what are you thinking? You look like you're lost in space."

"Sorry. My mind drifted. Sometimes it's hard for me to stay focused." I paused. "Sonia, I'm just your typical businessman trying to make an honest buck, and I'm not into deep thinking. But talking about Wellstone reminded me of a play that a client once told me about. These people die and end up in hell. There's a window that opens up whenever anybody back on earth remembers them."

"*No Exit*," she said. "By Sartre."

"Whoever. When I heard about it, I was reminded of what happened after my mother died a dozen years ago. At first I thought about her all the time. Then days would pass without my thinking of her. Then a week or more. And now there are only occasional flashes of remembrance. My mother and Wellstone are like those people in that play. Slowly disappearing. We're closing the window on them."

She reached over and touched her fingertips to the back of my hand as it was resting on the table next to my coffee cup. "Your mother is not in hell, Jake, waiting for some mythical window to open. And neither is Paul."

The coldness was gone from her eyes as she said that, and I was moved by the soft huskiness of her voice, the silky blackness of her hair, and the touch of her fingertips. She added, "The tragedy, though, is that we lost that voice in the Senate because of his death."

"He might not have gotten reelected in any case," I replied.

"He would have won in a mudslide," she said.

"A mudslide?"

"You know, a big victory."

"You mean a landslide." I started to laugh, then choked it off when I realized my laughing might offend her.

But she simply smiled for the first time since we'd sat down.

"Jake, you can laugh if I make a funny mistake with my English. I don't mind. Just make sure that you don't mock me. My in-laws did that all the time, and I vowed I'd never put up with it again."

"Do you want to talk about it? How did you meet this family in the first place? They were a long way from Brazil."

"In more ways than one," she said. "When I was in my last year at college, I went to an art exhibit at the Brazilian-American Institute in Rio de Janeiro and met a visiting scholar from Minnesota who swept me off my feet. We married and moved here where he does research at the Ag School in St. Paul. But something between us fizzled, and five years ago we divorced."

"But you stayed here. Didn't you miss Brazil?"

"Oh, yes. We have a word, 'saudades.'"

"What?" I asked.

"SowDAHgees," she laughed. It was the first time I'd heard her laugh, and I liked the sound of it. "Like this," she said. She mouthed the word, motioning with her hands for me to repeat.

"SowDAHgees," I said.

"Perfect," she smiled, flashing her white teeth. "You could be a linguist. It means sadness and longing and nostalgia all in one. I grew up in Rio. What I miss is the block where we lived in Ipanema, playing volley ball on the beach, dancing the samba with my friends at Carnival, and feeling the excitement of the street markets." A dreamy look came into her eyes as she shifted position on the bench across from me, and there was an erotic rustling of clothes beneath her. Then she looked me in the eye and smiled again.

"That's me. Now tell me about Jake Morgan."

"Well, this restaurant tells you the most important thing about me." I swept my hand in an arc toward the window overlooking the patio, the bare, brick wall behind her, and the rustic, pine book cases on the inside wall. She looked puzzled.

"It was started by a group of recovering alcoholics, and it's been a kind of gathering place ever since."

"You are alcoholic?" she asked, half shaking her head in discouragement, as though she'd had some experience with alcoholics and it hadn't been pleasant. It seldom is.

"A recovering alcoholic," I said.

"Recovering?"

"You never stop being alcoholic. You're wired for it, and all you can do is control it while you put your life in order."

She nodded her head once, motioning for me to continue.

"I started drinking when I was teenager in Queens, in New York. Things came to a head after I got older and had worked my way up to being a mutual fund manager. I was getting plastered every day. My boss and my wife pressured me into a treatment program here. When the treatment was over, the fund wanted me to take a demotion, but I wanted no part of that, and by this time, my wife wanted no part of me. So I stayed here. It was fall like it is now, with the trees changing colors. I got out of the business of helping mutual funds screw their customers and set myself up as a financial planner where I help people sort out the good funds from the bad."

"So, if you're wired for it, how do you stay sober?"

I picked up the menu from the table and pointed to the café's name on the front, Day by Day. "One day at a time," I said. "It's just a slogan, I know, but so far it has worked. I go to meetings. I keep up friendships. And I haven't had a drink since I came here from New York five years ago."

Nancy the waitress served our food then, a bagel with cream cheese for me, toast and a fruit cup for Sonia. There was a long pause until she broke the silence. "You were looking for Lars last night. Did he ever show up?"

"No," I said. "I called him at home to find out why he didn't show, but there was no answer."

"We could try his office." She pulled a cell phone from her purse and punched some keys. Odd that she would know his phone number off the top of her head. As she waited for the call to be answered, she flipped her head so that her long, black hair moved to the side, and she tapped her lacquered finger nails on the table top.

"Not there," she said. "But he left a message." She tapped in the numbers again, leaned forward, and held the phone out to my ear, holding it out just far enough that I had to bend toward her. I caught a whiff of her perfume and a sense of her breasts a short distance from my face. They were small breasts, but they were oh so close. The spell was broken by Lars' voice.

"This is Lars Johanson. I will be out of my office for the rest of the week, closing up my cabin for the winter. I will be back on Monday morning."

"Out of town? Doesn't he have classes to teach?"

"A full professor can take a Friday off now and then," she said, pulling back the phone and resuming her upright posture.

"There's something odd, Sonia. Why would he invite me to the dinner and then go up North without telling me?"

"Beats me," she said as she turned off the phone. "At least you know where he is."

"Yes. But I don't want to wait till next week to get these papers signed." In truth, there was no hurry to get his signature. I was just fishing for a reason to stay with Sonia a little longer. "I should drive up there. It's only a couple of hours, just a little past Taylor's Falls. Do you want to come?"

"I have classes this afternoon."

"Then we'll go tomorrow. We'll have lunch on the St. Croix River. Have you ever been there when the leaves are changing color?"

"Tomorrow is Saturday. I have to take care of Rodrigo."

"Your son?"

"You remembered I have a son." She smiled.

"Bring him. We'll stop at the apple orchard and he can pick out a pumpkin for Halloween."

A wary look crossed her face. She pulled the designer sun glasses out of her hair and held them in both hands, resting her elbows on the table. "Jake, you were up front with me about being alcoholic, and there is something I need to tell you about Rodrigo."

I nodded for her to continue.

"My son has a disability, Williams syndrome."

"I don't know what that is."

"It's a genetic condition that gives him distinctive physical features and uneven development. He is eight years old, and in some areas like music and language, his development is normal for his age, maybe even advanced. In some other areas, he is more like a five- or six-year-old."

I'm sure I looked startled. This was a lot of baggage for one person. Divorced. Homesick. A hothead who'd just insulted her employer's guest of honor. And now this.

But what I said was, "Well, he'll like the apple orchard and the woods and picking out a pumpkin, won't he?"

"I am sure he will," she smiled, indicating her assent.

"I'll pick you up at ten. You can call me if anything comes up in the meantime." We exchanged business cards.

She laughed when she saw my business name: J. P. "Jake" Morgan, CFA.

"J. P. Morgan?"

"Good name for a money manager, no?"

"Well, at least your nose isn't big and red."

"Not many people know that J. P. Morgan had a big, red nose."

"Not many people are art historians. He was the biggest art collector of his time."

As I paid the tab and we wandered out the door, she grinned and said, "Thank you for the breakfast, Mr. J. P. Morgan. When we started arguing about Paul, I feared that seeing you was a mistake. But you turned out to be very nice. Thank you." She gave me half a smile.

I tried to make a light response. "You turned out to be very nice, too."

We shook hands, and I watched the sway of her hips as she strode around the corner toward her car. Did all Brazilians walk like that? I pushed the remote key to unlock my BMW that I had parked in front of the restaurant just to impress her. But she hadn't even noticed it. She got into an old Ford Escort. On the rear bumper was a green and white sticker, "Wellstone Lives!"

III

I headed to my office in what, when I had started in the business, had been a low rent district on West Seventh Street. Since then the area had prospered and was now a chic blend of new medical facilities, gentrified eating places in refurbished brick buildings, and a smattering of old one- and two-story structures serving as consignment stores, small shops, and offices. It was in one of these two-story structures that my business was located, on the north side of the street overlooking the downtown skyline. My clients seemed to enjoy meeting there amid the ferns and Asian art work arranged in the reception area by my office manager, secretary, aide, and director of operations, Li Vang. Of course, it was a small operation; the only person she had to manage, aid and direct was me.

As I came through the main door, Li was standing on tip toe arranging the top drawer of a file cabinet. A grin lit up her face as she looked over her shoulder to greet me. "Good morning, Mr. Morgan."

"Morning, Li. Why don't you just call me Jake, like I've told you?"

"OK, Mr. Morgan. You got mail. I put it on top of that pile from yesterday that you haven't opened yet." She gave me a stern look. One of her tasks was to compensate for my inherent state of disorganization.

"I'll get to it right now."

In the mail was an envelope with Lars' return address, post-marked the previous Tuesday. It held a small key and a note.

Jake,

I am going to miss the banquet at the History Center on Thursday. I'll explain later why I didn't call. In the meantime, I need a favor. The key I've enclosed is for a storage locker at the Mall of America. Empty it and hold the contents until you hear from me. If anything happens to me, the contents are yours to use as you see fit.
Lars

PS:

At the banquet I reserved a place for you next to our art historian, Sonia Lindquist. If things don't work out for me, she might be in danger. Watch out for her.

Lars had a penchant for the melodramatic, which I normally discounted, but this sounded troubling. I yelled to Li in the outer office, "Li, did we get any phone calls from Lars Johanson?"

"No," she yelled back.

I called into my answering machine at home. No messages. I looked up his card in my rotary file and called his home, his office at the college, and his cell phone. No answers.

I crumpled Lars' note around the key, stuck them in my pocket, and went out to the reception area where Li looked up at me from some documents on her desk.

"Li," I said. "I left something at home that I have to pick up. I'll be back in an hour."

Heading out West Seventh Street toward the interstate, I drove past the airport, and turned toward the Mall of America. I parked on the lowest level and walked through the transit hub, where I had to wait for one of the sleek, yellow and gray light rail trains to pass, its bell clanging to warn people in its way as it began its trip toward downtown Minneapolis. Entering the mall from this angle always leaves me overwhelmed by the size of the place. The first things in sight are huge: the Aquarium and an indoor amusement park, complete with a roller coaster and other rides.

Surrounding the amusement park are four levels of retail shops, theaters, and restaurants catering to all manner of tastes and income levels. There's even a chapel. The mall is a cathedral of consumerism, and I loved it. With good reason. The earnings from many of those shops had helped enrich several stocks that I had stuffed into my clients' portfolios.

I took the glass elevator by the amusement park up to the fourth level, where the storage lockers are located, pushed Lars' key into the slot of his locker, and opened the door. The locker held two Kowalski Supermarket shopping bags and six shoe boxes bound with masking tape. They weighed a ton. I put the shoe boxes into the shopping bags, picked up the bags by the handles, and headed out, my shoulders slumped forward from the weight of the shopping bags.

Arriving back at my office, I gave a quick "I'm back" to Li Vang as I walked past her desk toward my inner office. She gave a blank look at the shopping bags. I pulled open a file cabinet drawer where I could store the shoe boxes until I contacted Lars. As I lifted the boxes up to the drawer, one of them slipped from my grasp and split open when it hit the floor. My jaw must have dropped a foot at the sight of what spilled out of the box: wads of fifty-dollar bills bound with paper wrappers.

To get some privacy from Li, I shut the office door, then cut through the masking tape on the other five boxes. Same thing. Loads of fifty dollar bills. I dumped one boxful onto my desk and counted, then multiplied by six. I was stunned. One million dollars. All in used bills, not new ones. I thumbed through a dozen bills and saw no sequence to the serial numbers. From all appearances, one million dollars of unmarked, unidentifiable, and probably untraceable money.

It's not illegal to stuff a storage locker with a fortune in cash, but it certainly is suspicious. What legitimate reason would Lars have for keeping this much money in cash? And did this have anything to do with his cryptic warning that Sonia might be in danger?

As a licensed financial adviser I am required by law to report any attempted large transaction of cash. Of course, Lars hadn't offered a transaction. He had merely asked me to hold some of his money until he got in contact with me. The best thing would be to return those shoe boxes as soon as possible.

With that in mind, I made one last attempt to reach him by phone. No luck. Not wanting to lug the shopping bags past Li again and pique her curiosity, I waited until noon when she put on her jacket to go out for lunch. She looked over her shoulder as she headed out the door.

"Did you finish with that mail?"

"I got a good start on it," I replied.

After she stepped out the front door and disappeared up the street in the direction of a small Asian café, I put the shoe boxes into the shopping bags and set them in the back seat of my BMW. A bank would no doubt use an armored truck to transport this much cash, so I was a little nervous driving around with it sitting on my back seat. But all in all, it was a more pleasant way to spend an October afternoon than sorting through that pile of correspondence back on my desk.

The route north on I-35 toward Lars' cabin was lined with trees in the early stage of changing color, and the golden orange tints starting to come out on the green trees made the trip a pleasant drive. It took two hours to reach the Moose Lake exit and find the gravel road that wound through the towering fir trees to Lars' clapboard cabin. It sat on a hill overlooking a small, isolated, algae-coated pond. Not knowing if he had already left and I'd made this trip for nothing, I was relieved to spot his pick-up truck parked next to the cabin. But my relief was short lived. There was no answer when I knocked on the door. I pushed it open and called, "Lars, it's Jake," as I stepped into the spartan room that served as kitchen, dining area, and living room.

IV

But Lars couldn't hear me. He was lying face down on the floor, next to the old wooden kitchen table, a big rip in the back of his checkered flannel shirt and a dark stain where the blood had flowed from the wound. I staggered out to the porch and puked into the dirt.

After wiping my mouth, I pulled out my cellphone and called 911. It wasn't till the call was finished that I remembered the million dollars sitting in the back seat of my car. Even though Lars' note in my pocket would show that the money belonged to him, it might be difficult explaining all this to a suspicious cop.

I started to transfer the shopping bags to the trunk when I realized that was not going to help. If the cop wanted to search my car he would just demand that I open the trunk. I set the bags on the back seat, pulled some financial brochures from a box in the trunk, and stacked them in the shopping bags on top of the shoe boxes so it would look like the bags held nothing but financial literature.

Just as I finished that task, a sheriff's car pulled up to the cabin, its siren blaring and its red lights flashing. Deputy Gunther, said the badge on the shirt of the deputy sheriff. He was big and looked intimidating in his brown sheriff's jacket, with a frown on his face as he listened to me explain that I had driven out to get Lars' signature on some papers. I pulled out Lars' documents from my briefcase.

He walked through the door of the cabin, then stopped. "Look at that hand," he said, pointing at Lars' left hand which was tied to a two-by-four and lay stretched out in front of his head. Four fingers were missing. And lying nearby was a pair of old pruning shears, with traces of blood on the blades. I almost threw up again.

"The reason they cut off your friend's fingers," said the deputy, "was to get information from him. And whatever that information was, they got it."

"How can you tell?"

"They didn't have to cut off the rest of his fingers." Deputy Gunther showed no more emotion than he would have if he'd said that Lars' shoes were scuffed. "Do you know what that information would have been?" He looked me squarely in the eye.

"I have no idea."

"Since you're his financial planner, you probably know more about his affairs than anyone else, except maybe his wife."

"He's not married," I said

"How deep was he into drugs?"

"Lars didn't even drink. Drugs are out of the question."

"Notice that smell, that smell of cat piss."

At first, I didn't notice anything. But as I concentrated and forced my mind off the sight of Lars' body, I could detect an unpleasant odor that could have been cat urine.

"Methamphetamine," said the deputy. "Somewhere around here, there was a meth lab. Perfect spot for it. Isolated, well off the highway, no other cabins nearby. Come over here." He led me back to the patrol car, took out a roll of yellow, plastic sheriff's line tape and made a big circle around the cabin.

After phoning headquarters for help that would be needed, he stood by his patrol car and asked me a million questions.

"Where were you this morning before you came out here?"

"I had breakfast with a friend. Then I was working in my office until noon. You think he was killed this morning?"

"Somebody else will have to determine that. But the body's still warm, so I'd guess it was sometime this morning."

"And I'm a suspect?"

"Not if you've got witnesses for where you were this morning. You're not so much a suspect as a person of interest."

My pulse was racing throughout this talk, and it must have spiked to 180 when he asked for permission to search my car. He leafed through the financial brochures sitting in the box in the trunk, then took a cursory look under the front seats. Turning to the back seat, he lifted a brochure from the one of the shopping bags. When he saw several copies of the same brochure beneath it, he tossed the first one back into place and slammed the door shut. I'd been holding my breath throughout this search, and I slowly exhaled, then inhaled, being as careful as possible not to look conspicuous.

Two more patrol cars pulled up at that moment, and Deputy Gunther said, "You can go now."

One part of me wanted to stay and watch the crime-scene investigators, but I learned long ago to leave as soon as you get the client's signature. Don't wait around and give him time to reconsider. And I sure didn't want Deputy Gunther to reconsider. I edged my car along the gravel road away from the cabin and headed back to the interstate.

The sight of Lars' body stuck in my mind throughout the drive home. I dreaded what I had to do next, but there was no way around it. Lars had been an old friend of Sonia's, and it would be callous in the extreme to let her find out about this from a newscast. At the junction where I-35 splits east for Saint Paul and west for Minneapolis, I pulled onto the shoulder and dug her business card out of my wallet. I programmed her numbers into the speed dial of my cell phone and punched the first button.

"Hello," came her husky voice into my ear.

"Sonia, it's Jake. I've got to talk to you."

"I'll be seeing you tomorrow. Can't it wait until then?"

"No. It's an emergency, and I have to talk to you now."

"Well, talk then," she said.

"I can't tell you this over the phone. I have to see you in person."

"Jake, it's five o'clock. I have plans for this evening and do not have a lot of time to get ready. Just tell me what it is."

I paused for a moment, trying to formulate the words in my mind.

"Jake?"

"Lars was killed. And you might be in danger."

"Oh, meu Deus!" I heard over the phone. Then silence.

"Can I come over and tell you what I know?"

"Yes." Her voice was muffled as she gave me directions.

Before heading toward her house, I phoned my lawyer, but he wasn't in. The most I could find out from the receptionist was that he and his wife were celebrating their anniversary in the Bahamas and did not want to be contacted until they returned the next week.

"Could someone else help you?" she asked.

"No. Just ask him to call me as soon as he gets in."

Sonia lived in the Midway, a neighborhood of apartment buildings, duplexes, and small, 1920s houses located midway between downtown Minneapolis and downtown Saint Paul. Once a white, working-class area, the neighborhood now housed Arabs, Hmongs, blacks, Somalis, Native Americans, and modest-income whites, all mingling in an uneasy but workable accommodation.

Her home was in a second floor duplex, just a block from Snelling Avenue, a street of gas stations, auto repair shops, tattoo parlors, and low-priced restaurants. In the front window of her duplex was one of those green and white signs that had dotted the Twin Cities for a year or more after Wellstone's death. It said, "Remember Wellstone. Keep Fighting."

She pushed the buzzer that unlocked the porch door, and the door swung open so fast it banged against the wall with a sharp noise. At the top of the stairs leading to her apartment, she opened a door to let me in. It was a marvelous old place, with a living room, dining area, and kitchen on the right side of the unit, and a doorway on the left side of the dining area leading to what was no doubt a bathroom and bedrooms. Prints and paintings hung on the walls. The tables and other flat surfaces were dotted with shiny, dark brown —almost reddish— wood objects, probably of Brazilian origin. Next to a side wall was what looked to be a very expensive electronic keyboard. The apartment was impeccably neat, even down to the row of cardboard boxes lined up between the keyboard and a cast iron radiator like the type I'd had as a child living in Queens.

She led me to the couch in the living room, and when I faced her to tell her what had happened, I could see red streaks in her eyes from crying. I told her everything that had taken place between my finding the million dollars in Lars' storage locker and the sheriff accusing him of running a meth lab. When I got to the part about the cut off fingers, she cringed.

"There's more," I told her, handing her the note from Lars. "I don't know what it means, but you might not be safe."

Ugly lines crept out from the corners of her down-turned mouth as she read the note. "This warning does not make sense, Jake. If it's the money they're after, it is you who is in danger, not me. I hope you got rid of it."

"It's in the trunk of my car, out in front of your house."

"You left a million dollars on the street? In this neighborhood? I hope it's an old, inconspicuous car that no one will notice."

"Not exactly," I said.

"Why didn't you just give the money to the cop?"

"If I had done that, then right now I would be sitting in some rural police station trying to convince some skeptical cop that the note was authentic." I pointed at the note she was still holding in her hand. Of course, there was another reason that I didn't want to mention to her. If the police got their hands on the money, I wasn't sure I'd ever get it back. She gave me a quizzical look, as though that thought was already passing through her mind, so I embellished.

"I'm already considered a person of interest, according to Deputy Gunther. And note or no note, if they found me with a million dollars cash at the scene of the murder, I would become a person of extraordinary interest. When the police come calling again, I want to have my lawyer present."

She squinted and took my wrist in her hand as she gave me a look of concern. "Oh, Jake. What are you going to do?"

"I'm hoping that my lawyer will hold the money in escrow while we report it to the police and whoever else needs to hear about it. Once it's out of my hands and the police know about it, the killers will leave me alone. The trouble is, my lawyer's out of town until next week."

For a moment she didn't say anything. Then a strange glint came into her eyes.

"Who else knows about this, Jake?"

"Nobody. Just you and me, and the killers."

I nodded for her to continue. But instead of saying anything, she stood up and walked to the kitchen, motioning for me to follow, her hips swaying with each step. She turned on one of the burners of the electric range.

"You are certain that nobody else knows about the money?"

"Yes."

She took the note that she was still holding, pinched it between her thumb and forefinger, her pinky sticking out, and held it above the burner that was turning red from the heat.

"We can assume that the killers will search Lars' house?"

"Yes."

"All you have to do is put the money inside Lars' kitchen where the killers will find it. Allow me to burn this note, and the only sign of you knowing about the money disappears. The killers will be satisfied, and the police will never know you had it."

"Destroying evidence is against the law."

"You didn't destroy evidence. You tossed the note into the trash can at the Mall of America before you opened the storage locker."

"How do I get into his house?"

"Once we were working together on a curricular project, and he sent me to his house to get something. He keeps a kitchen door key in his garage, hanging from a screw in the back of the light switch, just by the side door of the garage. He never locks that door. All you have to do is reach behind the light switch and take the key."

How did she know so much about Lars' habits? I wondered. But I asked, "What if he no longer does that?"

"Then just leave the shoe boxes inside the garage door. If the killers don't find what they are looking for in the house, they are sure to look in the garage."

I just stared at her for a moment in surprise. This devious gambit did not mesh with the delicate looking person in front of me, still wearing the same white sweater she'd worn to breakfast, still having those reddened eyes from crying over Lars' murder.

"Jake, in Brazil we call this a jaytoo, a way out. It is what you do in a desperate situation. You find the jaytoo, the way out. There is always a jaytoo. Use the jaytoo, Jake, and several of your problems disappear. You no longer face hours of interrogation by the police; you don't have aggressive newspaper reporters stirring up doubt among your clients by suggesting that you picked up a small fortune in cash from the meth trade; and best of all the killers lose interest in you. No interrogations. No killers on your tail. No complications."

She was still pinching the note over the burner.

"And Lars' killers get off scot-free."

She gave me a disturbed look, then asked, "Do you know anything about detective work?"

"No."

"Then don't be macho. Leave that to the cops. Your safety, and maybe mine, depends on the killers finding the money and getting away unseen."

She paused before going on.

"What do I do with the note, Jake? Give it back to you or drop it on the burner."

I was speechless for a second, stunned by her audacity.

"Drop it."

She led me out of the kitchen and turned to face me as she opened her front door for me to leave. Her shoulders shuddered. "Oh God, I do not want to be alone just now. But you have to get that money over to Lars' house before the killers show up."

She reached both hands behind her neck and unclasped a chain. It held a small, silver medal. "It's a Saint Jude medal," she said, handing it to me. "He's the patron saint of desperate situations."

I put the medal in my pocket and headed down her stairs. Desperate situations? My situation didn't seem that bad. But it would certainly turn bad if the police caught me breaking into Lars' house. Even though I could not think of a better plan, I was starting to regret having leapt so readily at Sonia's idea.

It was dusk by the time I reached his big, two-story house in Macalester-Groveland, a college neighborhood of bygone elegance that had curving streets with Ivy League names. Being new to the craft of breaking and entering, I circled Lars' block to scout the environment. There was nothing suspicious in front or on the side street at the end of the block. In the middle of the side street, I stopped to look down the alley that ran in back of Lars' house, but saw nothing. Continuing forward, I turned onto the street that ran parallel to Lars' and drove to the side street at the other end of the block. As I was about to turn onto that side street, I spotted an SUV pulling to a stop at the end of the alley. Two figures got out and walked up the alley in the direction of Lars' house, while the SUV driver turned off the engine and waited at the end of the alley. I did a U-turn, and doubled back to the other end of the alley just in time to see the figures disappear between two garages and go into a back yard.

What a plum! If I could reach 911 fast enough, the police would catch the killers on the spot, and my problems would be over. I did not want to use my cell phone, however, for fear that it could be traced, so I sped back to Snelling Avenue, the nearest commercial street, in search of a pay phone. The closest place was O'Gara's Bar & Grill, a former neighborhood tavern that had outlived its Irish clientele and become a sports bar for the young. It was packed with customers, and nobody noticed me as I came through the door looking for the pay phone. I found it and dialed 911.

"The men who killed Lars Johanson are right now searching his house in Macalester-Groveland. If the police move fast, they can catch them."

As I hung up, the smell of liquor and beer and wine in the bar washed over me. And for an instant I stood immobilized next to the phone. One little shot of bourbon couldn't hurt anything. I deserved one after all I'd been through that day, and the thought of it got my mouth to water. But I had to get out of the bar before the police came looking for the anonymous tipster.

When I got back to Lars' neighborhood, the SUV was still parked at the end of the alley. It took another fifteen minutes before police sirens could be heard approaching. A few moments later, one of the men came running out of the alley. Then came the second figure, slowed down by something clutched under his arm, a small briefcase maybe, or a laptop computer. The two men hopped into the SUV, which took off in the opposite direction of the sirens.

I slapped my palm on the dashboard. If those fucking cops had just left their sirens off they would have caught the killers red handed instead of scaring them away. I was now back to square one. Worse than square one. Thanks to Sonia's bright plan, I no longer had Lars' note to prove that the money had come from him. I cursed myself for having listened to her in the first place. Those misty, brown eyes and that husky voice must have addled my brain.

Reaching my condo building on Mississippi River Road, I lugged the shopping bags up to my twelfth-floor unit and stuck them in the hall closet. I slumped onto the couch, and the second my feet landed on the coffee table the urge for a drink washed over me like a tidal wave. Hoping it would go away if I went out and did something, I went down to the basement garage, walked past my BMW, and hopped into my old Plymouth Voyager van with the "for sale" signs on the side windows. Only with the logic of an alcoholic would a man think he could stay sober by leaving a spot that had no liquor and going out to where it was all over the place. I tried to drive around aimlessly, but suddenly, without realizing how I got there, I found myself back at the parking lot of O'Gara's where I had made my anonymous call an hour earlier. I sat with the engine idling, my mind remembering the smell of the bar, picturing a shot glass of bourbon, and relishing what it would be like right after the liquid burned its way down my throat.

But going back into the bar and running the risk of being identified as the person who made the anonymous call to the police made no sense. I put the gearshift in drive and edged over to Summit Ave, St. Paul's grand old boulevard that stretches five miles from the Catholic cathedral on the east to the Mississippi River on the west. In between are grandiose mansions built a century earlier by the city's industrial elite; the home of F. Scott Fitzgerald, St. Paul's most famous novelist; two colleges; a law school; several houses of worship; and, at the halfway mark, the Summit Avenue Alcoholics Anonymous Clubhouse, an old, rambling house with an immaculate lawn out front and several cozy rooms in which sub-groups could meet.

A meeting was just starting when I came through the door and took a seat in a circle of people. They were discussing Step Four of the AA Twelve Step program: conducting a fearless and moral inventory of ourselves. We went around the circle, letting everyone say what they wanted about the step or about anything else. I was the last to speak.

"I'm Jake, and I'm an alcoholic."

"Hi Jake," came a chorus of ten voices.

"I want to thank you guys for being here, because knowing you'd be here was the only thing that kept me from getting bombed an hour ago. But I can't relate to Step Four right now."

I leaned forward with my elbows on my knees, clasping my hands together to keep them from shaking. There was a collective dropping of jaws as I described the knife wound in Lars' back, the missing fingers, and the cop's suspicion of a meth lab.

"There's something else, too. I had to break this news to a mutual friend, a woman I've just met and find myself attracted to. I don't know if I'm feeling so crappy because of Lars or because I am worried that my being the bearer of the bad news might have turned her off on me. She's also a little volatile, and I can't figure her out. One minute she's as warm and tender as your fondest dream, and the next minute she's exploding."

I told the story of Sonia calling Moneybags a chicken shit and everything that had happened afterwards, except, of course, for the shoe boxes of money, the Saint Jude medal, and my misguided attempt to plant the money in Lars' house. Now that I was talking, the words were pouring out of my mouth like they had a life of their own. This made me uneasy, since I take pride in having absolute control over what I do or say. When I finished, no one said a word, or moved, or even scraped a shoe on the floor.

"Maybe this is a part of Step Four's moral inventory after all," I said. "I'm feeling guilty that I'm more concerned about making a bad impression on my new friend than I am about Lars. I guess that doesn't speak well for me, but that's the way I feel."

We brought the meeting to an end by joining hands and saying the serenity prayer. Sarah, on my right, said, "I don't think it's a good idea to get involved with someone right now, when you're going through this stress and are vulnerable to relapse."

I discounted that. We don't get to choose how much stress we'll be under when a captivating person walks into our lives.

Half of us then went for snacks at a local restaurant where something unexpected happened, something that could never have happened at the AA meeting itself, which by design is apolitical. Everyone had an opinion about Sonia and Wellstone. Joe, a grumpy, old, ex-union organizer started it off.

"I think your friend was right to say what she said. That piece of shit deserved to be told off."

"Well, maybe he wouldn't have said what he did if those Wellstone liberals hadn't gone overboard at that memorial service, booing the Republicans and turning it into a political rally."

This was from Bob, a young administrator at a big insurance company.

"Nevertheless, losing Wellstone was tough. I broke down like a baby and cried when I heard his plane crashed," said Paul, a handsome, athletic guy in a tight T-shirt.

"I couldn't get out of bed for days I was so bummed out," said Sarah, the same Sarah who had advised me to stay away from Sonia.

"My insurance plan now covers mental health," said Mary, her hands wrapped around a cup of decaf coffee. "If it hadn't been for Wellstone, that would never have happened."

"But he didn't get coverage for chemical dependency treatment for us," complained another.

"There wasn't any support for it. He did what he could."

It went on like that for some time before the topic changed. I seemed to be the only person there who lacked strong feelings about Wellstone. By the time we finished, it was midnight and my urge for a drink had abated. Sometimes that's all it takes. Keep busy, get outside of your own head, and wait for the burden to lighten.

As we got up from the table, I walked out with Joe, the grumpy, union organizer.

"Joe, I don't understand these powerful feelings about Wellstone. I don't understand them in Moneybags, who hates him. I don't understand them in you and Mary, who love him. And most important, I don't understand them in Sonia, who's probably destroyed her job over the guy even though she was only here a couple of years before he died. I admit that he did a lot for mental health and for veterans. But other than that, what did he accomplish? When something big gets through Congress, they name it after that guy that did it. The Fulbright Program. The Humphrey-Hawkins Act. Or in my field, the Scott-Rodino Act. If Wellstone was so great, why isn't some law named after him?"

"What he did," Joe the union organizer said with the kind of patient look that a teacher gives to a favored, if somewhat dense, student, "was master the parliamentary nitty gritty of the Senate. Nobody had his gift for amending bills, getting holds put on bills, or blocking something's passage by requiring unanimous consent. Maybe there aren't any laws named after him, but his record of using parliamentary tactics to block things that would hurt common working people is monumental. And for the past two decades, that's been the name of the game."

It didn't sound very convincing to me, but I put my hand on Joe's shoulder as we walked down the sidewalk toward our cars and said, "If you say so."

He gave me a hostile stare for a second, then softened it and said, "You know who you should talk to?"

"Who?"

"Jim Anderson."

"Half the people in Minnesota are named Anderson. What's special about this one?"

"He writes for *Street Scenes*." *Street Scenes* was an alternative newspaper that specialized in the post-adolescent entertainment scene and carried occasional pieces of serious journalism, almost all of it anti-establishment.

"He did several pieces on Wellstone's death, and he wrote a lot of stuff about money laundering for the drug trade."

Money laundering? Lars and money laundering was almost as off the wall as Lars and the drug trade. But how else would anybody get twenty-thousand fifty dollar bills?

"Give him a call. Maybe he can help you sort it out."

When I got home, I was so exhausted that I headed straight to the bedroom. Emptying my pockets, I pulled out the Saint Jude medal and looked at it for a moment before setting it on top of the dresser. I fell asleep thinking about Sonia.

V

When I phoned Sonia the next morning to double check if we were still on for the trip to the apple orchard, she said yes, and added, "Did you get rid of the shoe boxes?"

"I'll tell you when I get there."

Instead of taking the brand new BMW, I drove my old Plymouth Voyager van with the For Sale signs in the side windows. Not having any experience with disabled children, I had no idea what kind of damage her son might do to the upholstery.

I picked her newspaper off the porch and scanned it before pushing her doorbell. A small picture of Lars and a short article about the murder appeared on the bottom of page one, with a mention of me as the person who had found the body. I folded the paper inside out so she wouldn't see the headline about Lars when I gave it to her.

She pushed the buzzer to unlock the door and I pushed it open softly so it wouldn't bang against the wall as it had the last time. She was wearing a form-fitting pair of stone-washed blue jeans and a matching denim jacket. Her eyes still had red streaks and worry lines were spreading from the corners of her mouth.

Behind her and framing her was a dark, shiny, wooden arch that separated her living room from the dining area. A small boy sat at the electronic piano, playing a piece of classical music.

"Oh," she said when I handed her the paper. "Rodrigo is supposed to get the paper in the morning, but he is so excited about going to the apple orchard he must have forgotten."

Her son slid off the piano bench and came over to us. He was dressed in corduroy pants and a khaki, bomber pilot jacket, with little wings sewn over the right pocket. His face was long and narrow, a little asymmetrical, with long upper lips, a small chin, and widely spaced teeth that contrasted with his mother's perfect teeth. But his voice sounded normal as he said, "Can we go now, Momma? I want to go."

"Rodrigo, where are you manners? Say hello to Jake."

He beamed as he took my hand and said hello with that same beguiling smile that his mother had. Then he looked at her. "Let's go, Momma."

"Patience, Rodrigo. I need to finish talking with Jake first. Go to the bathroom so you'll be comfortable on the ride, and then we'll go."

She led me to the living room sofa and sank into it. I sat down beside her and told her what had happened at Lars's house the night before.

"So the killers got away and you still have the money?"

"For the time being. It's stuffed in my hall closet."

"What will you do now?"

"Well, just in case the police decide to search my condo, I'll hide the money for the next few days, probably with a friend that I trust up in Center City. Then when my lawyer gets back from his vacation, I'll turn it over to him.

She laid her head against the back of the couch and gave a blank stare at the ceiling. "I keep thinking about Lars," she said. Her right hand was reaching over to a candle on the end table, her lacquered nails picking at wax that had dripped onto the candle holder.

"He did not fit the mold of a college professor, what with his checkered shirts and his scruffy appearance. But his heart was in the right place, and I cannot believe he had anything to do methamphetamine. He is the one who put me in touch with Wellstone when I was desperate. I'm going to miss him."

Rodrigo came in and said, "Let's go Momma."

She gave the boy a warm smile and ran her fingers through his hair before getting up from the sofa. She tucked the designer sun glasses into her hair, took Rodrigo by the hand, and we went outside to get into the Voyager. Nobody spoke until we got onto the freeway.

"Well, I'm no longer at the college," she said out of the blue.

"They fired you?"

"No. I quit. I'm in the second year of a five-year contract. But after the other night, they won't renew it, and I don't want to spend three years begging for it. So I talked to the president and offered to quit right now if they would pay my salary through the end of the school year. He was so happy to get me off campus that he threw in an extra three months of pay. He even sent some student workers over to help pack the stuff in my office. That's why those boxes were in my dining room."

She seemed remarkably unworried about being out of work. "You've got chutzpah," I said, turning my head and grinning.

"What?"

"It's a Yiddish term that you hear all the time in New York. It means you've got balls."

"Watch your language, Jake. We have a child here."

"You realize," I said. "This would never have happened if it hadn't been for that pehDAHso gee bosta at the banquet."

Rodrigo leaned forward and shouted, "Jake said a bad word. PehDAHsso gee bosta! PehDAHsso gee bosta! Bad word. That's a bad word. PehDAHsso gee bosta!"

Sonia twisted in her seat and pointed her finger at Rodrigo, but I could see her holding back a smile. "Hush, Rodrigo. You can't say that."

"PehDAHsso gee bosta! PehDAHsso gee bosta! Jake said a bad word." Rodrigo was bouncing up and down with glee under the seat belt.

"Rodrigo, be quiet!"

"But Jake said it."

"Jake doesn't know what it means. So for him, it is not a bad word. But you do know what it means, and I don't want to hear it."

Rodrigo said one more time, "PehDAHsso gee bosta!"

Sonia waved her finger back and forth in front of his face and let loose with a string of words in Spanish or whatever it is the Brazilians speak. The boy finally quieted down and stared out the window as we drove on.

"Rodrigo is bilingual?" I asked in astonishment.

"To a point," she replied. She frowned at me, mouthed "No" with her lips, and began waving her finger at me as a sign that she did not want us to talk about him in his presence. She shifted the tone of the conversation.

"We speak Portuguese at home, because my father flies us to Rio each year, and I want Rodrigo to be able to talk with his cousins and grandparents."

"Your father flies you to Rio each year?" Her father must be well heeled.

"Except for that one time when we met in France."

Rodrigo bounced up and down again. "Remember that airplane, Momma. The one with the funny nose?"

"Plane with a funny nose? The Concorde? You flew on the Concorde?"

"Just that once, right before they took it out of service." She looked a little sheepish.

Well, her father was definitely well heeled. No doubt about it, a plastic surgeon. A mere dentist could never afford the Concorde.

Rodrigo took a Matchbox car from his pocket and began to drive it over the upholstery in the back seat. He hummed the song he'd been playing on the piano, humming the same notes over and over as he drove his car up one side of the seat and down the other. He did this all the way to the apple orchard. I thought I was going to go nuts from the humming. But Sonia did nothing to quiet him.

At the orchard, we rode the hay wagon, walked through the fields, and tasted the apple butter. Sonia's shoulder occasionally bumped against my arm as we walked. Rodrigo petted the sheep in the petting zoo and wandered through a maze that had been constructed from bales of hay. Sonia leaned on the hay bales and watched him wander through the maze. He looked over at us every few minutes to catch his mother's eye. When he was out of earshot, I said to Sonia, "I'm impressed that Rodrigo is bilingual. That's a huge accomplishment."

"It is and it isn't. He will imitate anything he hears and he responds to his environment. If the environment is English, that is how he responds. If it is Portuguese, he imitates and responds that way. To a certain extent this is true of me as well. The English seems to be one compartment of my mind, the Portuguese another, the Spanish another, and the French yet another. The difference is that I can shift back and forth between the compartments when I have to. It's very difficult for him to do that."

"So he knows what "pehDahsso gee bosta" means in Portuguese, but he couldn't give me the English word for it."

"I never know for sure, but I hope not, because I don't want him saying the wrong thing at the wrong time."

At that moment, Rodrigo got lost in the maze and turned his head frantically in all directions, searching for us, a look of panic on his face. Sonia ran to him, took his hand, led him out of the maze, and hugged him to her side. She sent him running over to the huge stack of pumpkins for sale. He ran with an awkward gait.

"What you are seeing, Jake, is the uneven development I told you about. He is a little behind his age on some motor skills, and he gets lost at the drop of a hat. You saw how panicked he was when he got turned around in the maze. So I have to keep my eye on him constantly. On the other hand, his language and musical abilities are superb. Music is very important to him. It is the center of his life. It is as if there is always some song going through his mind."

We caught up with him as he was pushing his way through the pumpkins until he found the one he wanted. It was so huge it must have weighed a ton. I'd probably get a hernia carrying it up to their duplex. Rodrigo said softly, "Momma, I'm hungry."

Sonia said, "Jake, could we stop for a bite on the way home? I am so sick about Lars that I would throw up if I tried to eat, but I must get some food into Rodrigo."

"Why not? There's nothing we can do about the shoe boxes right now anyway."

"What shoe boxes?" he asked.

"Just some new shoes I bought," I said.

She gave me an I-told-you-so look, which I interpreted as a warning to be very careful about what I said in front of the boy.

Grateful for the chance to drag out my date with her, I headed east toward the town of Stillwater. It is Minnesota's oldest settlement, founded in the mid-1800s as a point for shipping lumber down stream after it had been cut from the surrounding forests. The town sits in a valley of the St. Croix River, which feeds into the Mississippi, and as we drove down the hill into town, Sonia's eyes were fixed on the water and the restored 1800s brick buildings coming into view. The lumber business has long since disappeared, and the town's main street now specialized in dress shops, antique stores, restaurants, and other tourist attractions.

Spanning the river is a picturesque, steel girder, lift bridge, one of the few such bridges left in the country.

I pulled up to the Dock Café in the middle of the town and we sat outside on the patio looking out toward the lift bridge, the boats in the water, and the rolling hills on the other side of the river, with the trees changing into their golden orange colors of the fall.

"Would you mind if I had something to drink?" she asked, looking over at me with her dark eyes. "Now that I know you're alcoholic, it is hard to know what to do in front of you."

"Go ahead," I said. "You should have whatever you want." I didn't tell her, but the events of the previous day still had me longing for something to drink myself, and something a lot more potent than the dainty glass of Merlot she ordered. Despite saying she'd puke if she ate, she downed a cup of soup and half of a sandwich. I joined Rodrigo in having a cheeseburger. He pointed at the hills on the Wisconsin side of the river and burst out. "Momma, look at the hills. It's just like Rio."

"Is that true?" I asked her.

"Not really. In Rio the hills are mountains. And the river is a huge bay. It was discovered by the Portuguese on January 1, so they called it the River of January. That's what Rio de Janeiro means."

"Does talking about it give you a sense of . . . What did you call it? Sowdegs?"

She laughed for the first time since we had left her duplex, showing off those perfect white teeth. "SowDAHgees," she said. "How do you forget how to pronounce the good words and yet you pronounce the bad words perfectly?"

"PehDAHsso gee . . . ?

"No!" she blurted out.

"You ever going to tell me what that means?"

"Nope."

"Rodrigo will tell me."

He looked toward us at the sound of his name and Sonia gave him a warning glance. Then she turned her warning glance to me. "Please, Jake. This is not funny. I am trying hard to teach him the kind of manners he needs to get along in the world."

She turned her glance back to him and smiled. "And he is doing a good job of learning them. Aren't you, Rodrigo?"

He smiled and nodded his head up and down, basking in the attention. Then he took his Matchbox car out of his pocket again and started driving it all over the table and chairs, even using his mother's leg as a driveway, humming his song all the time. He wandered to the edge of the patio where he drove his car along the patio railing. Sonia watched him out of the corner of her eye, while we sat at the table under the warmth of the midday sun.

"But you do get sowdegs for Rio?" I asked.

"SowDAHgees," she corrected with a smile. "Of course. But you must have the same feeling about where you grew up in Queens."

"Very good," I laughed. "Lots of people here don't know the difference between Queens and the rest of New York."

"I visited New York right before taking my citizenship test, so I learned about Queens and Manhattan and Brooklyn."

"You became a citizen?"

"If I was going to make my life here, I was not going to be a foreigner. Some people will always see me as an immigrant, but I am not a foreigner." She looked a little testy about the distinction.

"In these days of globalization, it can't make that much of a difference."

She waited a second before replying and looked over at Rodrigo driving his car along the patio railing. Then she turned her head and fixed her brown eyes on me.

"Until Rodrigo was born that was true. My marriage was in trouble, Jake. Deep trouble. When we got to Minnesota, we had to live with my in-laws for awhile, and it was a huge culture shock for me."

I nodded.

"I grew up in a family where everyone got to talk, and we all listened to each other, but none of my in-laws wanted to hear anything I had to say. They looked down on anything to do with Latin American. They wouldn't even call Rodrigo by his right name. They insisted on calling him Roderick or Roddie, as though his name in Portuguese wasn't good enough for them."

Her lips turned down into a scowl as she said that, and she paused for a second before continuing.

"And on top of everything, my father-in-law was a drunk. One day he slapped Rodrigo, so I took Rodrigo and moved into a motel. I refused to leave until my husband found us an apartment of our own. It took a month."

"My God, that must have cost a fortune."

She chuckled. "Oh, Jake, every now and then the financial planner in you just pops right up to the surface. Just before we left Brazil, my father gave me $5,000 for an emergency fund, and that's how I managed."

"After we got out of the motel, things spiraled downhill. If I am going to live with somebody, I have a powerful need to talk and have that person talk with me, but these were not his strong points. We weren't getting what we needed from each other, and eventually he took up with a graduate student at the Ag School. I no longer blame him for that, because I can see now how cold I had turned toward him. But at the time, I was devastated. I can't tell you how painful it was, Jake. I wanted out of that marriage in the worst way. But I was afraid I wouldn't be allowed to stay in the country if I got divorced. So I put off the divorce until I became a U.S. citizen and got passports for Rodrigo so we could both have dual citizenship and fly to Brazil with no restraints."

"It makes that much difference?"

"You were born here, Jake," she said, pronouncing it Zhaak, as she does. "So you have no fear of being kicked out and being separated from your loved ones. I did."

I said, "Well, it must have pleased your husband when you became a citizen."

"He called me a calculating bitch. I went behind his back to get Rodrigo's Brazilian passport, and when he found out he was furious. He accused me of planning to take Rodrigo away from him."

She glanced over to her son again and added, "I wouldn't do that. Maybe I was a calculating bitch, but I would never deprive Rodrigo of his father."

Then she changed the subject. "Enough about me, Jake. Tell me something about yourself. Does your family still live in New York?"

"My mother died many years ago, while I was still drinking. She never got to see me sober up, which is a regret I carry to this day. My father lives at the Veterans' Home in Minneapolis."

"Why there?"

"He's a Vietnam vet who got a bad exposure to Agent Orange. He spent his entire life's savings on medical bills until the VA started owning up to their responsibilities for all the Agent Orange illnesses." I stopped, then went on. "It was Wellstone who pushed the VA into that."

She gave a smile at my admission that Wellstone had done something good. Rodrigo came back to the table from the patio railing, leaned next to his mother, and watched me as I went on talking about my father.

"After I sobered up I brought him to Minnesota, but living together was impossible. I was too messy for him, and we fought about everything. When a place opened up at the Vet's home he moved there. I had mixed feelings about it, feeling relieved that he was out of the house and feeling guilty that he'd left. But he's happier there. He gets better care and he likes hanging out with all the vets. In some ways he's more comfortable with the past."

She twirled her wine glass on the table top, ran her fingers through Rodrigo's hair, and then asked me, "Can I meet him?"

That startled me. I was leaning back on two legs of my chair and I momentarily lost my balance. She chuckled at the consternation she'd caused me.

"Sure," I said, "But why?"

She smiled again. "Jake, there is one thing you need to know about me. I don't kitty foot around."

"Kitty foot?"

"You know, kitty foot, what you are doing when you keep saying everything except the thing you mean."

"Pussyfoot, Momma. You mean pussyfoot, not kitty food," said Rodrigo with a big grin.

I chuckled at the exchange between Rodrigo and Sonia, and she shook her head back and forth as she smiled at him.

"Well, I don't pussyfoot around. Until you decide what to do about this situation and until we find out what Lars meant in that note, I am kind of stuck with you." She gave me an impish grin. "And it might be a good idea to find out more about you."

"Well if you don't like pussy footing, you're going to love my father. Before he got incapacitated by the Agent Orange, he was a truck driver, then an organizer for the Teamsters. And pussy footing doesn't get you any place with the Teamsters. I've got to warn you. He's gruff, and he's got a bizarre sense of humor."

"So I can meet him?"

"I see him tomorrow. I can pick up you both at, say, twelve thirty?"

"You want Rodrigo to come?"

"Yes," I said.

"Why?"

"You'll see."

Just before we got up to leave, she pulled a digital camera from her purse and sent Rodrigo back to the railing at the edge of the patio so she could snap a picture of him, with the river and the hills and the steel girder lift bridge over his shoulder in the background.

Her glass of Merlot was still half full and I could smell it. How anybody could leave half a drink behind always mystifies me, and I gave it a wistful glance as I pulled out some bills to leave on the table for the waitress. We drove back to Sonia's place in silence, and, after I carried Rodrigo's pumpkin upstairs, she shook my hand and said "AhTEH logo."

"What?"

"It is what you say when you are leaving."

"You're teaching me Portuguese?"

"It won't hurt you to learn a few words." She gave me that impish grin again and softly closed the door.

VI

The date with Sonia had put me back on cloud nine, and I decided to celebrate by going on my daily run. I jogged across the Ford Parkway bridge and ran north on the Minneapolis side of the Mississippi to the Lake Street bridge, crossed it, and headed south on the St. Paul side. As often happens when I'm running, the problems I'm working on churned in and out of my subconscious, and by the time I got back to my condo, I had figured out how to ask my friend in Center City to hold the shoe boxes for me for a few days.

"Bob Vukovich," he answered after the third ring.

"Bob, it's Jake, and I need a favor. Can you hold something for me for a few days? I can't keep it at home or in my office, and I need someplace to park it until I figure out what to do."

"No problem. I'll be here all day tomorrow. Just bring it out."

"I kind of need to get rid of it right now."

"I was going to go over to the casino at Hinckley tonight. But I'll wait for you. Maybe you'd want to come along to the casino?"

Not likely, I thought, but didn't say. I remember the rush I had felt on my twenty-first birthday when a slot machine in Atlantic City poured out a bucket of quarters to me. It had been a minor version of the rush from my first drink of booze. And today,

I can never get out of my head the fear that I might trade my addiction to alcohol for an addiction to gambling. So I stay away from the casinos for the most part.

Bob was the one person I trusted not to peek into the shoe boxes, but I nonetheless took the precaution of wrapping them in duck tape. Setting the boxes in the trunk of my BMW I headed north on Mississippi River Road where the sidewalks teemed with joggers, cyclists, and young parents pushing infants in strollers. The late afternoon sunshine pouring through the leaves of the overhead trees made bright splotches on the pavement, and it was so peaceful that I continued along the river until I reached I-35 on the other side of the University of Minnesota. At the town of Forest Lake I turned off the interstate onto Highway 8, and headed out to Center City. It is home of the Hazelden Institute where I had spent a month in treatment five years earlier, and where I had made some close friendships and picked up several clients.

I went straight to Bob's little house on Lake Chisago. He had been the counselor I'd grown most close to. Not at first. I hated him at first. After all, he took away my best friend, Jack Daniels. And during those first few days of treatment, I wanted Jack Daniels more than anything. But once I committed to staying sober, Bob became a great friend. He was a gnarled, Serbian ore miner from the Minnesota Iron Range who is convinced he'd be dead by now if he hadn't stopped drinking. He takes me ice fishing and snowmobiling on his lake, and I treat him to a Timberwolves game each year.

He greeted me with a bear hug that knocked the shopping bags out of my hands onto the floor of his porch. We picked them up and tucked the shoe boxes behind some sauce pans on the bottom shelf of his cupboards. We then sat in his living room for a coffee, and I told him about the elegant Sonia Lindquist.

"A typical sultry Latin?" he asked.

"Well, I'm not sure there's anything typical about her. But

she's certainly got a playful side, and she's impossible to ignore. If you're sitting down talking with her, she'll occasionally lean forward so you pick up the scent of her perfume. She's always reaching out to touch you with her hand when she wants to make a point. And when you walk, her shoulder brushes against your arm every now and then. She's like some kind of human magnet that draws you into her space." I paused. "And it's nice."

"Does she have anything on the ball?"

"She speaks four languages and until yesterday was a college professor of art history. But sometimes she does things that just don't make sense for a person like that." I told about her outburst at the president's dinner. "Why would she blow up like she did and wreck a good job like that just because of what some slob had to say about Wellstone?"

"I don't know, Jake. She sounds like one of those erratic Latin woman, the kind you'd be better off staying away from before she explodes in your face."

"I haven't been laid in weeks and you're telling me to stay away from the most sensuous woman I've seen in ages?"

I didn't plan to tell him about Lars. But my name had already been mentioned in the newspaper story, and Bob would learn about it soon enough. So I laid it all out for him.

"Your friend was in the drug trade?"

"Impossible."

"But they found a meth lab."

"It was planted."

"How do you plant a meth lab?"

"Well, maybe not planted," I said as I set my coffee mug on the end table and stood up to leave. "But you spill a few chemicals around maybe you can make it look like a meth lab was there. I don't know. I'm out of my element here. Meth wasn't my drug of choice."

"Sure you don't want to go over to the casino with me? I got to do something to supplement my income."

"You could go back to your union job on the Iron Range."

"Not me. I had my fill of pulling horse's cock."

"Horse's cock?"

"That's what we called those long copper cables that carried the electricity out to the equipment. It took a thick cable to handle the juice. And it's wrapped in rubber insulation, so if you cut off a piece, it looks like a horse's cock. When the machinery has to move further out, somebody's got to put on those insulated, rubber boots and drag the horse's cock out to the equipment. So half the time you're slogging through the muck with a live cable." He grimaced. "No wonder I became a drunk."

Bob walked me to the front door overlooking the lakefront, which was lit up by a full moon hanging in the sky. He reminded me of a date we had coming up to take a group of children of his clients to the amusement park at the Mall of America.

"Why don't you bring your girlfriend's son?"

"Two minutes ago you were warning me to stay away from her. And now you want me to bring her son to the amusement park?"

"Well, you've already got that dopey look of a teen-ager in puppy love, so I doubt that you'll listen to my advice. You might as well show the kid a good time."

I'd barely gotten back to my condo when the telephone rang. Hoping it might be Sonia, I picked it up on the first ring.

"Listen, Morgan. We want that stuff Johanson gave you."

"You want the money?"

"Money? I don't give a shit about your money. I want the stuff Johanson gave you to hide."

I glanced at the caller ID, but it showed nothing.

"He didn't give me anything. I don't know what you want."

"Don't give me any shit. Just take what you've got and bring it to me. Right now. At the Eastern edge of Lake Vadnais, that spot where the Hmong go fishing. I'll be sitting there with a fishing pole."

"Fishing? In October?"

"Just show up. Alone. Get out of your car and hold whatever you've got out in front of you with both hands. I'll sort through it for what I want and give the rest of it back to you."

"I'll tell you what I'm going to do, my friend. I am going to call the police."

Click. The phone went dead. I punched star 69, to show the last call, but nothing came up.

I slumped onto my couch. They didn't seem to know about the money. So far as the money was concerned, I was off the hook. Except for Sonia and me, nobody in the world knew that it existed.

"Where are you now?" said the voice on the other end of the line when I called the police.

"Home. It's a condo on the twelfth floor in Highland Park."

"Stay there. Whatever you do, don't go anywhere near Lake Vadnais. We'll send somebody to look around."

"He won't show. I told him I was going to call the police."

There was a pause at the other end of the line as though the person there was trying to figure out why I would have said something so stupid.

"We'll check it out anyway. If we need anything more from you, we'll call."

VII

The next morning I called the news organizations that had phoned after seeing my name in the sheriff's report about Lars. Most of my calls reached answering machines where I left messages that said I had nothing to add to what had already been reported. One call was answered by an actual, live person instead of a machine. The young man seemed upset that I'd disturbed him. "People don't usually bother us only to say they don't know anything."

"I'm just returning a call," I said. "It seemed like the polite thing to do."

My last call was to Jim Anderson of *Street Scenes*.

"I've been reading about you," he said. "Anything you can tell me?"

"Maybe. Could you meet for lunch tomorrow? Say at the Day by Day. At noon?"

"That's OK," he said. "But I'd think a financier could afford a better place than that."

He apparently hadn't heard of "Minnesota nice."

At Sonia's building, I rang the bell, but no one answered. It wasn't likely that she would have stood me up, so I sat on the old, wooden, porch steps to wait and watched two Somali girls clad in long grey robes and head scarves play hopscotch on the sidewalk across the street. A few minutes later, Sonia's Ford Escort pulled into the driveway. It was one of those old driveways with concrete strips for the tires and grass between the concrete strips, and somehow she managed to get all of the car's tires halfway onto the grass. Flashing her ear-to-ear grin, she pushed the car door open and stuck her left leg out of the car. She was wearing a long, tight, denim skirt with a slit up the side that exposed several inches of her thigh. Hanging from the silver chain around her neck was a polished, dark-reddish, wooden pendant, a human fist with the thumb sticking out between the index and middle fingers.

"I'm sorry for making you wait," she said, "but church ran late. And then I had to get Rodrigo a bite to eat."

"Church?"

"After the last two days, I needed it. You should try it, Jake. You look a little nervous."

"I am nervous. And you should be, too. This might not be a bad time for you to take your annual trip to Rio."

"I considered it after you showed me that note from Lars. But I can't go right now. My divorce decree only allows Rodrigo to leave the country sixty days each year, and we already went last summer." She slammed the car door, waited for her son to come around from the other side of the car, put her arm around his shoulders, and ambled toward me.

"Besides, I start a new job tomorrow."

"You got a new job? Already?"

"Not new, to be honest. I was working part time at the New Dimensions Art Gallery in Loring Park. When I told them I had quit the college, they asked me to come on full time."

"Is it possible to make a living doing that?"

"I have a year to find out," she said cheerily. "My first project is going to be an art show in December."

I said, "There is something new I need to tell you before we go, but you might not want Rodrigo to hear it."

She said something to him in Portuguese, unlocked the door to their duplex, and sent him up the stairs, apparently to do an errand for her. Then we sat down on the steps. I told her about the mysterious phone call I'd received the night before and my reporting it to the police.

"On the bright side, the killers don't seem to know anything about the money. However, they think I've got something that belonged to Lars and they want it back.

"What is it?"

"I have no idea, and that's what makes all this so menacing."

Her right hand went up to the shiny wooden pendant hanging from her necklace, and she fingered it absentmindedly for an instant.

"What's that?" I pointed to the pendant.

She twisted it with her fingers and glanced at it for a second. "It's an Afro-Brazilian religious symbol. I haven't gotten around to replacing the St. Jude medal I gave you, so I've been wearing this. It's called a feega." She turned her smile to me. "Do you still have the St. Jude?"

She had me perplexed. A sophisticated, multi-lingual PhD who seemed to think she'd be protected by superstitious medallions. I pulled the St. Jude medal from my pocket to show her, and she smiled again. "It's meant to be worn around your neck, Jake, not carried in your pocket."

But before she could pluck it from my hand and hang it around my neck, Rodrigo came out to the porch and handed her a yellow cardigan sweater. She draped it over her shoulders and we headed down to my van that was parked on the street in front of her house.

Her heels clicked on the tiled floor of the Veterans' Home as we walked to my father's room, and Rodrigo gawked at the re-

cruitment posters from World Wars I and II that dotted the corridor. The door to my father's room was open, but I rapped on it
with my knuckles to draw his attention. He was sitting upright
on his bed playing solitaire, the cards spread out on a tray that
swung over his lap. As he looked up, his eyes shifted from me to
Sonia to Rodrigo and back to me, his sunken cheeks giving him a
wasted look.

"I brought a couple of friends, Pop," I said as I put my fingertips on the small of Sonia's back to nudge her forward. "This is
Sonia Lindquist. She's from Brazil, and this is her son, Rodrigo."
Pop broke into a huge grin as he bent over to shake hands with
the boy.

"I seldom get such young visitors," he said, beaming at the
boy. "I've been sitting here bored to tears getting ready to work on
my will and suddenly I'm in the presence of a beautiful angel and
her charming offspring."

"Your will?" Sonia asked without blushing, apparently accustomed to being called a beautiful angel. I had told her about
the devastating effect that coping with Agent Orange had on his
finances, and she must have wondered what possessions he
would have left to put in a will.

"Don't ask," I said.

"Jake, you need to be more sociable," said Pop. "She asked a
reasonable question and she deserves a reasonable answer." The
corners of his lips curled in glee as they do when he is pulling
somebody's leg. That was one of his few endearing traits that I
could remember from my youth when our relationship had been
hostile. He took the grin off his face and, with a look of complete
seriousness, said, "I'm willing my body parts for organ donations."

"I think that's very generous," she said, pronouncing it
theenk, and Rodrigo corrected her.

"It's think, Momma, not theenk."

She looked at him, but didn't admonish him for correcting
her in public. She just shook her head in bemusement. Judging

from the grin that came to the corner of my father's lips, he was just as amused by this exchange as I was. But Sonia didn't skip a beat. She simply replied to my father, "Why do you need a will for that? Can't you just put organ donor on your driver's license?"

"Don't ask," I repeated.

Pop scowled at me, then smiled down at Rodrigo who was standing in front of him, and then lifted his smile to Sonia. "I'm willing specific body parts for specific purposes," he said, the roguish grin returning to his lips.

She looked puzzled. "I didn't know you could do that," she said, more as a question than a statement, suspecting that he was putting her on, but not quite certain of it.

"Since they're your body parts, you have the right to send them wherever you want." The upturned corners of his lips broke into a big grin as he relished the put-on that he was concocting. "My brain, for example, goes to the White House. They seem to have lost their's."

Sonia giggled, bent backwards, and put out her fists in a double-thumbs-up gesture. Pop noticed that and went on. "This is a very astute young lady, your Chilean friend is, Jake."

"Brazil, Pop. She's from Brazil, not Chile."

"And the heart goes to Wall Street. No offense to you, Jake, but Wall Street could use a heart."

Sonia turned to me and tittered. "Your never told me how charming your father was, Jake."

"Listen to your Chilean amigo, Jake. She's very wise."

"Brazil, Pop, not Chile." I turned to Sonia. "Don't encourage him."

"Jake, I'm just answering her question about my will, and I've only gotten down to the heart. We've still got a ways to go."

"Pop, we don't want to hear what comes next."

He faked a serious look and said to Sonia, "I apologize for my son's formality. You need someone a little more playful. What's he got that I don't have?"

"Fewer wrinkles," she laughed.

I handed Pop the paper sack. He thanked me as he took it, reached inside, and pulled out a deck of playing cards along with a bottle of red wine. "The silver lining of your affliction, Jake, is that you developed excellent taste in wine." He looked at Sonia. "He did tell you about his troubles, didn't he?"

"He did."

"Not that my conversations with Sonia are any of your business," I said, attempting to get him to back off. He ignored me and continued talking to Sonia.

"I'm very proud of my son," he said. He stared into her eyes. "Not everyone visits his father on a regular basis and not everybody gets cured of this affliction."

"Nobody gets cured of it, Pop. You just live with it day by day. I'm sober now, and I'll be sober for the rest of the day. Tomorrow I have to do it all over again." I said this more for Sonia's benefit than his. Even though she'd lived with an alcoholic father-in-law, I wasn't sure that she understood the process of recovery. Then to change the subject, I said, "Why don't we take advantage of the sunshine and go outside by the picnic table."

Pop put on his bathrobe, slid the bottle and playing cards into the robe's pocket, and put some paper cups from the tray by his bed into the other pocket. I helped him into his wheelchair and his eyes were on the same level as Rodrigo's. "And you, my young friend," he said and smiled, "can be my motor. Jake, help him push me."

I guided Rodrigo behind the wheelchair and put his hands around the handles. Although Pop had been a big, heavy man, he was now so shriveled from the Agent Orange exposure that Rodrigo was able to push him along the tiled floors without help. At the end of the corridor, Rodrigo stopped in front of a huge ceramic flower pot that blocked his path. "What is that for?" he asked.

"So we don't fall down those steps." Pop pointed at a stairwell behind the flower pot. "Some of the guys here don't drive their wheelchairs very good." He reached over to push a button next to a nearby elevator door.

Outside, the chair did not move smoothly across the grass, so I had to place my hands on top of Rodrigo's and push Pop over to the old, wooden picnic table about fifty feet from the chain link fence that overlooked the Mississippi River.

Pop pulled three paper cups from his pocket, filled two of them with wine, pushed one over to Sonia and pulled one in front of himself. "And for you, my young chauffeur," he said, smiling at Rodrigo, "a treat." He pulled a can of soda pop from his bathrobe pocket. He popped the can open, poured some into a paper cup for me, and handed the cola can to Rodrigo. Lifting his paper cup in a toast, he asked Sonia, "How do you say 'Toast!' in Chilean?"

"Brazilian, Pop. She's from Brazil, not Chile."

Sonia laughed and said, "Saude." Then she mouthed the word for us. "SowOOHgee."

"SowOOHgee," we all said, lifting our drinks.

"What's that noise?" asked Rodrigo, tilting his head toward a faint hum in the distance over by the river.

"It's the lock and dam," I said with a smile. "You've got good ears." The sound was so faint that I had to strain to hear it.

"His hearing is extremely sensitive," said Sonia. "That is common among children with Williams syndrome."

I brought them to the chain link fence overlooking a sharp drop off to the Mississippi River which flowed about a hundred feet below. When Sonia spotted the drop off the other side of the chain link fence, just a few steps away from her feet, a look of panic came to her face. She grabbed Rodrigo by the arm and pulled him back a few paces. I looked at her, puzzled.

"It's the height," she murmured. "I'm terrified by heights."

But Rodrigo wouldn't stay back from the fence. He broke loose from his mother and leaned against the fence to watch the water roaring over the dam below. She grabbed him by the shirt

collar to pull him back, but his fingers clutched the chain links of
the fence. I gently took Rodrigo by the shoulders and turned his
attention toward a barge that had just entered the lock on the
upstream side. I pointed to the huge doors of the lock that were
closing behind the barge and explained how the barge would sink
to the downstream level, where the doors on the other end would
open and the barge would move out to continue its trip down the
river. It wasn't clear that he understood anything I said. The
barge was sinking slowly and he soon lost interest. Just then Pop
called out from the picnic table.

"Rodrigo. Come over here. Let those two love birds alone for
a minute and I'll teach you how to play war."

As Rodrigo moved toward the picnic table and Sonia was
able to step back from the fence, the petrified look eased off of her
face. "Love birds?" she said.

"I'm embarrassed," I replied. "I warned you that he's got a
bizarre sense of humor. That's why he called you Chilean and
made up the stuff about his will."

"Let's sit down, Jake. It won't be so scary if we're sitting."
She grabbed my hand and pulled me down to the grass in front of
her. I sat facing upriver with my shoulder touching the fence, and
she sat facing me looking down river, but a little bit away from
the fence. She didn't let go of my hand and we sat holding hands
quietly on the cold grass, watching the barge slowly sink as the
water poured out of the downstream side of the lock.

"Can I ask you something?" I said. "Something out of the
blue and totally unrelated to what we've been talking about?"

"What?" she said.

"It just came to me as I was watching the arches of that old
bridge It's very picturesque."

She glanced over her shoulder at the arches of the Ford
Parkway bridge and nodded.

"I've never known an art historian before. How did you get
into it?"

She let go of my hand, clasped her hands together on her lap, looked down for a moment, then gave me a warm smile. "When I was sixteen, my father took the family to Sao Paulo for a visit. To a child used to playing volleyball on the beach in Rio, Sao Paulo was a terrible place. It was just one boring office building after another. But my father got opening night tickets to the Biennial Art Show, which is the biggest art show in Latin America. I was enchanted, Jake." She gave a wistful smile, her eyes bright from the memory.

"You should have seen the women in their beautiful gowns! My father wore a tuxedo. The artists all had shabby clothes. The son of one of the show officials took me on a tour to show me the highlights, and my mother trailed close behind. She wouldn't let me out of her sight for fear of what that boy and I might do if left alone. Sonia chuckled. "I don't even remember that boy's name, but he made the world of art look so glamorous that I told my parents that art was what I wanted to study in college. After I came to the U. S., my father paid tuition and babysitting costs so I could get my degree at the University of Minnesota."

"That's a fantastic story. Your husband must have been very pleased."

She gave me a stern look. "Pleased? Would you be pleased if your wife was getting money from her father that you couldn't afford to give her? And getting a PhD that was going to make her less dependent on you?"

"Of course I would have been pleased."

She looked skeptical, like she wanted to believe me but she couldn't quite manage to.

"How did you get into selling art?"

"The first time we went back to Rio for a visit, I borrowed money from my father to buy some paintings, and when I got back here, I was able to sell them at a good profit right off the bat. The Hispanic and Indian art is more popular, and I have a lot of competition there, but I am the only one in town with good Brazilian art. I sell other art as well, of course, because I didn't want to be stuck with only one thing, but it's my Latin American art that people like the most."

We sat quiet, facing each other. In the corner of my eye, the ugly coal barge floated in the lock, and it was the most beautiful thing I'd seen in years. That's how spellbound I was. Glancing at the picnic table to see that we were not being watched, she bent forward and leaned toward me, the Afro-Brazilian feega dangling from her necklace. I leaned toward her, and just as our lips were about to touch, Rodrigo shouted out, "Momma! I won!"

He pulled the digital camera from his mother's purse and ran toward us, stopping about fifteen paces away. He lifted the camera and snapped our picture while we were still sitting on the grass, holding hands and bending forward toward each other.

When we got back to the picnic table, Pop said, "Are you going to tell me about that newspaper story?"

"I don't know much, and there are only a couple of things to add to what you've already read. The killers seem to want something that they think Lars gave me." I told him about the phone call, my reporting it to the police, and Lars' suggestion that Sonia might be in danger. I leaned forward to whisper the last part, so that Rodrigo couldn't hear it.

"God," he said. "This sounds like I'm back in the Teamsters again fighting off the mob." He stared me in the eye. "What's your plan of action?"

"I don't have one. None of it makes any sense to me. If they'd just tell me what they want, I'd give it to them tomorrow. But until then, we're just trying to stay out of sight and keep the cops informed. Got any ideas?"

"No," he said. "But I'll think about it."

We got Pop back to his room and prepared to leave. I guided Rodrigo through the door and just as I was to go out, Pop said, "Jake?"

I looked back.

"That is a very classy lady, Jake," he said in a quiet voice. "Make sure you treat her better than you did the other one."

"I will, Pop. I will."

Sonia belted Rodrigo into the back seat of the van, then got into the front seat, pulled her own strap over her shoulder and snapped it into place. I headed back toward the graceful bridge that had prompted me to ask about her beginnings in art history.

"Jake," she said, looking at me. "What did he mean? 'Treat her better than the other one.'"

"My ex-wife," I said. "That's who he meant. Can you wait till some other time to hear about it?"

She nodded yes and closed her eyes as we moved onto the bridge, a structure not that high to my mind, barely 100 feet above the water. She didn't open her eyes or say a word until the car turned onto the exit ramp on the other side of the river. Then she said, "I forgot to ask if your friend took the shoe boxes."

"He did. But he said something a little strange."

She turned her head toward me. I described Bob's work in the iron mines, without, of course, repeating his phrase horse's cock. "What was strange was his statement, 'No wonder I became a drunk.'"

"Why is that so strange? That kind of life would drive anyone to drink."

"The drunk always rationalizes his drinking by blaming it on some external factor like other people or an unpleasant job. One of the first things I learned from him in treatment was to stop blaming other people for my drinking. Now it almost sounded like he was reverting to the drunk's logic."

"You think he has gone on the wagon?"

That stumped me for a second, then I chuckled. "You mean off the wagon. When you start drinking again, you fall off the wagon, not onto it."

She shook her head slowly. "First Rodrigo corrects my English and now you're doing it. You can laugh if I make a funny mistake with English, Jake, just so you don't try to ridicule me. I won't put up with that."

"Your English is perfect," I said, trying to mollify her. "It's just that some phrases come out funny. Anyway, no, I didn't see any sign that he was drinking. It was probably just an innocent phrase that doesn't mean anything."

I walked her up the stairs to her duplex and we said good-bye at the top of the stairs. She looped her hands around my neck and completed the kiss she'd started to give me by the fence overlooking the lock and dam.

"Rodrigo likes you," she said with a warm smile.

"How do you know?"

"That's why he took our picture."

It was barely six o'clock and I was back at my condo, lounging on my sofa flicking channels between a football game and a golf tournament, with my mind in a fog, fantasizing about Sonia, when the telephone jarred me to my senses.

"Is this the J. P. Morgan of Morgan Capital Management?"

"Yes."

"This is the St. Paul police. There's been a break-in at your office on West Seventh."

"Do you have an officer there now?"

"That's where I'm calling from."

"I'll be right there. It'll take about twenty minutes."

VIII

Patrolman Joe Samson was swinging back and forth in Li Vang's swivel chair when I arrived. He pointed to the back door lock that had been picked and the file cabinet padlock that had been broken by a bolt cutter.

"They obviously cased your office in advance," he said "since they knew exactly where to go and didn't waste any time. They got in, went straight to that filing cabinet, took what they wanted and got out. Can you tell what's missing?" He pointed at the file cabinet drawer that was still pulled open.

I fingered through the file folders in the second to top drawer that the burglars had left open and came to a gap where Lars Johanson's file should have been. I explained to Officer Samson about Lars' murder, the threatening phone call I'd received the night before, and now the pilfering of Lars' file.

"What was in the file that they wanted?"

"Nothing of any use to anyone. Just copies of a will, a trust, and investment records."

"I have to get back to my rounds," said Patrolman Samson. "We'll send someone out tomorrow to examine the scene, so don't touch anything. In the meantime, keep your security alarm connected, and we'll come out again if we get another call."

After he left, I plopped into Li's swivel chair and swung myself back and forth. I logged onto her computer and printed out Lars' files. Then I burned his computer file onto a CD in case the police wanted a copy of his records. I put one of the sets of paper documents into the file cabinet, then stored the other set of papers and the CD in my safe so I'd have them handy to give to the detective in the morning. On the off hand chance that the police might seize my computers, I copied all my data files onto a CD, made an extra copy to put in the safe, and brought the other one home with me.

The next morning I got to the office early so I could brief Li on what had happened and call my lawyer before the police got there. The lawyer told me how to deal with the police when they showed up, then asked, "Anything else? This got anything to do with that call you left for me while I was on vacation?"

This was my chance to turn the million dollars over to him. But now that it didn't look like this was what the killers were after in the first place, I wasn't totally sure I wanted to part with the money. I said, "Just that the sheriff's deputy up in Moose Lake thought I was a person of interest in Lars' murder."

The police arrived at nine o'clock in the form of investigative Sergeant Brian Olson and a patrolman who immediately set to work dusting for finger prints. It took an hour for the detective to grill Li and me about the break-in, what the burglars were looking for, what our security procedures had been, and what we knew about several other things. The questions jumbled together in my mind.

"We'll need everything you've got on Lars Johanson."

"I pulled together all his files, but my attorney warned me not to turn over anything to you until you come up with a warrant identifying exactly what has to be seized."

Sergeant Olson rolled his eyes to the ceiling and looked over at the patrolman who had finished packing his equipment and was sitting in an empty chair. He responded to the sergeant by also rolling his eyes.

"Mr. Morgan, your client Johanson was mixed up in the meth business."

"I don't believe that."

"Well, the sheriff in Moose Lake believes it. There's also the business of him hiring illegal Cubans a few years back."

"He got them their green cards."

"And in addition to the meth and illegal Cubans, he operated a string of laundromats that would be an ideal cash business for disposing of money gotten through the drug trade."

"The day-to-day management was done by somebody else. He just owned it and monitored the operations."

"Don't split hairs with me. He owned a perfect business for money laundering, and you, Mr. Morgan, handled his finances."

"So I'm a suspect for murder and money laundering?"

"Murder, no, as long as you can prove that you were in fact where you said you were Friday morning."

I turned to Li. "When did I come in and leave on Friday?"

"You got here about ten. You were still here when I left for lunch at noon."

"And before that?" asked Olson.

"I had breakfast with Dr. Sonia Lindquist at the Day by Day Café. The waitress was Nancy."

"What is Nancy's last name?"

"I don't know. Some people I only know by their first names. That's common among recovering alcoholics." Although you're never supposed to volunteer information to the police if they're investigating you, it didn't seem like a bad idea to volunteer something that he'd undoubtedly find out anyway.

"If your witnesses confirm that you had breakfast where you said, then you're not a murder suspect."

"And the money laundering?"

"As his financial adviser, let's just say you're a person of interest. And those files of Johanson might give us clues about both the murder and the money laundering."

"Searching his house might be a better way to get clues."

"Don't tell us how to run our business, Mr. Morgan. What we want from you is anything else that might shed some light for us."

"I've already assembled everything I've got." I pointed to the folder of Lars' stuff sitting on Li's desk. And I'll happily give it to you as soon as someone shows up with the warrant."

"We could get a warrant for everything here."

"That would be a fishing expedition, according to my lawyer, clearly unconstitutional, and quite upsetting to my other clients, some of whom are very prominent. They would stir up a shit storm if they thought their confidential records were being given to the police because somebody they'd never heard of got murdered."

I walked over to the file cabinet, pulled out three folders, and tossed them one after the other onto Li's desk. "A college president and a TV vice president." I didn't have to identify the folder of the third person. She was a vocal member of the St. Paul City Council.

Sergeant Olson focused on the third folder.

"I'm eager to cooperate with you in anyway I can," I said, "and I'll gladly give you anything about Lars Johanson that you specify in a search warrant. But my lawyer said he'd resist a fishing expedition among the rest of my clients."

I paused for a second and tried to mollify the detective. "Sergeant, whatever Lars did, he was still an old friend of mind, and I want to do whatever I can to help you find his killer. But I have to follow the advice of my lawyer, and I have a fiduciary obligation to guard the privacy of my clients."

He gave me a blank stare.

"Could you just get the warrant for Lars' stuff and think it over for a day or two about the other clients' stuff? It's not as though I can just erase anything from the computer drives. Your computer people could restore whatever files I deleted any time they wanted to. What's the harm in waiting?"

"Here's the harm," he said. "If your security system didn't stop those burglars yesterday, it also won't stop them if they come back tonight to get your computer. If you think your customers would be pissed by you cooperating with the police, just think how pissed they would be if their social security numbers and brokerage account numbers got into the wrong hands."

That stopped me for a moment. "Well, just tell me what extra security precautions to take, and I'll set them up immediately. If I do that, could you just leave my clients' records here for the time being?"

"We can wait on your other clients. But we want Johanson's stuff now. Patrolman Smith here," he nodded toward his partner, "is going back to headquarters for a warrant, and the rest of us are going to sit here and wait until he returns with it."

"What should I do in the meantime to assure you that my other clients' records aren't going to be stolen?"

"I'm not in the security business," he snapped. "Just hire someone who is. But I'd replace those old locks on your doors with digital combination locks. Get somebody to build a concrete block closet for your paper files, and put a digital lock on the door to that, too." He pointed to the file cabinet and the broken padlock on the floor. "Get rid of those desktop computers and work off of a remote server so your files can be stored offsite. Install a motion detector floodlight out back and a surveillance camera that will record everybody coming through the door. If you'd had that yesterday, we'd have a picture of whoever it was that cased your office before the burglary."

I was chagrined at how lax I'd been with my security precautions. I looked over at Li who was sitting in her swivel chair, wearing a bright yellow sweater and a billowing, felt skirt, an I-told-you-so look on her face. She'd been hounding me for months to upgrade our computers and improve our security arrangements.

Li," I said, "you've got a relative in the construction business. Could he do a rush job of building a secure closet for storing our confidential materials?"

"It's my brother," she said. "He's out of work and he's broke. He'd start this afternoon if you paid him enough."

"If he can get the blocks up today so we can lock up our stuff tonight, offer him twice his regular wage, sixty cents a mile to transport his supplies here, and a reasonable markup over what he pays for the materials. And after you get him lined up, see what you can find out about the other security measures that Sergeant Olson mentioned."

She punched some numbers into her telephone, and I turned to the sergeant. "Is that satisfactory?"

"It's satisfactory to me, but I can't promise you it'll satisfy the chief."

He picked Lars' folder off Li's desk and leafed through it. His eye rested on the most recent summary sheet that showed Lars' total assets under management and the rate of return that I had earned for him. His eyebrows raised and his chin nodded.

"He did OK for a college professor."

"He had a good financial manager," I said.

Sergeant Olson looked up at me and then back down at the rate of return Lars had earned, and he got that look on his face that I'd seen so often in prospective clients. Within days of this case being closed he would be on the phone with me to discuss managing his retirement savings. Sometimes this job is so easy I don't even have to work at it. Sometimes people just sell themselves to me.

We sat looking at each other and making small talk until Officer Smith returned with the warrant. He and the detective no sooner left with Lars' materials than Li's brother showed up to start the project. Like her, he was short, but he was very muscu-

lar and looked like he would have no trouble swinging the concrete blocks into place. They discussed several things, but I had
no idea what they were planning since they were speaking
Hmong.

"What do you want the finish work to look like?" she asked
as they both came into my office.

"You have a better eye for that than I have. So you decide.
Your penchant for Asian motifs is OK. But if you do it that way,
keep it simple. I don't want it looking like a Chinese pagoda."

"We're not Chinese," she said tartly. "We're Hmong."

"I stand corrected. Anyway, until that stuff's installed, don't
be here alone. I'd hate to think of what could have happened if
you'd been here when they broke in last night. There's no rush for
the finish work. But I want those concrete blocks up as fast as
possible, in case that asshole cop comes back to see if we've done
what we said."

Li laughed. "That asshole cop not bother you anymore."

"How do you know?"

"Did you see that look on his face when he saw how much
money you'd made for Mr. Johanson? He's going to ask you to
manage his money as soon as he can. And the last thing he'll
want is to alienate you in advance. I'll bet you a hundred dollars
on that."

"I don't bet," I said. "And if you still intend to get a financial
planning license and go into business with me, I don't want you
betting either."

"Mr. Morgan, what I do on my own time is my choice."

"And who I train to go into business with me is my choice."

"You think all Hmong people gamble. You need to have
more respect for us."

"Well, I've seen those purple casino buses cruising through
Frog Town on the first of the month trying to pick up people for
free rides out to the casinos." Frog Town was a small, low-income

neighborhood in St. Paul that had a substantial Southeast Asian population.

She scowled. "White people ride that bus, too."

"I know that. And I agree with you. If all those whites and Hmongs and others want to gamble away their monthly checks, it's none of my business. But gambling and investing don't mix. You are the best aide I've ever had, and you've got everything it takes to become a first rate financial advisor. But if you and I get seen hanging around the casinos, we'll lose credibility." I picked up the college president's folder that was still sitting on her desk and waved it at her. "People like this are not going to want us managing their money if they think we're gamblers."

I picked my jacket up from where I'd tossed it on the floor and, as I headed out the door for my lunch date with Jim Anderson, she called out my name. She was livid with anger.

"Mr. Morgan. You are a prude!"

Jim Anderson was already seated at the Day by Day when I arrived. He was nursing a cup of coffee and looked put out at my being late. He was huge, at least two hundred fifty pounds, and most of them looked like they had been put on by eating pizzas rather than pumping iron. His hair was thinning and a widow's peak was starting to form above his forehead. "Sorry to be late," I apologized, sliding into a bench across from him. "There was a cop at my office, and I got delayed."

He sat quiet, studying me for a minute, like a chess master trying to psych out an opponent. Then he said, "How much do you know about your friend?"

"Apparently, not as much as I thought. His killers think he gave me something they want. And the cops think I was helping him launder profits from a meth business they think he ran."

"So what do you want from me?"

"You've written about money laundering, and I was hoping you could describe how it works and how or if it could be done by a guy like Lars. I'm still skeptical."

"Well, the police did find traces of meth at his cabin."

"Yes."

"And he did have a string of laundromats in Minneapolis."

"It was an investment."

"Strange investment for a college professor, don't you think?"

"Lars had his quirks."

"And then there were the illegal Cubans working for him."

"Only for a short time. He helped them get their green cards. And he was a model of cooperation with the immigration people, who aren't very easy to cooperate with, by the way."

"Now let's review this. A guy who runs a cash business, hangs out with illegal Cubans, and operates a meth lab up north. And you don't see any potential for money laundering?"

Jim Anderson was getting on my nerves. "You sound like the cops. You had to know Lars. He was so honest he wouldn't even deduct his church contributions on his income taxes. It would be like taking money from God, he said. It's inconceivable that a guy like that would under report his income."

Jim Anderson gave me a disbelieving look, like I'd just said the earth was flat or something. "The problem with money laundering," he said, "wouldn't be Lars under reporting his income. It would be over reporting. He's got all that cash coming in from the meth he sells. But he can only spend so much of it before the feds start to notice. So he deposits it along with his cash receipts from the laundromats and, presto, it all becomes legal income. You're his financial planner. Any evidence of this?"

"How would I know how many quarters a laundromat takes in?"

"You see my point then," said Jim. "Clever when you think of it. Using a laundromat to launder money." He grinned, then went on. "And if you're the guy who did his income tax returns, you can't exactly blame the cops for suspecting you."

"Actually, it was my accountant who did them. I feed a lot of my clients' income tax returns to him. But how do you know all this stuff about Lars? It's not like he's on TV every night."

"Until I saw his picture in the paper, I'd never heard of him. But your phone call got me curious, and I spent yesterday afternoon calling people. That's what reporters do. We call people, and they tell us things. Pretty soon thinks start to snowball. A college professor gets murdered in suspicious circumstances. Somebody tells you he was a weird duck for a college prof, because he owned a bunch of laundromats. You call the college dean, who's a little pompous by the way, and you find out that the laundromats were a bit of an embarrassment to the college. Lars himself was a bit of an embarrassment, especially his hobbies."

"Photography?"

"No. His other hobby."

"Ham radio? Why would that embarrass the dean?"

"Beats me. I guess he wants his faculty to have more dignified hobbies than eavesdropping on peoples' conversations."

"So the dean was embarrassed by Lars' talking on short wave radio. So what? What does that have to do with money laundering."

"Nothing that I know of. I was just using that as an example of how things snowball when you start talking to people. One call leads you to somebody else who leads you to a third person and so on. Before you know it you find out about the laundromats, the illegal Cubans, the ham radios, and, most fascinating, this guy who's legendary for never passing up a free dinner fails to show up at an elegant banquet at the History Center. But his financial advisor is there making goo goo eyes with a Brazilian bombshell who jumps up and makes a fool of herself in front of four hundred people. I wish I could have seen it." Jim finally had a sincere grin on his face. "Did she really call Radezewell a chicken shit?"

"Several times," I said, pausing, waiting for him to continue. "Is she really as good looking as they all said?"

"More so," I said and added as icily as I could. "But I'm sure you'll find out for yourself."

He gave me that stupid grin again, then plopped a fat, yellow envelope onto the table and said, "I brought some background stuff you can read." It contained old *Street Scenes* articles from his money laundering series. I fingered them, then set them aside when Nancy the waitress brought our plates. A burger with fries for Jim and a salad for me.

"You eat like a woman," he sneered, taking a big bite out of his burger. Then he returned to the subject of Sonia. "Sounds to me like she's either got a lot of guts or a screw loose."

"Well, her going ballistic on Moneybags wasn't totally unprovoked," I said.

"Moneybags?"

"That's what Lars and I called Radezewell. Anyway, she has some powerful attachment to Wellstone that I don't understand. When Moneybags said he'd gotten that chicken shit Wellstone out of the Senate, she thought he meant that Moneybags himself had gotten rid of Wellstone. And that's when she started calling Moneybags a chicken shit."

Jim's face opened up in a huge grin. "I haven't even met the woman yet, and already I love her."

I shook my head a couple of times and said, "You're not another Wellstone groupy?"

"You had to love the guy," said Jim.

"Why do I have to love him? He did a few good things and I respect that. But I don't understand why I have to love him."

Jim looked at me, grinning, with a glint in his eye. "Let me tell you a story. There's this Middle Eastern cab driver in Minneapolis who had a big Wellstone sign on his taxi. A cop writes him a ticket, claiming that there's a city ordinance against licensed public conveyances displaying political ads. The cabbie objects and refuses to accept the ticket, so the cop impounds the car. The cabbie complains to Wellstone's office, and they say they'll look into it. When the cabbie goes to court, guess who shows up from out of the blue?"

Jim looked me in the eye and lifted his hands for me to respond. I refused to take the bait.

"Wellstone himself! He talks the judge into dismissing the charge and forcing the City to pay the cabbie for all his expenses and lost wages."

Jim folded his hands on the table and sat back in the booth, a look of triumph on his face.

"You don't really believe that?" I said.

"It doesn't matter whether I believe it. Half the people who hear this story believe it. It's like the stories of slaves during the Civil War who saw Abraham Lincoln walking through the cotton fields."

"You're equating Wellstone with Abraham Lincoln?"

"You're missing the point," said Jim. "It's the way people eat up the story that's comparable. Whether Lincoln ever really took a stroll through a cotton field or Wellstone really took the trouble to show up in court is immaterial. What matters is that people want to believe it. And then when they both get bumped off by their enemies, they become legends."

"Hold on a minute," I said, my fork poised, ready to stab a cucumber. "We don't know that anybody bumped off Wellstone. All we know is that his plane crashed."

Jim pursed his lips into the kind of slight smile one gives a child who says something naive. "The plane was brought down, Jake," he said softly. "They put out his lights."

"Jim, the plane crashed. It's unfortunate, but it happens every now and then, especially to small planes flying in bad weather to remote places. Wellstone wasn't the only politician to get killed in a plane crash. There was Heinz from Pennsylvania. Carnahan from Missouri. Boggs from Louisiana."

"And they were all Democrats. You ever notice that?"

"Heinz was Republican."

"A liberal Republican."

"The National Transportation Safety Board spent more than a year studying the wreckage. They ended up concluding it was pilot error."

Jim rolled his eyes. "You're gonna believe the NTSB?"

"Until a better explanation comes along."

"Well, try this one. Somebody was out in the woods with a transmitter that overrode the signals the plane was getting from the airport."

"That's crazy." My fork was still poised over the cucumber in my salad bowl. I stabbed it viciously and put it into my mouth. "You sound like one of those conspiracy nuts who say the CIA bombarded the plane with electromagnetic waves."

"That's science fiction." He took another bite of the burger. "But the radio signal from the airport would be easy to override. The radio frequencies are not secret, and there'd be no way after the fact to find a record of the signal."

"Wouldn't it be illegal to transmit on a radio frequency that was reserved for aircraft communication?"

Jim rolled his eyes again, then looked out the window at the pond in the patio before turning back to me. "If someone wanted to assassinate a U. S. Senator, do you really think he'd worry about a small legal technicality like transmitting on a forbidden frequency?"

"But, Jim. This would take a powerful transmitter and a big generator to provide the electricity. How the hell would they get all this stuff out to the woods? I've seen pictures of the spot. It looks like a wilderness area. And how would they remove all that equipment without being seen?"

"I don't know," he admitted. "That's the mystery. Maybe they had a helicopter. There's a lake nearby. Maybe a plane with pontoons flew in. Maybe the transmitter didn't have to be as big as you think. Maybe it was operated from a truck on a highway several miles away. I don't know how it was done or who did it. All I know is that it was possible and up to this moment nobody has proven it didn't happen this way."

"But who would do it?"

"Could be anybody. He was just about the only one speaking out against invading Iraq. Maybe the CIA or the Pentagon was afraid he'd galvanize opposition to it."

"That's nonsense." I stabbed at a cherry tomato and it slid off the dish onto the table.

"Could be. I admit that I don't have a good theory about who was behind it. But I do have a theory about how the plane was brought down. Do you have a better one?"

"The pilots just made a mistake."

He rolled his eyes at that remark.

Nancy came by to refill our coffees and pick up the dirty plates in front of Jim. I pushed my salad bowl toward her. "You're not going to finish it?" she said.

"I had a big breakfast."

She took away the dirty plates and dropped off our checks. Jim looked at her nose ring as she worked and then at her hips as she walked away with the dishes.

"I don't know what more to say, but I'll read your articles. Let's stay in touch." I handed him my business card.

"J. P. Morgan?"

"It fits, don't you think?" It must be a character flaw, but I get a kick out of people's reactions to my J. P. Morgan schtick.

"There's one more thing. I need a financial planner."

"That's all I need as a client, Jim. An investigative reporter who thinks I launder money for the drug trade. How about if I refer you to someone?"

"I want you."

"Why?"

"As I said, I talked to a lot of people yesterday, and they all trust you. They all think you're pretty good."

"Two minutes ago I was helping launder money. And now I'm trustworthy?"

"Jake, some of the people I talked to are your clients, and they are ecstatic at what you've done with their retirement savings. No neutral person would think that a guy as successful at that as you are would screw around with money laundering."

"The police seem to think so."

"They're not neutral. It's their job to think the worst of people. Look, I got $10,000 from a law suit, and I need someone to invest it for me."

"You're not making your case any stronger, Jim. An investigative reporter with a penchant for suing people?"

"You say that as though it's something bad," he said, putting a hurt look on his face.

"Jim, my fee for handling your money would barely be $100 per year. That wouldn't even cover my expenses."

"Well, double my money and next year you make $200."

"Nobody can double your money in a year."

"I gotta do something, and you're the only planner I know."

I paused as I looked over at Jim with the conspiracy theories rattling around in his brain. Normally I accept the world as it is and don't pass judgment about other people's philosophy of life, no matter how bizarre it might be. But that didn't mean I had to get entangled financially with them. On the other hand, in finding out what he had about Lars and me and even Sonia in a very short period of time he had shown an extraordinary ability to dig up information. It might be useful to keep on good terms with him.

"You got any dependents?"

"No."

"How about this," I said. "I'll fill out the paperwork for a no-load index fund. You leave enough emergency money in your bank account to cover expenses for a month or two, and write a check for the balance to the fund. That way you won't have to pay my fees, but you'll have some money invested." And, I left unsaid, we could both pretend he wasn't my client.

"What's an index fund?"

"Your money will go up and down with the market. It's where I'd put anybody's money if they only had $10,000. Once in a while you'll lose money, but over the long haul you'll come out ahead. You won't be Mark McGwire hitting seventy home runs a year. You'll be more like Wade Boggs, if you remember him, hitting a lot of singles, but ending up with a terrific batting average."

Jim Anderson gave me a skeptical look. He didn't seem to know any more about baseball than he knew about investing. But he said, "OK. Here's my address." He wrote it down on the folder of newspaper clippings he had given me.

"Do you want some of it in an IRA or do you want all of it in a cash account?"

He looked puzzled, but he listened carefully to my explanation of the relative merits of the IRA versus the cash account for a person in his circumstances.

"The IRA," he said.

"A regular IRA or a Roth?"

The blank look came back to his eyes, and I launched into another explanation. "If you're in a lower tax bracket now than you will be when you pull the money out, a Roth makes more sense. Otherwise the regular IRA would be better."

"The Roth," he said.

I said goodbye to Nancy, got onto I-94, and headed to Loring Park in Minneapolis to look for Sonia's art gallery. On the way, I called Li Vang on my cell phone. Her voice became so icy when she realized it was me on the phone that it's a wonder she didn't freeze my ear.

"Would you download two application forms for our Total Market Fund and send them to Mr. Jim Anderson?" I gave her the address. "Fill out the first one for $4,000 going into a Roth IRA and leave the amount black for a cash account. After you've got the information filled out, use those little red plastic markers we've got to indicate where he has to sign his name.

"Should I send a prospectus with it? Or should I gamble that he won't know he should have gotten it?"

With all my other distractions, the last thing I needed was Investigative Reporter Jim Anderson complaining to the SEC that I hadn't sent him a prospectus along with his fund application. But her gambling comment told me that she was still angry. "Send a prospectus," I said, "and thanks for reminding me. I owe you a lunch. What did you find out about security systems?"

She gave me a cost estimate.

"That's a lot of money," I said.

"Mister Morgan. This place is not safe. I will not gamble my life here without some kind of security system."

"OK," I said. "Go ahead."

I needed to apologize if I was going to have any hope of her getting over my lecture on gambling. "Li, I'm sorry for some of those things I said before. I have the highest regard for you and did not mean to insult you or the Hmong people. It's just that we have to be careful about the public image we present." She didn't seem totally mollified, but at least her voice warmed up from ten below zero to, maybe, five above. Before hanging up, I also asked her to have an alarm monitoring system installed at my condo and at Sonia's address.

IX

Sonia gave me a slight smile and a dainty wave of her fingers as I came through the door of the New Dimensions Art Gallery. She was busy with a customer, so I browsed the artwork that hung on the white walls. But most of it was so abstract that it meant nothing to me. Every now and then the customer asked a question, and Sonia would nod her head and point out details as she stood up straight in a tight, long, blue skirt that clung to the curve of her hips. It was hard to keep my eyes on the art.

A man emerged from a back room. He had several earrings and wore a shiny silk shirt. "Can I help you?"

"I'm just browsing while I wait for Sonia," I said.

"Enjoy," he said and returned to the back room.

Sonia excused herself from her customer and went to a desk at the back of the room where she picked up a shiny, patent leather purse. "I will be awhile," she said as she came over to me. "This could be a big sale." She emphasized the word big and her eyes sparkled.

"When can we talk? I have to update you again."

"Come by my place about six, and I'll fix us something to eat. We can talk then."

"OK," I said, flashing a big appreciative smile.

"But before you go, I have a present for you."

From her purse she plucked the photo that Rodrigo had snapped of us sitting on the grass by the fence overlooking the lock and dam on the Mississippi. We were holding hands and our bodies were bent toward each other. She had a shy grin on her face as she gave me the photo. Then she gave her dainty wave with her fingers, turned back toward her customer, and said over her shoulder to me, "Rodrigo will be back late. He is with his dad."

That gave me four hours to fill before getting her alone in the duplex. I went jogging along my Mississippi River route, then showered, put on my best slacks, a new shirt, and a tan sweater. Still two hours to kill before seeing her. I got a brilliant idea. Jim Anderson had raised troubling questions about Lars, and Sonia had told me where to find the key to Lars' house. No harm in driving by to see if anyone was watching the place. They weren't. No harm going inside to see what I could find. I parked a quarter mile away and sauntered toward the alley behind Lars' house just as though I belonged in the neighborhood.

I hid for a moment in the alley to see if anyone was watching, before I slipped inside his garage. Then I plucked the key from behind the light switch that Sonia had told me about, strode quickly to the kitchen door, and stepped inside. China and silverware were strewn on the floor. In the living room, sofas and easy chairs were turned over and the upholstery cut through. Pockets from coats in the entry closet were slit open and the clothes thrown on the floor.

The second floor was just as much a shambles. Next to Lars' bedroom was an office, and scattered all over the office floor was his huge collection of photographs, some of them of Sonia, which caught my attention. Despite his technological proficiency, Lars had never digitalized his photographs. He always used an old, thirty-five millimeter camera. Strangely, despite the hundreds of photos strewn on the floor, I did not see a single negative.

The drawers from his desk had been dumped on the floor and his computer removed, leaving the printer sitting on the desk unplugged to anything. My eyes lit on the printer's paper tray, where a bulge was pushing up the stack of paper. Absentmindedly, I pushed down with my finger to smooth out the bulge in the paper, but it wouldn't disappear. Lifting the paper, I spotted a small flash drive, no longer than my thumb. Thinking it might be his backup drive, I stuck it in my pocket, then knelt down to sift through the photos and documents on the floor. The only thing remotely interesting was an envelope filled with old credit card statements. I stuffed the statements into my pocket and went downstairs.

Next to the back living room wall sat Lars' upright piano. The bench had been upended and the sheet music scattered on the floor, but the top piano lid appeared to be untouched. For some reason, the movie *Casablanca* popped into my mind. Lars and I had once see it together. He was as much of an old movie buff as I was. It didn't seem likely that he would have mimicked the movie's star, Humphrey Bogart, who hid critical documents in the top of the piano in Rick's Café Americain. It seemed even less likely that the burglars would have missed such an obvious location. But it was worth a try. Given the nation's historical amnesia, maybe they'd never heard of *Casablanca*. I used my handkerchief to cover my fingertips as I pried open the top lid of the piano. It set off a pinging sound as it came loose and the noise echoed off the soundboard. Sitting on top of the piano hammers was a sealed, white envelope. I stuck that in my pocket next to the other envelope and headed back to the kitchen door.

It was then that I spotted two large men in dark jackets walk into Lars' back yard from the alley. My heart pounded as I slipped into the kitchen pantry and closed the door. Thank God for these old houses with all their nooks and crannies. I pushed my hands into my pockets in search for something to use as a weapon and felt the Saint Jude medal that Sonia had given me. I looked around the pantry for something with more punch, but the only possible weapon in sight was an old, wooden rolling pin. I wrapped my handkerchief around the handle, picked it up and held it by my side.

Then I heard voices. "Check out the kitchen one more time, while I go up to take another look through those photos."

One set of steps receded toward the stairway and another set tromped into the kitchen. Then the steps came toward me in the pantry. I raised the rolling pin over my head and, just as the door pushed opened, I brought it down hard against the man's head, just above the right eye. He slumped to the floor, stunned, blood gushing from his forehead. I scrambled out the kitchen door and sprinted down the alley, looking over my shoulder to see if anyone had followed me. When nobody appeared, I slowed to a brisk walk and headed back to the car.

As soon as I got out of the neighborhood, I pulled out my cell phone to check in with Li Vang. It was well past four thirty, but I knew she would leave a message on the answering machine if anything had come up since we last spoke. Just two messages.

"Mr. Morgan, someone will stop by your condo at two o'clock tomorrow to set up the security system you want. They will be at Doctor Lindquist's house on Thursday. Who is Doctor Lindquist anyway? Also, a Ms. Erika Bergstrom from Radezewell Enterprises wants to talk with you." That was interesting. Radezewell Enterprises? Why would Moneybags be contacting me?

It was still too early to show up at Sonia's duplex, so I took the envelopes from Lars' house to the nearby Saint Clair Broiler to examine while I sipped coffee in a booth beneath a huge photo of a century-old Twin Cities scene. If Lars' materials contained nothing, which was what I expected, I could just drop them in a trash can and no one would be the wiser. But it didn't work out that way.

X

Sonia let me in and brought us to the kitchen, where she had placed two soup bowls on a small table. "Is something light OK?"

"It's perfect," I replied. "Sonia, let me get this out of the way first." I told her about the break-in at my office, my confrontation with the intruder at Lars' house, and my ordering the installation of security systems at my office and home.

"Since Lars' note said you were in danger, I'd like to have one installed here, too."

"How does it work?"

"It's a sound alarm, triggered by anyone breaking glass trying to get into your duplex or moving around once they're inside. When the alarm is set off, it sends a signal to a twenty-four-hour monitoring service. When you come into the house, you have a few minutes to punch your password into a keypad, and if you fail to do that somebody phones you to ask for the password. If they don't get it, they call the police."

"What will it cost?"

"I'll pay for it. If you're not comfortable with that, you can have it removed after we get out of this mess. They can put the keypad on the wall by that door that goes to your bedrooms, and

I'll have a motion detector light put on the stairs leading up to your back porch. They can do it Thursday afternoon."

"I work on Thursday."

"If you'll trust me with a spare key, I'll come over while its being installed. With my laptop and my cell phone, I can work out of your living room."

She went to a desk drawer to find a key, but as she handed it to me she had that uneasy look of someone giving their signature to a used car dealer.

"The other troubling thing is that it's getting more and more difficult to believe in Lars' innocence." I gave her the envelope I had plucked from his piano.

"An e-ticket to Costa Rica?" she said. "Why would he go to Costa Rica?"

"Probably as a jumping off spot to someplace else. If he flew to two or three places it might be harder to find out where he finally ended up. The key thing is the date of the flight."

I pointed to the date on the e-ticket. "It was last Saturday, the day after he was killed. He knew he was in danger and put his money someplace where I could pick it up and give it to him before he left the country."

"How would he do that? Since nine-eleven it has become almost impossible to sneak large sums of cash through customs."

"Impossible for you and me. But money launderers do it all the time."

"So you are persuaded that he was laundering money?"

"Not quite persuaded. But most of what we've seen points to that. And what makes me very uncomfortable is that the police think I was helping him."

"What else did you find?"

"Nothing suspicious. Just some old credit card statements and a flash drive I can look at later on my computer. Maybe he used it as a backup drive."

"What's on the credit cards?"

"He rented a motel room in Eveleth on October 24. That was the day before Wellstone died. And the plane crashed in Eveleth."

"Maybe he was working on the campaign or trying to mend fences with his brother up there," she said.

"Lars had a brother in Eveleth? I never heard him mention a brother in Eveleth."

"One day at Lars' house I overheard a bitter fight they were having on the phone about finances. So far as I know, they never talked after that." She pointed at the credit card. "What's this on the slip from the previous month, where he wrote transceiver?"

"It's a radio device that both sends and receives signals. Since he was a ham radio operator, maybe he was just adding to his collection of radio equipment."

"What are you going to do now?"

"Well, I don't want to get caught with this stuff in my possession. So after checking out the flash drive, I'll crush it somehow and toss it in a trash can. The other stuff I'll just burn, like we did with Lars' original note."

She took me by the hand to her stove. "Let's burn it now," she said.

We sat across from each other at the small table where she had set out the two soup bowls. She bent forward to fill our bowls with rice and a thick black bean soup with small bits of meat, and her dark hair shifted with the motion of her body. One of the buttons on her blouse had come undone, and each time she bent forward, a small slit would open and give me a glimpse of a lacy, beige bra. I took my eyes off the white blouse and lifted a spoonful of soup to my mouth.

"This is delicious!" I said, smiling at her while putting a piece of the meat into my mouth. "What is it?"

"Tongue."

I gagged, spit the meat into my napkin, and hid it on my lap. I sipped the rest of the soup, taking care to avoid the pieces of meat, and when I finished, the bottom of my bowl was speckled with chunks of tongue.

Over Sonia's right shoulder on the wall behind her, I spotted a small framed photo. She and Rodrigo were standing on each side of Paul Wellstone beside his green campaign bus. His arms were draped over their shoulders and they all had wide smiles.

"How did you get that photo?" I asked.

"Paul was a big help when I got divorced and was feeling desperate. I knew there was something wrong with Rodrigo, but the doctors had not yet diagnosed him as having Williams syndrome. My husband and his family wanted to deny anything was wrong. After I got divorced, Lars introduced me to Wellstone and told him about Rodrigo. Paul's staff got me into the Mayo Clinic for a diagnosis and helped me find resources for support groups, special education, and children's activities. A child like Rodrigo does not get invited to many parties with other kids, so it helps to have group activities to give him a sense of belonging."

She paused, but I refrained from saying that any congressman would have done as much for a constituent. It's a low cost way to win votes.

"I have treasured that photo. But the thing that sticks most in my mind was his last week. I remember it like it was yesterday. I talked with him on Monday. On Friday he was dead."

"You talked with him? Right in the middle of the campaign?"

"At a coffee party. One of the African-American women at my church set it up so he could meet with some local blacks."

"But you're not black."

"Sometimes they include me. Since most Brazilians have some African genes, maybe they think I'm less racist that the typical Minnesotan."

"Are they right?"

"That's for them to decide, not me. Anyway, there were a few Somalis at the party. They brought little pieces of bread that were wrapped around little pieces of beef. They were in a wicker basket that they passed around. Paul and Sheila took some and we all did. It was like the Last Supper."

I must have looked skeptical, because she said, "Don't raise your eyebrow, Jake. I'm telling you what happened. At the end before he left, I shook his hand and thanked him for all he had done. I said 'God be with you.' That is not something I normally say. But it seemed right at the time." Her eyes were misting as she paused to think about it. "And four days later he was dead."

She had me mesmerized by the power of her feelings, as she sat so straight, the photo of Wellstone hanging behind her on the old, painted wall of the small kitchen. She absent-mindedly used her spoon to scoop out pieces of the tongue that were speckled over the bottom of my soup bowl. And she put them in her mouth. Then she got up and brought us each a demitasse cup, which she half-filled with sugar before pouring coffee up to the brim. It was the strongest coffee I'd ever tasted, but all that sugar took out the bitterness and gave it an almost syrupy flavor.

"I know you have trouble understanding why I feel so loyal to Paul," she said as she sat back down in her chair. "It's just that I'm indebted to him for the help that he got for Rodrigo and me. And there are lots of other people indebted as well. He helped your father and the other veterans. He helped the mentally ill get health insurance coverage. He helped lots of people who were desperate. He was doing in our lives what St. Jude did in his life."

"St. Jude?"

"St. Jude, the patron saint of desperate situations. Don't tell me you threw out that medal I gave you."

I pulled it from my pocket for her to see. "Are you telling me that Paul Wellstone was the reincarnation of St. Jude?"

She laughed, her husky voice dropping a notch. "Jake, You are too literal. Think symbolically. They both brought hope to desperate people. They both suffered a violent death. And they both died in the month of October."

"Sonia, I told you I'm not a deep thinker. I *am* a literal

person. That's how I make my living." I added with a grin, "Symbolic reincarnation?"

She laughed again, her hair shifting slightly as she did so. "Oh, Jake. Don't be so harsh with me. We're just starting to learn about each other. Let's enjoy the process." She tilted her head downward, and her Afro-Brazilian feega swung back and forth on the chain hanging from her neck. She looked up from the corners of her eyes and flashed that coy smile she'd given me when she'd started flirting the very first time we'd met. "You're just getting to know me. I'm just getting to know you."

"That was a great song."

"What was?"

"'Getting to Know You.' It's from an old Broadway musical, *The King and I,* way back in the 1940s. It's about a woman just like you, with a small child, adapting to a new culture half a world away from home."

"How did you know that?" The corners of her mouth turned up as she said in a teasing voice, "Practical-minded businessmen don't keep up with sixty-year-old Broadway musicals."

"I got it from my mother. She started as a dancer, and she loved it, but she didn't have the charisma or whatever it takes to make a living at it, so she worked at a talent agency. She used her position to finagle free tickets to every musical revival she heard of."

"Finagle? What does that mean?"

"She'd arrange auditions for dancers and singers. When one of them would get a role, my mother would ask for free tickets. My father wouldn't be caught dead at a Broadway musical, so she'd get matinee tickets and take me. Since it'd get me out of school for an afternoon, I loved it. So you name it. If it had a revival in New York between 1975 and 1985, I saw it. *The King and I, Pajama Game, Damn Yankees, West Side Story.*

Sonia gave her big ear to ear grin. "Do you remember me telling you about the jaytoo?"

"Finding a way?"

"That's what your mother was doing when she finagled those tickets. She understood the jaytoo. She could have been a Brazilian, Jake. And I'll bet that somewhere inside that practical, literal mind of yours is a playful spirit just waiting to get out."

And then, as if to give me a lesson in playful spirits, she took my hand, stood up, and led me to the living room where we sat on the sofa. She brushed her lips against my cheek, and in seconds we had our arms around each other and her mouth was pressing against my lips. She let herself slide onto her back on the sofa as I pushed against her. I undid the top button of her blouse, but she pushed my hand away. She placed the palm of her hand on my face and looked into my eyes, and when my fingers went for the buttons again, she pulled away from me and stood up. I feared that I had pushed her too far too fast. She slowly began to undo the rest of the buttons. As each button came undone, a little more flesh and a little more of the beige bra came into view. She opened the blouse and gave a self-conscious smile as she dropped the blouse to the floor, so she was wearing nothing from the waist up except the lacy beige bra and the feega suspended between her two small breasts. In back of her, framing her, was the shiny, dark arch separating the living room from the dining room.

Just as she reached behind her waist to undo the clasp on the long blue skirt, BAM! The door at the bottom of the stairs slammed open and banged against the wall.

"Nossa Senhora! Rodrigo!" she exclaimed. She snatched her blouse from the floor and rushed over to the door at the top of the stairs, holding it shut until she could get her blouse back on and rebuttoned. I looked in resignation as each button got fastened, closing off more and more of this vision from my sight.

Rodrigo walked softly up the stairs, and I could hear another pair of heavier footsteps tromping along with him. Just as the footsteps reached the top of the stairs, Sonia opened the door and bent over. Rodrigo burst into her arms. "Momma, estou de volta!" He grinned at me and added, "Hi Jake. Meet my dad."

I grabbed a newspaper from an end table to hold against my lap as I stood up to greet Rodrigo. The father dallied long enough to give a goodbye handshake to his son. Not a hug, a handshake. As he darted out the door, he smiled in a funny, mocking way at Sonia. It was only then that I noticed she had mis-buttoned her blouse. There were two extra holes at the top and two extra buttons at the bottom. She looked down at them and broke into an embarrassed laugh. It started as a giggle and then broke into a belly laugh. Her laughter infected me, and I started laughing too, and my laughter infected Rodrigo. In a moment all three of us were sitting on the floor roaring with laughter.

Finally, our laughter died down and she gave me a sheepish grin that morphed into a frown. "Jake, you can wait?" She said it as a question, pleading for understanding. "Please say you can wait."

When you haven't been laid in several weeks, you really don't want to hear "Please wait." I just sat there on the carpet in the middle of her living room, unable to think up anything to say.

She told Rodrigo to put his backpack in his room while she finished talking with me, and when he left, she turned to me. "Jake, I let myself get carried away. I am sorry, but we can't go on."

We were still seated on the floor in the ridiculous poses we'd slid into during the giggling fit, her with her buttons all mis-aligned and me with the newspaper covering my lap, although there was no longer any need for it. She furrowed her brow and tilted her head forward in an anguished gesture.

"Please understand, Jake. I am not saying, 'No.' I am saying, 'Not yet.' Can't you see that?"

"See what, Momma?" asked Rodrigo, returning to her side. She twisted around and hugged him to her chest.

I was still without words, wondering what was going on in her mind. If it was just a matter of Rodrigo bursting in to break the spell between us, that was one thing. But since she knew he was going to burst in at some point, why had she led me to the couch in the first place and then voluntarily begin to strip? Was it all just a big tease? But that wasn't a question I could answer at the moment, and it's not my style to pressure people into something they're not ready for. Even in my business, if clients aren't ready for what I'm trying to persuade them to do, I never make a hard sell of it. Just be patient, I've learned, and usually they come around to seeing it your way. I nodded my head in resignation and told her about the upcoming weekend.

"On Sunday, Bob Vukovich and I are taking some kids to the amusement park at the Mall of America. Can you and Rodrigo come?"

Rodrigo's eyes lit up, but Sonia said, "I have to work at the gallery on Sunday."

Rodrigo jumped up and down. "Can I go Momma? Can I go?"

Sonia gave me a nervous look.

"Why not?" I said. "I've been telling Bob about you. He wants to meet Rodrigo."

"We can talk about it on Thursday after you oversee the installation of the security equipment. If you're still coming."

"I'll be here," I said curtly.

She looked uneasy as she handed me my jacket and held the door open for me to leave. She tilted her head up for a kiss. But I was still unsure whether it had just been a matter of the spell between us having been broken or whether she'd been setting me up for a big tease all along. So, instead of kissing her, I merely pecked my lips on her forehead before I headed down the stairs. She looked hurt.

XI

Back at my condo, I dropped my jacket in the corner and checked for phone messages. Only one, from the Erika Bergstrom Li Vang had told me about, asking me to call her at home, which I did. After listening to Sonia's husky and languorous accent for the previous two hours, Ms. Bergstrom sounded crisp and efficient. Could I pick up a packet of materials Lars had left behind at Radezewell Enterprises?

"Now? It's nine o'clock at night." When you're forty years old and you've jogged five miles that afternoon, you're limp by the time nine o'clock rolls around.

"Well, not just this minute," she laughed. Maybe Sonia was right, maybe I am too literal. "Tomorrow morning will be fine."

"Couldn't you just send it to my office by courier?"

"There are some things we need to discuss."

"I'll stop by on my way to work. Say eight thirty?"

"That's a little early for the office. Why not just come to my apartment, and we can talk here."

She gave me the address. Classy location. It was in the Riverplace Complex, tenth floor, just across the Mississippi from downtown Minneapolis.

She wore a cheerful smile as she let me into her apartment the next morning. Tall, thin-faced, and big-breasted with long blond hair, she wore a chic tube dress that came just above her knees. She led me to the living area which had overstuffed, dark leather couches facing each other across a glass coffee table. Big picture windows looked out on the nineteenth-century arched stone bridge that crossed the river.

She ushered me to the leather couch and took a seat across from me. As she sank into the leather chair, her dress crept up her thigh. I saw more of Ms. Bergstrom's legs in the first sixty seconds than I'd yet to see of Sonia's. On the glass table top was a coffee serving set and a plate of strange looking pastry wafers. She poured coffee and handed me a pastry.

"These are good," I said after a bite. "What are they?"

She was all smiles. "You obviously aren't Norwegian."

"No," I said.

"They're krumkake. I get them from a Scandinavian store over on Lake Street."

She handed me a big, manilla envelope. "These things belonged to Lars. You can look them over and give whatever is appropriate to the executor of his estate."

"You had some things to discuss," I said.

"Yes," she paused, as though she was choosing her words carefully. "I know that Lars was an old friend of yours, so I don't want to say anything shocking or offensive about him. But we think he took something that Mr. Radezewell wants back."

"I seem to be learning all sorts of shocking things about Lars lately," I said. "What did he take?"

"That's the problem. Mr. Radezewell didn't tell me what it was. He simply thought that Lars might have given you some things to hold for him."

"Why would Lars have done that?"

"You were his friend and financial advisor."

"Well, the few things we traded over the years were only

things of sentimental value. It would be easier to help you out if you gave me a better idea of what you are looking for. Documents? Corporate plans? Money?"

"I told you, I don't know. Mr. Radezewell was secretive about it. But I can tell you we would be very grateful if you helped us out. We're looking for another financial advisor to help with some clients and our corporate portfolio."

I didn't say anything and I must have looked skeptical, because she smiled. "What's that raised eyebrow for?"

I laughed. "Let's face it. After that banquet last week, with your boss trashing Wellstone and me giving moral support to Wellstone's biggest fan, it's hard to see why Radezewell would want to work with me."

"You're not another Wellstone groupy?"

"Not me. I'm just your typical investment guy trying to make an honest buck. I don't care much about my clients' political views one way or the other. But a good share of the people in that room were indeed his groupies, as you put it. Probably half the staff at the college are Wellstone sympathizers. If Radezewell hates Wellstone so much, why would he make a big contribution to a college that's loaded with Wellstone supporters? And a college that bills itself as the Stanford on the Mississippi? Stanford is not exactly a hotbed of conservatism either."

She rolled her eyes at the mention of Stanford on the Mississippi, then said, "He's a generous man."

"Generous? The man started out as a slum landlord. I've never heard of a generous slum lord."

"He was not a slum lord. He was an entrepreneur of low-income housing. Many people don't have the excellent credit rating that you have, Jake. And you take on a lot of risk when you rent them an apartment."

"Whatever it's called, what does he get out of donating big bucks to the college?"

"Respectability," she said.

"He's giving away millions of dollars just for respectability?"

"Well, the college probably won't get as much as they think. The point is that a lot of the movers and shakers are stuffy, and they snub him because of the way he got started. That shuts off a lot of avenues for him. So he's shifting into new areas of business and stepping up his charitable giving."

"That makes sense," I said. "But tell me. If he wants to associate with this center of Wellstoneism or whatever it's called, why did he trash Wellstone in public? That's what I can't figure out."

"He has powerful feelings about this country. It's been very good to him. And to you. He doesn't want everything he's worked for torn down by the terrorists."

"Paul Wellstone, a terrorist?" I left the question hanging. The previous night, Sonia had made him out to be a saint, and today Erika was painting him as a terrorist.

"Not a terrorist," she said. "But somebody who is too soft on the terrorists. He opposed the war in Iraq."

"Lots of people opposed the War. I didn't, but they did. The pope opposed it. Does that make him a terrorist sympathizer?"

"Jake, I'm not calling Wellstone a terrorist sympathizer. I'm just trying to explain how Mr. Radezewell sees things."

All this talk about Wellstone reminded me of Sonia's insistence that he'd been done in by Moneybags. So it was on her behalf that I made my next comment, and it must have seemed out of the blue to Erika.

"There is one possibility of figuring out what Lars might have taken. Could you find out what Mr. Radezewell was doing on October 25, 2002 and the week before that?"

"What for?"

"I just want to know who he saw that day and where he was just before then. It might help me figure out what to look for if the executor asks me to help him go through Lars' stuff." Thankfully, she didn't remember that October twenty-fifth was the day of Wellstone's plane crash.

"That was a long time ago. How I am going to find out that?"

It was apparent that Erika's duties did not involve much secretarial work. "His secretary would have kept his calendar on her computer, and, unless she's deleted it, it's still there. When she goes out for lunch, just look it up."

"I'll see what I can find," she promised.

She got up and walked over to the floor-to-ceiling windows where she adjusted the blinds. When she returned, she sat down next to me on the leather couch.

"I understand that Lars didn't give you anything that might belong to Mr. Radezewell. Maybe he hid it someplace. Do you have any idea where he stashed things for safe keeping?" She inched closer to me and turned at a slight angle so that her right breast was touching my arm.

"Probably in his safe deposit box, just like the rest of us."

She frowned.

"Erika, I was his financial adviser, not his secret confidant. That means I ran his retirement portfolio and linked him with the specialists who did his trust and will and taxes. I had a comprehensive view of his overall finances, but I don't know where he hid things and I knew very little about the details of things like his laundromats or whatever it was he did for Moneybags."

"Moneybags?"

"Mr. Radezewell," I smiled. "That's what Lars called him, and I got into the habit."

"You should be more respectful, Jake." She withdrew her breast from my arm. "As I told you, Mr. Radezewell is looking for some investment help."

"It still seems unlikely," I said, being careful not to raise an eyebrow. "But tell me, what would be the price of being his financial planner?"

"Price? You are a strange businessman, Jake Morgan," she said. "Most financial advisors would drool at the chance to manage a portfolio the size of Mr. Radezewell's."

"I'm not saying it's out of the question. I'm just skeptical that it would work right now."

She responded by moving a little closer until not only was her breast pressing against my arm but our hips were touching.

"Jake, let's forget about Mr. Radezewell for the moment."

"Erika, what are you fishing for? I want to help as much as I can, but you have to give me something to work with." If she only knew how much her proximity made me want to help her and how long it had been since I had helped any woman.

"A place where he could hide a small collection of documents, letters, memos, receipts, or even photographs."

"So you want me to pinpoint where Lars hid things that, for whatever reason, he wouldn't put in a safe deposit box."

"Yes."

"I have no idea."

"What about your girl friend? Would she know?"

"Sonia? How would she know where Lars kept his stuff?"

Erika paused. "She and Lars were close, Jake." She looked again like she was trying to choose her words carefully so as not to offend me. "Very close. A lot closer than you might realize."

"Why don't you just call her up and ask?"

"Be serious. After last week, Mr. Radezewell would not be able to get the time of day out of her, much less a little help. You, on the other hand, seem to be on her good side. You could find out easily. And we would be grateful." Suddenly her breast was pushing more firmly against my arm. The pitch of her voice dropped a notch and I could feel her breath on my neck. "Very grateful."

"Erika, I'm not going to spy on her. There's all kinds of people who knew Lars. If you can't get her to talk with you, try somebody else. Try his brother in Eveleth."

"Lars had a brother in Eveleth?"

"Yeah, but they didn't get along very well. So he might not know much either."

"Jake, I don't want to push you into doing something that

might make you uncomfortable. Forget that I asked about your girlfriend. But if she ever happens to mention anything, we'd be very grateful if you would just point us in the right direction."

My left calf started to cramp as it sometimes does if I sit too long in one position. It's probably a consequence of all my jogging. I excused myself to stand up and stretch. "Erika, could I trouble you for a glass of water?" That had nothing to do with the cramp in my calf. The coffee and the krumkake had made me thirsty.

"Jake, you can have anything you want," she said with a suggestive smile, as she went to her kitchen, leaving me to stare out the picture window at the downtown Minneapolis skyline. She came back in front of me, handing me the water. She stepped back, and in a flash, she reached behind her back, unzipped her dress, let it fall to the floor, and stood before me wearing nothing but a silky black teddy, dark shiny tights, and high heeled shoes. With her feet spread apart she looked just like Lola in the movie *Damn Yankees*. The old stone arched bridge showed between her thighs in the window behind her. I'd never seen a bridge framed quite this way, and my mind started playing a song from that movie, "Whatever Lola Wants, Lola Gets."

"As I asked before, what would be the price of teaming up with Mr. Radezewell?

"Price? What are you talking about?"

"Well, when people entered into a pact with Lola, they paid a price."

"Who's Lola?"

"You never saw the movie *Damn Yankees?*"

"Never heard of it."

How could anyone be so successful as to afford an apartment with this magnificent view and never have seen *Damn Yankees*?

"Anything you want," she repeated.

XII

When Li Vang gave me an icy goodbye at four-thirty that afternoon, I hung back. I needed to talk with someone badly. But since her nose was still out of joint because of the lecture I'd given her on the evils of gambling, she could hardly be the one to hear my confession of just having laid the beautiful Erika Bergstrom.

I lifted the phone and called Simon G. "How about getting something to eat. I gotta talk to somebody."

Simon G. was my AA sponsor and we agreed to meet at The Kirkuk Café, a Kurdish restaurant where we got a booth in the back. As Simon studied his menu, I gazed at the huge photos of Kurdish scenes that dotted the brick walls. It was a good place for two alcoholics, because Mahmoud, the owner, had lost his liquor license for failing to pay the license fees on time. The waiters insisted that it was just an oversight on his part, but I always suspected that the owner, a Muslim, simply did not want to serve alcohol. Whatever the reason, he wasn't going to get any complaints from Simon or me. We closed our menus and gave our orders to the waiter.

I told Simon most of what had happened over the previous week. He looked at me with piercing eyes sunk in a gaunt face and asked me something unrelated to Lars' murder. "How do you feel about her son?"

"I've somehow become suspected of money laundering and all you can ask about is Sonia's son?"

"No reasonable person is going to believe that you laundered money for anyone. And even if you had, there's nothing that your AA sponsor could help you with about that. So I focus on what's important for your recovery. How do you feel about her son?"

"Before I met him I was nervous, and he drove me nuts running his toy car all over everything and humming all the time. But the kid's a charmer. Do you know what he did?"

"Not unless you tell me."

"We're sitting on the patio of the Dock Café in Stillwater looking out at the old lift bridge. Rodrigo pulls this hairbrush from his pocket and starts running it through his mother's hair. She does nothing to stop him, as if she likes him doing that. Then he picks through the hair in the brush like he's looking for something. He suddenly starts giggling and holds up a long strand of grey hair for me to see."

"What'd she do?"

"She just laid it on her lap and shooed him over to the patio railing to play with his car there. Like she didn't care one way or the other if I saw she was starting to get grey hairs."

I was smiling and feeling warm at the remembrance of it, when Simon said something that wiped the smile from my face.

"Jake, what the fuck are you doing?"

"What do you mean?"

"You're supposed to be in recovery and you're screwing two different women."

"Actually, I've only screwed one of them. Besides there's nothing in the twelve steps about being celibate." But I knew what Simon was leading up to. Pretty soon he'd tell me I was stepping close to that slippery slope. That was his favorite metaphor.

"This woman Sonia has been up front with you about her son's handicap, her first marriage, her political views, and her grey hairs, even her curiosity about your father and your background. She's clearly fishing for a sign that you'd be open to something deeper than just a one night stand. Then you turn around and screw somebody else."

"Don't be a prude, Simon. That Erika is a beautiful woman. No man in his right mind would have turned her down when she stood there with her legs spread, in her spiked heels, the shiny tights, and the black teddy, looking like Lola."

"Lola?"

"You've never seen *Damn Yankees?*"

"Never heard of it. Don't get me sidetracked. I'm trying to get you to ask yourself something. Are you behaving toward this woman Sonia as a man in recovery or as a dry drunk."

"Dry drunk? I'm a dry drunk because I went to bed with a beautiful woman? Like I said before, there's no rule against that in the twelve steps."

"Well, there's an unwritten rule that you don't go around recklessly hurting people. How is this woman Sonia going to feel when she finds out that you're sleeping around with the woman who's recruiting you to spy on her."

"Spy is a little harsh," I said. "Besides, I refused to do it."

He shook his head. "The key issue, Jake, is staying focused on your recovery. If you manipulate somebody you're pretending to love, you're defocusing and you're stepping toward that slippery slope. You've almost poured your first shot. You haven't drunk it yet, but you've got it sitting in front of you. It's just a small step from rationalizing your treatment of Sonia to rationalizing your first drink. Remember, the twelfth step of the program is to practice the principles in all aspects of our lives. Are you doing that?"

At that moment, I hated Simon. Why had I asked him to dinner in the first place? But I knew he was right.

"So I'm a dry drunk?"

"I'm just posing the question. The drunk manipulates his loved ones. The person who's serious about recovery treats them with respect. Which are you going to do?"

"You're infuriating, Simon," I said as the waiter brought our check and I reached into my pocket for my wallet. "I come to you for a little support and all you do is ask me questions."

"Isn't that what a sponsor's supposed to do?"

On Thursday I took my laptop to Sonia's duplex to meet the installer of her security system. He dragged his equipment up to her unit, and I showed him where to put the alarm control pad. Then I went to the living room couch, placed my laptop computer on the coffee table in front of me, and inserted the flash drive I had pulled from Lars' printer tray.

I had been right about the flash drive. It seemed to contain Lars' entire life. Internet passwords, college projects, spreadsheets, correspondence, you name it. The item that leapt out at me was a personal journal with entries going back ten years.

I resisted the temptation to look up the references to Sonia and instead looked for what Lars had to say about Moneybags, me, Erika Bergstrom, and potential trips to Costa Rica.

Lars raved about Erika Bergstrom in her black teddy. But their affair was not gratifying, judging from succeeding references to her as manipulative, greedy, bitchy, snoopy, and double-crossing. Just who was being double-crossed, however, I couldn't figure out. Maybe it was Lars. Or maybe it was Moneybags.

If Erika was a strike-out on getting useful information, Moneybags was a treasure trove. Frequent mentions of trips up north, cash exchanges, Cuban illegals, and rental real estate. As I had suspected, it was Moneybags who'd put up the money for Lars' laundromats. Also, it was for Moneybags that he'd bought the transceivers, and Moneybags had reimbursed him twice what

Lars' credit card slip indicated they had cost. Why would Money-bags want a transceiver in the first place?

I closed the journal and began searching the spreadsheet files. I looked first at his calculations for his income taxes in 2000, which was before I'd taken over his financial management and he'd still been doing his income taxes by hand. Sure enough, Lars did not declare that cash he had gotten from Moneybags to start up the laundromats. There were other cash payments as well. Since 1998, hundreds of thousands of dollars had passed through Lars' laundromats, rental properties, and other real estate trans-actions in a mind numbing array of numbers. If the IRS ever got their hands on these files, Lars would have a lot of explaining to do. Of course, he didn't really have to worry about the IRS any more. He must have been awfully confident that his computer would never be subpoenaed. Or maybe these files only existed on the flash drive which could be disposed of easily. None of it made much sense.

The installer came in and said, "I'm all done. Just let me get you to sign some papers and show you how to work the system. Then I'll be off."

What I did after he left doesn't speak well for my character, since Sonia's earlier relations with Lars were none of my busi-ness. But Erika had dropped hints about an affair between them, and Sonia herself had shown a fair amount of knowledge about Lars' habits. Why the dazzling Sonia Lindquist would get in-volved with a guy she had called scruffy was a mystery to me. And not pursuing that mystery was just as impossible as keeping my fingers off her blouse buttons had been earlier in the week. I opened Lars' journal again, tapped Control-F, typed in "Sonia," and went to the first reference.

Tuesday, September 5, 2000. Beautiful new art histo-rian introduced at faculty meeting today. I talked with

with her during the mid-morning coffee break. It turns out she's a recently divorced Brazilian, whose ex teaches at the Ag Campus.

Friday, September 15, 2000. Hosted a dinner for the entire Art Department so I could get a chance to know Sonia better. Spending an entire evening with those people wasn't easy. A bunch of temperamental jerks pretending to be geniuses. Except for Sonia. She stayed on to talk after the others left, and she seemed impressed that I had organized the Professors for Paul Wellstone committee. With that cashmere sweater and short skirt she was wearing, she drove me nuts. She must be a fantastic piece of ass.

Lars had a crude way with words. I deleted the reference to skirt and ass, just in case Sonia ever got her hands on this flash drive and saw these journal entries..

Thursday, October 5, 2000. The president put on his annual banquet last night at the University Club. I sat next to Sonia, who was a knockout. We hit it off. She said she had the evening free, because her young son was spending the night with his father. When I invited her for a night cap at my house she accepted, and nature took its course. Although it was boring listening to her rattle on about Brazil, it was worth the effort. Sonia is a first class fuck.

DELETE!

Tuesday, October 10, 2000. Sonia and I were both free in the mid-afternoon, so we met for coffee. The faculty lounge was empty then and I had her all to myself.

She's lonely and having a hard time handling her son by herself.

Thursday, October 26, 2000. Sonia and I have started taking our coffee breaks at my house. I showed her where to find the house key so she can come and go as she wants.

By Thanksgiving, Sonia's romance with Lars was dying out and he was no longer getting to see her very much. On December first he wrote:

Haven't had a coffee break with Sonia for two weeks. Thank God for that massage parlor on Snelling Avenue.

DELETE!

By Christmas she was planning a vacation in Rio, and using the trip as a means to break off her romance with Lars. How she managed to do that and remain friends with him, I don't know. The only entries about her after that were sporadic and gave no hint of any more romance. There was, however, one significant entry just before she left for Rio in 2000, and it was a doozie, as my mother used to say. I almost fell off the chair when I read it.

Thursday December 14, 2000. Sonia stopped by, but not for a coffee break, unfortunately. She asked if she could keep some jewelry and documents at my house while she went back to Rio. She was afraid to leave them in her apartment. I took her to my secret storage place, and we stashed her stuff there. She agreed that it was a brilliant storage place. No burglar would ever find it. Not in a hundred years.

Maybe Lars' secret storage place held whatever it was that was wanted so badly by both Moneybags and Lars' killers. With Lars' computer in their hands, the killers would soon find out that Sonia could lead them to whatever it was that they wanted. If they would cut off Lars' fingers to get what they wanted, I hated to think what they might do to Sonia.

She had to be told this. But how was I going to do that without her exploding when she realized I had just snooped into her private affair with Lars? Just then the door at the bottom of the stairs banged open and Rodrigo's unmistakably soft steps came trudging up the stairs. Sonia was back, and I still didn't know how to tell her about my prying into Lars' journal.

XIII

She came through the door wearing her big, ear-to-ear grin, as though we'd never had a minor tiff three days earlier.

"It's time to celebrate, Jake." She walked over and threw her arms around my neck.

"Wow," I said. "My presence seems to have a good influence on you." I reached behind my back and pushed down the laptop lid so she couldn't see it. Then I put my hands on her waist.

"That, too," she laughed, and her eyes sparkled. Still holding her hands on my neck, she swerved her hips like a teenager about to tell a juicy item of gossip. Then she let go, backed up a step, and spread out her hands in a ta da gesture.

"What?" I asked.

"Remember that woman I was talking to when you came to the gallery last Monday? Today she bought the most expensive painting I've ever sold. Tonight we eat out, and I pick up the tab."

"Where?" Asked Rodrigo.

"The Lexington," she exclaimed and looked over at me, still wearing that huge smile.

"That must have been one hell of a sale," I commented. The Lexington was a moderately expensive, wood paneled restaurant in St. Paul that catered to an older generation of retired priests, former politicos, and one-time social gadflies.

"It was," she said. "I'll tell you about it at dinner. Rodrigo, how about going to wash up while I go find a dressier necklace."

The silver chain with the feega looked dressy enough to me, but she disappeared into her bedroom and came back carrying a string of pearls. She turned her back to me, held up the pearls with one end of the strand in each hand, and said, "Please fasten this for me, Jake." Her back was touching my chest as I hooked the pearls in place and slid my hands down to her shoulders. She let them rest there for a second, then turned away just before I could slide them over her breasts.

I stuffed the flash drive into my pocket, stowed the laptop under the front seat of my van, and we headed toward the restaurant. Rodrigo ordered a hamburger, I ordered veal marsala, and Sonia got the walleye filet, Minnesota's tastiest fish. She gave me a pleading look. "Do you think I could have a glass of wine?"

"Sonia. You've got to stop worrying about me. You can't stop me from drinking if I have a relapse. And you can't drive me into a relapse by having a drink yourself. It's my problem, not yours. Have a glass of wine. Have champagne if you want."

"That sounds good," she said.

I turned to the waiter, "A glass of champagne for my baby. A glass of plain water for me."

"I'm not your baby," she said, giving me an amused look, tilting her head down to the side, and looking at me from the corners of her eyes. "I'm not anybody's baby."

"It's a variation of an old Louis Prima song."

"Who's Louis Prima?"

"Oh, how quickly the great ones pass from memory!"

But she was too hyped up by the sale she'd made to have time for my views on yesterday's pop culture. I couldn't get in a word about Lars' journal because she was so effusive about the sale she'd just made, how it stemmed from her knowledge of art, how she herself had found the painting on a trip to Brazil, how the sale would help expand her clientele at the gallery, and how much more rewarding it was to work with adults who appreciated art rather than with twenty-year-olds who just took classes to fill out a graduation requirement. Her hands were in constant motion as she emphasized what she was saying or brushed the hair back from Rodrigo's forehead or touched her fingertips on the back of my hand. I was engrossed.

Then, without warning, she folded her hands on the table and changed the subject. "I am forgetting my manners, Jake. You must be getting bored listening to me babble like this."

We were sitting at the back of the restaurant next to the dark paneled wall and surrounded by people with grey and white heads. The three of us were the youngest people in the room.

"Jake, I need to ask you something I should have asked earlier."

So it wasn't about her manners.

"You seem to be a very ethical person, but you once said you had been in the business of helping mutual funds screw their customers. What did you mean?"

I drummed my fingers on the white table cloth in irritation. Every time we approached a deeper level of intimacy, some new hurdle seemed to pop up in her mind. I took a deep breath.

"Well, I didn't mean me personally. I just ran a small growth fund in a family of funds, so most of the practices were beyond my control. Say you bought $10,000 of XYZ Fund. You probably paid too much in fees. You paid too much in commissions if you bought it through a stock broker. You're probably paying for ill-disguised kickbacks masquerading as marketing costs that you don't know about. And you paid the closing price on the day you bought it. But big hedge funds might have bought it at the previous day's close, which dilutes the worth of your shares. Or the fund manager might use front running to trade his personal holdings in a stock before he makes the trades for the fund. All these hidden costs are microscopic and they are spread among thousands of share holders, so the extra cost to you each year might only be $20 or $30. You won't even notice it as long as the fund keeps going up in price. And that was my job, to keep the price going up. I shouldn't brag, but I was a very good at that." I scrutinized her face to see if she was impressed with my prowess, but she looked like her mind was wandering.

"I never had a down year. I beat my benchmarks every year, and the rewards were intoxicating. Good salary. Huge bonuses. Prestige. Awards for being Money Manager of the Year."

"So you didn't personally cheat your customers?"

"The worst thing I did was use letter stock to goose the price of my fund if I was in danger of not beating my benchmark."

"Letter stock?"

"Suppose, for example, you want to start your own art gallery and you need a million dollars to get it off the ground."

Her eyes lit up. Finally, I had her attention. "You incorporate and sell my fund a million shares at one dollar per share. Now the stock in your gallery, unlike something like, say, Exxon, doesn't flash by on the TV screen a hundred times a day. So there isn't any way to know what my stake in your gallery is worth at any given moment. Let's say that for me to beat my bench mark, the value of your gallery has to go up to three million dollars by year end. So I get somebody to buy a thousand of my shares at three dollars each, and presto; I can say that the rest of my shares are worth three million."

"Why would anybody pay you three dollars for a stock that is only worth one dollar?"

"Maybe he owes me a favor. Or maybe I just give him the money. My bonus in a good year is well over that $3,000."

She gave me a disappointed look.

"I'm not proud of it. But remember, I never did anything illegal. And nobody who bought my fund and held it for a year ever lost money. Some people made a lot of money. And those who bought in at the beginning made an enormous amount of money. Even if I hadn't goosed my returns with letter stock, my fund still would have been one of the best performers on Wall Street."

"Then why did they demote you?"

"I made a very expensive mistake. I was drinking heavily. I'd have a drink in the morning, then two or three at lunch, and one or two in the middle of the afternoon. When my wife would smell the liquor, she'd give me the cold shoulder, and I'd use that as an excuse to have more drinks. I must have been putting down a fifth of bourbon a day. I got careless and entered into one of those letter stock deals without checking it out thoroughly. The company I'd bought went belly up, and ten million dollars went down the drain. My fund was up so much that it still ended the year with a gain, but ten million dollars is a lot of money to lose just because somebody can't hold his liquor. My wife staged an intervention and my boss threatened to fire me unless I went to the treatment program here. But after I finished the program, they said they wanted to demote me to a lower position. So I quit."

"Would you have accepted that demotion if your wife would have taken you back?"

"She wasn't going to do that."

"Why not?"

"Would you have taken your husband back after what he did to you?"

"Are you telling me you had a mistress on the side? I will not live that way again, Jake. You have to understand that."

"My only mistress was booze. What I did was worse than having a mistress. It was the worst thing I ever did to anyone."

She stayed quiet, waiting for me to go on.

"Are you sure you want to know?"

She nodded her head yes.

"She invited two nieces to spend a weekend with us, and we

brought home a pizza. But before serving it, she wanted to do something else first. I can't even remember what it was. I got mad, because I wanted us to eat the pizza right away while it was hot. I guess I was one of those mean drunks you've heard about."

"I lived with one," she said. "My father-in-law."

"Anyway, we had a terrible fight, and I threatened to kill myself. I went into the bedroom where we used to keep a pistol, slammed the door shut, pulled out the gun, and fired a shot at the outside wall. It sounded like a bomb. I'll never forget the look on her face when she opened the door expecting to see a bloody mess and instead saw me sitting on the bed in perfect health."

Sonia's jaw dropped a notch, and Rodrigo stared wide-eyed.

"She took her nieces home and a few days later set up the intervention that coerced me into treatment. I don't know what happened to the gun. I've never had one since then."

Sonia didn't say anything. I don't know what I expected her to say. There wasn't a whole lot she could say.

"Outside of my family and AA, you're the only person I've ever told this to," I said. "And if you weren't getting serious about me, I wouldn't have told you."

We sat quiet for several minutes, and I was the one who had to break the silence.

"I'm no saint, Sonia, and I'm not trying to hide anything from you. But what I've become is just an ordinary businessman doing the best he can to stay sober and improve the financial lives of his clients. I don't know what more you want from me."

"I also don't know what I want from you, Jake. What you did to you wife appalls me, but I respect you having the courage to share it with me."

It wasn't until we were driving back to her duplex in the Midway neighborhood that I figured out how to tell her about Lars' secret storage place. I toyed with the idea of saying that

Lars had once told me of a secret storage place and asking her if she knew where it was. But after Simon accusing me of being a manipulative dry drunk, and after my admitting to Sonia how badly I'd treated my ex-wife, I wanted to avoid any shred of duplicity. I'd just have to tell her about the diary and let her react any way she wanted.

I parked in front of her duplex. "Could you let Rodrigo go ahead? I need to tell you something in private."

She gave Rodrigo the key and watched him go through the door, into the stairway, and up to their apartment before she turned to me. It only took me a moment to hand her the flash drive and tell her, but waiting for her to respond felt like an hour.

"You looked at Lars' private diary?"

"Yes."

"Did he talk about our coffee breaks?"

"Sonia, you've got to read the diary yourself. There's important information for you. You're in great danger."

"Did he talk about our coffee breaks?" She repeated the question, louder,

I paused for an instant.

"Did he talk about our coffee breaks?" She shouted it this time.

"Yes," I said sheepishly, looking down at the floor mats.

"Look at me, Jake."

I looked up. Her brown eyes no longer looked so enchanting.

"Why did you pry, Jake? That was my private life. Who gave you the right to snoop on me? Why did you do it?"

"Sonia, I'm sorry. But it wasn't your diary. It was Lars' diary, and it's now in the hands of the people who killed him."

But the more I talked, the madder she got.

"Maybe it was Lars' diary, but it was my life."

"Sonia, I'm sorry. I feel terrible. I was looking for clues about Lars' murder. What I found is that you might be the key to the whole mystery, and that puts you in great danger."

"Fuck the keys, Jake. All you wanted was to find out how to get me into bed. That is all you have been doing since you met me." She looked like she was about to say something more, but was holding back from crossing a line she wouldn't be able to cross back again.

"Why did you do it, Jake? I would have told you about Lars. I was planning to. I just hadn't figured out how. When you found out it was a journal, why didn't you just skip over the parts about me? That would have been the decent thing to do."

"I'm sorry, Sonia. I'm sorry for hurting you. But Lars' computer is now in the hands of the killers. And if that computer contains the same files that were on this flash drive, you are in great danger. You should not stay here alone."

"Forget that, Jake. You are not staying here tonight." She threw the flash drive on the floor, but she paused before she completely shut the door on our relationship.

"You did something terrible, Jake. I cannot trust you. Do not call me. I will call you when I am ready." She stepped out of the van. "I mean IF I am EVER ready." With that she slammed the door and the last thing I noted before she turned and marched toward her duplex was the hard, angry look in her eyes. I felt like I'd been kicked in the stomach.

I rolled down my window and stayed parked in front of her house until I saw the lights come on in her apartment bedroom. Through the open window of my car came the sound of Rodrigo playing his song on the piano.

If the killers were going to kidnap her or Rodrigo, would they break into her place through the front door or the kitchen door? When they'd burglarized Lars' house they'd gone in through the back. I drove to the alley behind her house and found a spot where I could keep an eye on the outdoor wooden stairs leading up to her second-floor kitchen door.

Sometime after midnight my eyelids started shutting on me, so I drove around to the front of her house in an effort to stay alert. Rolling down the window to let in some cold air that would keep me awake, I forced myself to keep watching the street and sidewalk. No black SUV came into sight and no one walked by. Feeling exhausted and useless, I finally gave up the vigil and went home.

XIV

Just before seven I phoned. "Don't hang up. You are in extreme danger on the streets and I want to follow you to your gallery to make sure that you get there in one piece. You don't even have to talk to me. Just tell me what time you leave."

Nothing but silence.

"Sonia?"

"Seven-thirty." The phone went dead.

Skipping my shower, I slipped into a business suit and no sooner arrived at her duplex than she and Rodrigo emerged on the porch and headed toward the garage at the back of her driveway. A thick fog hung in the air, and I had to stay almost on her rear bumper to keep her in sight. I parked right behind her at the James J. Hill Magnet School while she took Rodrigo inside. Since this school billed itself as an incubator for gifted youth, and drew criticism for that billing from some people whose children were denied admission, I was curious how Rodrigo had gotten admitted, given his Williams Syndrome. Of course, he did have a bent for music and he was bilingual, so maybe he fit right in with the other kids. But somehow I doubted it. While I was still pondering that, she came out of the building, stepped into her car, got onto I-94 and headed west toward Minneapolis.

She pulled into a curbside parking spot across from the art gallery, and I stopped on a crosswalk behind her. Instead of going directly to the gallery, she came toward my car. Wearing a tight, tan leather skirt that came down to the top of her knees, brown boots zipped up over the calves, a matching leather jacket curving over her hips, and a dainty silk scarf with little green and yellow images, she looked like an apparition coming through the fog that was hanging over Loring Park. She slid into the passenger seat of my car. Behind her, outside the car window, the skyscrapers of downtown Minneapolis rose and disappeared into the gray fog. She eyed me for half a minute before saying anything.

"You need a shave."

"I keep an eye on you halfway across town and all you can think to say is I need a shave?"

"I'm just trying to break the ice, Jake. It's awkward. Tell me what's going on. You call me with a scary message when I'm barely out of bed, before you even shave. And you spend half the night watching my house. What is this all about?"

"Who said I was watching your house?"

"I woke up about two in the morning and saw you sitting in your van."

"What makes you think it was me?"

"You were parked right under the street light, and I could see those for sale signs in your window." She smiled. "Jake, you're not very good at this dagger and cloak stuff."

I reached into my pocket and pulled out the flash drive she had thrown on the floor of the car the night before. "Will you please look at it, Sonia? You know something that Lars' killers want to find out, and it puts you in great danger."

"Just tell me what it said."

"Lars showed you his secret storage place, and that's what the killers want to pry out of you."

"They don't have to pry it. I will gladly tell them just to get them out of my life."

"It's not that easy. We don't know who they are, and they will assume that you have already looked at whatever it is in that storage place that is so threatening to them. If they got rid of Lars because of it, they might want to get rid of you as well."

She finally seemed to understand the danger she faced, because she slumped down in the passenger seat.

"Oh, meu Deus, Jake. What am I going to do?"

"I don't know yet," I said. "You're probably safe once you're in your apartment, what with all that security stuff we installed. Just don't be out anyplace alone. What time do you get off work today?"

"One-thirty. After that I'll be working at home until I pick up Rodrigo at school."

"Is it all right if I come back at one-thirty to follow you?"

She nodded, her chin tucking into the elegant silk scarf as she did so. The green and yellow images on her scarf were miniature Brazilian flags. Before saying anything more she stared out the windshield for a moment at the iron girder bridge over the pond in the middle of the park, barely visible in the fog.

"Jake, please forgive me for last night. I overreacted. I was very uneasy about what you did to your ex-wife, and I couldn't get rid of the idea that you might do the same thing to me some day. Then when you told me about that diary, I just lost my composure. I don't want to push you away, but I need some time to figure out if I am ready for a relationship with you."

"You did seem to be ready when we were on your couch the other night. Or was it just a big tease? Because that's what it felt like."

Her chin jerked up a little in shock, like she'd never been confronted so directly before.

"Jake, I wasn't teasing you. I just got carried away. Sometimes I get so lonely. It is hard raising a child by myself, and you don't realize how charming you can be. Then when Rodrigo came home and broke the spell, I realized that I wasn't ready yet."

"And if Rodrigo hadn't come home early?"

"If I wasn't ready, then something else would have broken the spell."

"Sonia, I don't want to push you away either, but there's a couple of things we have to get straight between us. First, there were extenuating circumstances when I did that to my wife. I was drunk then, but I've been sober for the past five years. The trouble is, I can't promise you I'll never get drunk again. All I can promise is that I won't touch a drop of alcohol for the rest of today. That's how I live, one day at a time."

"This is a big issue, Jake, and I need more time to think about it. What's the second thing?"

"When you described your marriage, it sounded like sex was your tool of choice to manipulate your husband. The other night you left me feeling like I'd been manipulated, and to be honest, I didn't like it. Then last night I felt like I'd walked into a buzz saw. If you end up being ready for me, is this the way it's going to be? Because if it is, I'd just as soon not go that direction in the first place."

She looked me directly in the eye, but her voice was soft and subdued. "No, Jake, that is not the way it's going to be. Just like there were extenuating circumstances for you, there were also extenuating circumstances when I did that to my husband. I was young and had no idea of the disaster I was creating. You have to understand how infuriating it was to live with a family of people who looked down on me. Even that might have been bearable if he'd only been able to engage me with the frankness that you're showing now. No, I was not teasing you the other night. It was intoxicating to have a man in my arms for the first time in ages, and I got carried away."

"What about the buzz saw I walked into last night?"

"Sometimes I overreact. I'll try to control it."

"You've got me confused, Sonia. You seem to want some kind of intimacy that you didn't get in your marriage, but every time I get too close, a wall goes up. I know I pushed the envelope when I read that diary, and I understand your reservations about my addiction. But have you ever known me to take a drink? Or try to hurt you? Or even to be callous to you?"

"Jake, except for reading that diary you've been wonderful to me. You never look down on me or on Brazil, like my ex did. And Rodrigo likes you. I would like to have a relationship with you, if it could be a serious one. But I don't know what you want. Is it a serious relationship, or just a one night stand?"

"Sonia, if all I wanted was a one-night stand, I never would have told you all those things about myself. This is already a serious relationship. The only question is whether we want to move it forward."

She paused for a long moment before responding. "We can move it forward, Jake. All I'm asking for is just a little more time to get comfortable with you. At least a few days or a week. Can you give me that?"

I raised my hands, palms out. "It's your call. I won't pressure you."

"Will the affair I had with Lars make any difference to you?"

"No."

She didn't look persuaded. "Jake, I had just left my husband and I was new at the college and Lars was friendly and . . . "

I interrupted. "Sonia, you don't have to explain. It doesn't matter to me. If I had an affair, would it matter to you?"

"I don't care about what happened in the past. What matters is what happens from this point on. Can I count on that?"

"Yes."

She pushed open the car door, but before stepping out, she said, "Could you work out of my apartment this afternoon?"

"What's changed?" I asked. "Last night you wanted to dump me and today you want me to spend the afternoon with you."

"This conversation helped."

"So we're OK?"

"We're OK." Then she smiled and added, "Meu amor."

"What's that mean?"

"It means whatever we want it to mean. Don't try to translate it. Just say it."

"Amor," I replied.

She leaned over for a kiss, then stepped out of the car and walked through the fog to the gallery entrance, her hips swinging seductively as she walked.

It was nearly two o'clock when we got back to her duplex that afternoon. She pulled a huge briefcase to the living room, sat in the middle of the floor, and began spreading out photographs. "These are photos of pieces for the art show in December that I told you about. It will feature undiscovered artists that we want to promote, and I need to sort through the photos."

I loosened my tie and sank into her couch to watch, but the lack of sleep from the night before caught up with me, and the hissing radiators lulled me into sleep. The next thing I knew my watch said three-thirty and I had the miserable, groggy feeling that comes with waking up from an afternoon nap.

She was still sitting on the floor, leaning against the dark wood post that separated the living area from the dining room, staring at the photos sorted in piles in front of her. The brown leather skirt had slid so far up her thighs I could see the soft bulge in the beige underpants she was wearing. When she spotted my eyes on her, she crossed her legs, shifted positions and tugged her skirt lower, giving me a frown as she did so. I couldn't tell if it was a frown of embarrassment at having accidentally flashed herself to me or a frown of annoyance at my looking.

"What are you doing now?" I asked.

"I'm trying different combinations of where I want to hang the art pieces. These are the walls of the gallery." She pointed to the arrangement of photos spaced out in four different spots from her far left side to her far right side. She shifted another photo from the side wall to the front. "What do you think?"

"You're asking the wrong guy. What I know about art you could put in a thimble and still have room left over. Do you mind if I get a glass of water?"

"There is some cola in the refrigerator if you want it."

I got the cola, came back to the couch, and watched her shift the photos around. It felt good lying on the couch, watching her work, and hoping the skirt would climb up her thighs again. My mind wandered.

"Sonia, I just thought of something."

She looked up.

"Earlier this week I had a conversation with Moneybags' administrative aide, a woman named Erika Bergstrom. She had a lot of questions about Lars' secret storage place and she was convinced that you know where it is."

"I do know where it is. So what?"

"Until now I just thought she was fishing around to see what she could find out. But what if somehow the killers got that information from Lars' computer, passed it on to Moneybags, and he prompted her to ask me about it?"

I thought she would hit the roof when I told her that, but she just grinned. "In that case, Jake, our troubles are over. I just tell you where the storage place is, you tell Erika Bergstrom, and we get the killers off our backs."

"Except that you haven't told me where the storage place is. And even if you did, I wouldn't pass the information on to Moneybags. I'm not going to be a spy."

"Not even if it meant getting us out of this mess?"

"Passing this information on to Moneybags wouldn't help. If he's not linked to the killers, they'd still be on our necks. And if he *is* linked with the killers, that means he *was* involved in Lars'

death. In that case it would be a grave mistake to let him think
you know anything at all about Lars' hiding places."

"You think that Radezewell is behind all of this?"

"Until this moment, it hadn't even occurred to me. All we
know is that Lars had something that is badly wanted by both
Moneybags and the killers. But the fact that both of them are
fishing around at the same time trying to get something out of us
makes me wonder."

"Jake, we have to tell the police."

"How? I can't accuse one of the state's most prominent businessmen of being a killer just because his administrative aide
wanted me to spy on you."

"But you have the flash drive with the diaries."

"Stolen property. I'd be up shit creek if I handed that over to
the police. Which reminds me, I've got to destroy it and get rid of
it. Do you have a hammer?"

"Under the sink."

Placing the flash drive on her counter top, I smashed it with
the hammer, tossed the pieces into her trash can, pulled out the
plastic liner, tied it, and replaced it with a fresh one. She
appeared in the doorway and asked, "What are you doing?"

"Getting rid of the flash drive."

She pulled her digital camera from her purse and took several pictures of the photo layout on the floor. Then she stuffed the
materials back into the leather case, leaned it against the desk,
and asked, "Are you coming with me to pick up Rodrigo?"

"Let me follow you. We need more practice at keeping close
to each other when we're driving."

We were standing under the wooden archway that divided
the living room from the dining area. She asked, "Do you still
have the Saint Jude medal I gave you?"

I pulled it out of my pocket and she smiled.

"You keep it around your neck, Jake, not in your pocket. I
told you that before."

She took the chain, placed it over my head and closed the clasp. "That's better," she said, almost as thought she was talking to a child.

"Do you really believe these charms will protect us?"

The warm smile slipped off her face and she gave me a serious look. "These are not charms, Jake." She lifted her fingers to the feega lying against her pink sweater. "This is a sacred religious relic to the Afro-Brazilians." Then she touched the St. Jude medal she had just draped over my neck. "And St. Jude has always heard my prayers, always helped me find a jaytoo. I don't ask that you believe in St. Jude, only that you not mock him and that you wear his medal until we find our jaytoo."

She tucked the medal under the collar of my shirt, then went to activate her security alarm.

"Before you do that," I said, "let me dump this stuff in the garbage. I'll meet you by the front porch."

I skipped down the back steps, walked to a neighbor's garbage can, and stuffed her plastic bag under a pile of trash. With that done, I jogged back to Sonia's building. As I came up to the front of the house, she was already walking to her car, and a large man in a leather jacket was striding toward her. But she got into her car and locked the door before he could reach her. He ran back to a green van and jumped inside. When Sonia spotted me stepping out from the side of the house, she waved and pulled out of her parking spot into the street. She hadn't seen the guy who was stalking her, and he apparently hadn't seen me. He let one car get behind her and then pulled in behind the two cars.

"Jesus." I sprinted to my van and took off in pursuit of the other van. She was headed west and would have to turn around to go toward the school. When she turned left at the next intersection, the van followed. Then when she turned left again to head east back toward the school, the van followed.

XV

I punched Sonia's number on my cell phone, but there was no answer. I punched it again. Still no answer. What's the point in having a cell phone in your car if you don't use it? The phone must be in her purse where she couldn't reach it. Finally she came to a red light, and seconds later she answered the phone.

"Sonia, it's Jake. You're being followed."

"Oh, meu Deus!" she said.

"It's a green van. Turn right onto Snelling Avenue when the light changes and see what he does."

The van waited at the red light long enough for another car to get behind Sonia and then turned right again to pick up her tail.

"He's still there," I said. "Do this. Before you reach I-94, leave enough room for me to pull alongside you in the curb lane."

She edged forward, making it easy for me to get beside her. I dropped back far enough to read the license plate on the green van which was now right on her tail. RET 873. I had nothing to write with, however, and I had to keep repeating the number so I wouldn't forget it. RET 873. I looked over at the driver who had a bandage over his right forehead, precisely in the spot where I had cracked the thug back in Lars' house. I pulled even with Sonia so she could see me, then backed off. RET 873. The freeway ramp was just ahead of her.

I shouted into the phone. "Sonia, cut in front of me and make a sudden turn onto the freeway. I'll block him from following you. And don't turn off the phone."

She stepped on the gas, shot in front of me, and roared down the entrance ramp. I jammed on my brakes, coming to a stop at the top of the ramp and blocking the van from following her. But there was a second ramp entrance only a few yards ahead to serve the crossover traffic. The van driver sped toward that entrance, made a ninety degree turn onto the ramp, skidding his wheels in the process, only to have to stomp on the brake to avoid hitting a big pick up truck that was moving leisurely down the ramp. Impatient, he jumped the curb and tried to pass the pickup on the left side. He bumped the door of the pickup to nudge it out of the way, but the weight of the truck pushed him back to the left. Just at that moment one of his front tires hit a broken concrete block lying by the side of the road. The combined impact of hitting the truck and the concrete block sent the van out of control. It rolled side over side down the grassy incline toward the freeway, coming to rest upside down on the pavement where a fast moving car in the right lane smashed into it, pushing it into the middle lane. Vehicles braked and swerved as they sought to avoid the accident, and in minutes the westbound side of I-94 ground to halt as the pile of cars around the accident grew.

I pulled off the pavement onto the shoulder of the ramp and picked my cell phone off my lap. She answered immediately.

"He had a bad accident, so you can slow down and head back to the school. Pick up Rodrigo, but don't go home. Bring him to my condo until we figure out what to do."

"Where do you live? You never told me."

I gave her the address. "Wait by the front door where the security guards can see you. I'll call and tell them to keep an eye out for you."

Sirens were wailing in the distance as I walked down the embankment and found several people pulling victims out of cars. The green van was lying upside down, its roof crunched, the driver hanging from his seat belt. I couldn't tell if he was alive, but his head was twisted at an odd angle against the roof of the vehicle. One bloodied woman was lying on the pavement, moaning. I took off my suit coat, folded it, and tucked it under her head. But other than trying to get that one woman a little less uncomfortable, I was totally useless. Disaster preparedness was not my strong point, and I sighed in relief when the paramedics showed up. They moved into a triage mode, giving their attention to the cases in which they could make the biggest difference.

Several police officers arrived and began directing traffic around the bottleneck. One cop was looking for witnesses, so I gave him my statement.

"So this guy who caused the pile-up was stalking your girlfriend?" the cop said.

"Yes."

"Where is she now?"

"Picking up her son at school. That's where she was headed when this guy got on her tail. It's probably the same guy who broke into my office."

"Your office was broken into?"

"Yes. Sergeant Brian Olson is investigating it."

"Look, we've got our hands full with this accident right now. Your break-in is going to have to wait. Give me the addresses for you and your girl friend and tell me whatever else you can about the accident and the guy in the van."

When I reached the condo, Sonia was parked by the main entrance, and I led her to the guest parking slot in the garage. She was so tense that her hands were squeezed into fists. As we stepped into the elevator, she whispered through clenched teeth, "Jake, what are we going to do?

She clasped an arm around Rodrigo's shoulder and held him tight to her side until the elevator came to a stop on the twelfth floor. Rodrigo ambled over to my living room window overlooking the Mississippi. She stepped after him, as if she was afraid he would fall through the window if she didn't catch him, but she came to a stop a good three feet away from the window. When she finally trusted that her son wasn't going to plunge through the glass, she looked out at the view in the distance. It wasn't Rio or Manhattan, but it wasn't shabby by any means. She directed Rodrigo's attention to downtown Minneapolis in the distance, the University of Minnesota, the bridges over the river, and the old nineteenth-century stone water tower that's shaped like a witch's hat. As she turned to join me she spotted the Thomas Kincaid picture on the wall across from my sofa. Her head moved almost imperceptibly back and forth in a puzzled gesture, but she didn't comment about my taste in art.

I walked to my phone sitting on the kitchen island counter, and as soon as I punched the message button, Erika Bergstrom's crisp voice came into the room. Hearing the name, Sonia came over to listen to the message with me. Next to the phone was the picture Rodrigo had snapped of Sonia and me by the lock and dam on the Mississippi. She gazed at it absentmindedly as she listened to the phone message.

"Jake, this is Erika Bergstrom. I was calling to see if you had anything for me. It might be useful for us to touch base again and compare notes. I hope you enjoyed yourself the other day."

Sonia gave me an icy look. "You said you had a conversation with her. This sounds like a lot more than a conversation."

I replied immediately. "This morning you said you didn't care about what happened in the past. Do you still stand by that?"

She looked over at Rodrigo to make sure he was too far away to hear our conversation. "Yes. After what happened today, whatever you or I did in the past is of small importance. I do care, however, whether you're still involved with her, and I'm asking that you be frank with me about that."

"I am not involved with Erika Bergstrom, even though we went to bed once. There is no possibility that I will ever get involved with her under any circumstances. And despite how she sounded on the phone, the only thing she really wants from me is for me to spy on you. Is that frank enough?"

"Maybe a little more frank than I wanted. Don't be mad at me, Jake. I'm petrified next to that window, and my hands are still shaking from the car chase. You are my only hope at the moment, and I need to know if I can count on you."

"I promise that you can count on me. And that chase, as horrible as it was, might turn out to be a blessing."

"I don't see how."

"After that guy who stalked you gets patched up, the police are going to get a lot of information out of him. By the time they are finished, they could have this case solved."

"Oh Jake, I hope so," she said.

I reached over to the kitchen island counter top and picked up the envelope that Jim Anderson had given me earlier in the week.

"Would you take a moment to look over this stuff on meth and money laundering that Jim Anderson gave me the other day? It would be nice to get your take on it. While you look at that, Rodrigo and I will throw something together for dinner. Is that OK?"

"That would be nice," she said, slumping onto my couch and dumping the contents of Jim Anderson's envelope into her lap, right on top of that tight, brown leather skirt that had ridden more than halfway up her thigh.

I led Rodrigo into the kitchen and pulled a box of steaks from the freezer. "Think your mother would like this?"

He looked at the picture of sizzling steaks on the box and nodded yes, a big smile on his face. "OK," I said and pointed to the bottom cupboard. "Look in there for something we can put these in to thaw."

He hunted out a baking dish, while I pulled out three potatoes, washed their skins, and got three skewers to push through them for baking. Meanwhile, Rodrigo was softly piling pots and pans on the kitchen floor as he searched for a baking dish. I was struck by the quiet and meticulous way that he worked. He finally brought a metal pie tin over to me and held it up with an expectant smile.

"Perfect," I grinned as I put the steaks in it to thaw. "Can you find us another one?"

Back he went to the cupboard. More pots added to the pile on the floor. He bumped his head backing out of the cupboard and brought another pie tin. I handed him the potatoes to put in the tin. We set them into the oven and turned on the timer.

"Now," I said, "we need something special to go with this." I bent over and whispered so Sonia couldn't hear. "Something Brazilian." After my first breakfast with Sonia at the Day by Day, I had scoured the supermarket for something Latin American, and had discovered hearts of palm, imported from Costa Rica. If the Costa Ricans eat hearts of palm, other Latin Americans must do so as well. To make sure, I showed Rodrigo the picture on the can and asked, "You ever eat these?"

"Oh yeah," he said, smiling. "Vovaw gives them to us all the time when we go to Rio."

"Vovaw?"

A slight smile came to Rodrigo's face as he seemed amused at my language deficiencies. "That's what we call a grandma in Rio," he said.

I noted that he didn't say that's what they call a grandma in Rio. It was fascinating to me that, whereas I thought of him as American, he obviously considered himself Brazilian, or at least part Brazilian. I handed him a can opener to open the hearts of palm. While he was busy winding the can opener around the lid,

I washed several leaves of lettuce, broke them into bite sized pieces and mixed them with slices of green onion. Rodrigo finished opening the can of palm hearts. He didn't spill a drop of the juice, but I spilled quite a bit of it on the floor as I put the palm hearts on a cutting board to slice them. Putting all the ingredients into a plastic storage container, I sprinkled lemon juice over the top and shook the container to mix up the salad, and put it in the refrigerator to keep until dinnertime. Then I pulled out a cookbook, mixed a cup of tarragon french dressing and put it aside to pour over the salad when it was ready to serve.

Rodrigo wandered back to the living room and stared out again at the downtown skyline. Sonia appeared in the kitchen doorway, shaking her head when she spotted the mess on the floor. She edged close to me as she returned Jim Anderson's envelope. "I can't concentrate, Jake. I am so frightened. What if they try to kidnap Rodrigo?"

"That's probably what they were up to. If they could kidnap the both of you and get their hands on Rodrigo, you'd be forced to do anything they wanted."

She shuddered. Between the whiff of her perfume and her face only inches away, I wanted to stand next to her like that for eternity. But I got back to the task at hand. "We've got to get him some place safe until the police get some useful information out of that guy who stalked you. Could he stay with his father for a few days?"

"I could call him and see what he thinks."

"Why don't I take Rodrigo down to the exercise room and give you a little privacy to make the call?"

She nodded, and Rodrigo beamed when I invited him to try out the exercise room with me. I tried to lighten the mood, so I said to the boy.

"Do you want me to call you Rodrigo or Roderick?"

He looked surprised, as if it was the first time he'd ever been given a choice of what to be called. "Rodrigo," he said. "But you have to say it right."

"I did. I said 'Rodrigo.'"

"No. You said 'RODrigo.' You have to say 'RowDRIgo,'" he said, pronouncing the letter R almost like an H. He looked me straight in the eyes, like a teacher correcting a student.

"RowDRIgo," I repeated.

"That's better," he replied.

Sonia was smiling at this exchange. "Well, as long as he corrects my English, it's only fitting that he should also correct your Portuguese."

I led him out the door. "Let's go, Champ."

XVI

In the exercise room I helped Rodrigo adjust the weights on the machines to a level that he could lift for a dozen repetitions. He tried out the elliptical machine and almost fell off the treadmill when it got going too fast.

Watching him got boring after a few minutes, so I pulled out my cell phone and called directory assistance for Jim Anderson's number. The weight room was a dead spot, but when I moved into the doorway, the reception got better. Just then I had to run over and catch Rodrigo as he started to fall off the treadmill again. I set him up on the stationary bicycle and picked up the phone I'd dropped on the floor.

"Where'd you go," demanded Jim. "First, you call me, then you disappear."

"I hit a dead spot," I said. "Did you get the stuff I sent you?"

"Yeah. But I might have to get a new financial advisor."

"Well, I win some and I lose some. But you wanna give me a reason why?"

"I told you. I need to double my money fast. You apparently can't do that."

"That's true. So good luck on finding your new advisor. But that's not why I called."

"What do you mean, good luck? Aren't you going to try and keep me as a client? Make me a better deal?"

"What better deal is there? I gave you my honest advice and didn't charge you anything."

"Well, OK. I'll think about it. Did you read those clippings I gave you?"

"I did. They covered what you told me earlier, but in a lot more detail. You did a tremendous amount of work." It's a good idea never to pass up an opportunity to give someone an honest compliment, especially if you might need his cooperation.

"So, why'd you call?"

"A couple of things. First, did you ever do any stories on the fake drivers licenses that the kids under the drinking age get?"

"Yeah, why?"

"Can you lead me to anybody involved in that? I'm not asking you to betray a source. Just tell me somebody who's done it or knows somebody who's done it."

He took a moment to look up something and then said, "Call this number and ask for Sonny. But don't let him sell you a thirty-footer."

"A thirty-footer?"

"That's what they call a phony ID that's done so badly the cops can spot it from thirty feet. You gonna tell me what this is all about? A recovering alcoholic isn't the kind of guy to help underage kids buy their booze."

"I just want to talk to someone who can tell me how it's done. It might help me make some sense out of some things that have happened lately."

"Like what kind of things?"

"Let me run through them for you."

I sat on the floor and leaned back against the door jamb to keep an eye on Rodrigo while I brought Jim Anderson up to date on the events of the last few days, without, of course, mentioning that I had broken into Lars' house and swiped his flash drive.

"What do you think?"

"I think you ought to tell the police about the secret storage place."

"Then they'd want to know how I found out about this, and that could put me in deep water. Very deep water."

There was a long pause on the other end of the line. Then Jim said, "Jake, don't say things like that over the phone. You wouldn't be the first guy whose phone was bugged by the police, and I'd like you you to stay out of jail until I get these two stories nailed down."

"Two stories?"

"Well, the first is a gas. Millionaire philanthropist murders his money laundering, drug running, blackmailing accomplice and terrorizes a lonely immigrant trying to raise a disabled child."

"Blackmailing?"

"Why else would they kill Lars? If it had just been something he stole, they could have recovered it without the publicity and police investigation that a murder unleashes."

"In any case," I said, "We've got nothing more than a coincidence to link Moneybags to the murder. So it's a stretch. What's the second story?"

"Paul Wellstone's plane is brought down by a transmitter operated by a money-laundering, drug-running college professor and a millionaire philanthropist."

"You're in fantasy land. Not only is there no evidence that Moneybags did that, we don't even have any reason to suspect it."

"If a reporter waited until he had proof to follow up on a lead, he'd never have a story. We start with suspicions and then follow up until we get proof or the story falls apart. From what you've just told me, these two stories aren't even close to falling apart. And you, since you're not willing to tell the police what you know, are going to be lucky if you and your girlfriend aren't forced to watch each other's fingers get cut off. Or worse yet, watch the boy's fingers get cut off."

I glanced over at Rodrigo who was spinning away on the bicycle.

"How'd you find out about the fingers?"

"I told you. I'm a reporter. People tell me things. Even you are starting to share things with me, for which I'm grateful."

"Hold on a second!" I dropped the phone on the floor to catch Rodrigo who looked like he was about to fall as he got off the stationary bicycle. I put him on the treadmill and then picked up the phone. "I'm back. I've got one more piece of news for you."

"What?"

"Lars had a brother who lives in Eveleth. He might have some idea of what Moneybags and the killers wanted so badly from Lars. The trouble is that he and Lars had a falling out over finances, and since I was Lars' financial planner, I don't think he'd open up to me. An experienced interviewer from the press, however, might be able to get him talking."

"I've always wanted to see the Iron Range. Could you help me with the gas?" he said.

"Help you with the gas? I thought you just got $10,000 from a law suit."

"You told me to put that aside for a rainy day."

What a leach, I thought. "When can you go?"

"I'll leave right now, talk to him tomorrow, and be back by Monday."

"Could I reimburse you on Monday? I've got my hands full right now."

"I can only imagine what you've got your hands full of. Monday's fine. What are you going to do while I'm gone?"

"Maybe I should see Erika again. Get her someplace where she might talk more freely. She seemed a little inhibited the last time."

"That's not how you described her a minute ago."

"Well, not inhibited in what she was doing, more in what she was telling me."

What'd she say to make you think that?"

"It was more what she didn't say. When I mentioned Money-bags' links to a school that was calling itself the Stanford on the Mississippi, she just rolled her eyes. It was like she wanted to tell me something, but she was afraid she'd be overheard."

"Maybe you're right. Talk to her, and let's keep in touch."

"We will. We've got the basis of a good partnership here," I said.

"How so?"

"Well, if you are right and we prove it, you get your Pulitzer Prize story. And I get something even better."

"What's that?"

"I get to stay alive."

"One other thought," said Jim. Your girlfriend's not going to like it when she finds out you revisited Erika Bergstrom who, it sounds like, has already spent an hour rubbing her tits against you."

"Are you threatening to tell her?"

"Nope. I make it a cardinal rule to stay out of my friends' personal lives. But you wouldn't want to bet a lot of money that Erika Bergstrom has any such rule."

"No go," Sonia said solemnly when I brought Rodrigo back to the condo. She put him in front of the television and then came back to the kitchen to talk with me while I put the steaks onto the broiler rack in the oven and finished preparing the dinner. Now that she'd accepted the need to get the boy some place safe, she was disappointed that her ex-husband had failed to come through. "He is going to a conference and will not be back until Thursday. I asked him to cancel it, but he is presenting a paper and chairing a panel."

"Did you tell him Rodrigo's in danger?"

"Of course," she said, exasperated that I hadn't given her credit for thinking of that. "He accused me of just wanting to get rid of Rodrigo so I could be alone with you. He even mentioned my blouse being buttoned wrong when he saw you in my apartment."

Sonia's ex was either a nasty piece of work or was still carrying a torch for her. Or both. But that was an issue for the two of them to deal with, not me. "Sonia, until the police identify that guy who was following you and find out what he was up to, I don't think you and Rodrigo should stay alone in your apartment. You could stay in my guest bedroom here. And I will not pressure you into anything."

"I'm not sure that would be any safer. I called a women's shelter to see if Rodrigo and I could get in there. But it's full. So I called my friend Dora. She will put us up tonight and tomorrow until I can figure out something."

"Well, let me follow you over there."

"Thank you," she said. "I'd feel safer."

"I shouldn't tell you this, but my knocking out that thug at Lars' house was a fluke. I'm a jogger, not a fighter. So I don't know how much safer you'll be with me."

"So why shouldn't you tell me that?"

"Well, you're Latin. You might want your men to be macho."

"I've had my fill of macho men," she said, staring me in the eye. "Whatever you do, Jake, do not turn macho on me."

We sat at the table and Sonia beamed in delight at the hearts of palm salad, but she just picked at the steak and baked potato.

Not bothering to clean up the dishes, I moved to the sofa in the living room to switch on the TV news. There was graphic footage of the pile-up on I-94. The narrator attributed the accident to road rage. "The van caused a collision when it tried to pass a pick-up truck on the entrance ramp to I-94." The camera panned over to the pick-up with a dent in its left door, and the narrator continued talking. "After striking the pick-up, the van spun out of control and rolled down the incline into traffic. The driver, who was pronounced dead on arrival at Region's Hospital, had no identification, and the van had been reported stolen earlier in the day."

Sonia and I sat on the sofa staring open mouthed at the TV screen. "Oh, Jake," she said. "The cops don't know any more now than they did at the beginning. We are back where we started."

I followed Sonia's Escort back to her duplex where she filled a suitcase with a two-day supply of clothes and toiletries for herself and Rodrigo. I carried it down to her car and followed her to Dora's house by Lake Harriet in south Minneapolis.

Before she could get out of her car, I went to the driver's window, and she rolled it down. "Before you go in, there's a couple of things I need to bring up."

She waited for me to go on.

"I told my friend Bob that Rodrigo would be coming with me to the amusement park at the Mall of America on Sunday. Can I bring him?"

"Will he be safe?"

"There will be two of us next to him all the time. And Bob is a huge, powerful guy from the iron mines. Nobody in his right mind would mess around with him."

"We'll be out of church about eleven-thirty. You can pick him up there." She gave me the location. "And if you need to reach me in the meantime, you have my cell phone number."

"There's one more thing I have to do, and you're not going to like it," I said.

She gave me that suspicious look I'd seen so much of over the past twenty-four hours.

"I'm telling you now, because I don't want you finding out about it after the fact." I was still shell shocked from the ferocity of her reaction to my looking through Lars' diaries, and I didn't want a repeat treatment.

"Well, tell me," she said, turning off the car's ignition.

"I have to have another talk with Erika Bergstrom."

"You don't need my permission to speak to another woman," she said testily. "But why that woman?"

"I'm not asking your permission. I'm just trying to be up front with you. She could help us find out if Moneybags is linked to the killers."

"If she didn't tell you anything before, why will she tell you something now?"

"If I find out anything at all, we'll be in a better position to protect ourselves than we are in now."

She just gave me a cold stare without saying anything.

"All right. If you object, I won't do it. But if you do object, then you have to come up with a better idea."

That made her pause, as I knew it would, because there was no better idea. It was a long pause. She just sat staring out the windshield, her hands clutching the steering wheel at the ten and two o'clock positions. When I didn't say anything else, she turned her head to me and said in a voice quiet enough that Rodrigo, in the passenger seat, could not hear, "Jake, from the tone of her voice in that message she left for you, there is no doubt that she wants to seduce you. And that makes me very uneasy. But after the conversation we had this morning, I can't dictate who you talk to or don't talk to. That's no way to start a relationship. I have to trust you."

That didn't sound like a wholehearted trust.

"But you are going off to talk with a woman who is clearly bent on getting you into bed again. I need to be blunt about one thing, and then I'm never going to say another word about this. I won't share you, Jake. You can have me, or you can have other women. But you can't have both. I will not live that way again. It was the most painful thing in my life. And I'm begging you, don't do that to me, Jake." She turned her eyes back toward the windshield as a signal that she had no more to say.

I waved to Rodrigo in the passenger seat. We'll see you Sunday, Champ." I leaned my head inside the car window until my face was just inches away from Sonia who was still staring out the windshield. She didn't turn her lips toward me, so I gave her a kiss on the cheek. I was struck by the realization that her last word to me was not "Amor." I pushed away from the door and went back to my van, not exactly prancing with a skip in my step.

XVII

At noon on Saturday, I called Erika. She wasn't in, so I left a message and went jogging, taking my five mile run out the Minneapolis side of the Mississippi and back the St. Paul side. The trees had lost most of their leaves, the air was crisp, and the sky was overcast. It seemed more like November than October. While I was gone, Erika had left a message on my machine instructing me to call her back, which I did.

"Erika, we've got to talk. I've found out some things you might find interesting, and I need your reaction. Where could we meet?"

"How about the Black Forest? Do you know where it is?"

It was a German restaurant on the edge of the Uptown area of Minneapolis, the one neighborhood in the entire region with the most aura of a big city. Three story brick apartment buildings, a multitude of shops lining the sidewalks, a wide choice of ethnic restaurants, and a population drawn from every conceivable sexual preference, lifestyle choice, and political ideology. A neighborhood, in short, to awaken nostalgia in a transplanted New Yorker like me. But the restaurant wasn't right for the business we needed to conduct.

"We need a place with more privacy. Would you come to St.

Paul?" A long pause on her end of the line suggested to me that she didn't find the idea very appealing, but she didn't reject it outright.

"What did you have in mind?"

"The grill at the St. Paul Hotel."

I got there before Erika and slipped the hostess a sizable tip in exchange for a good table. When Erika came in, the hostess led us to a spot overlooking Rice Park. With the classic facades of the public library and the nineteenth century courthouse on the sides of the park and the lights of the contemporary, glass fronted Ordway Theater across from us, we had a front row view of the horse drawn carriages toting couples under thick blankets through the crispy night air. I hoped that the atmosphere of the locale would make Erika feel it had been worth the effort of driving all the way over from Minneapolis. But she didn't comment.

She ordered a black Russian and looked surprised when I ordered a cola. "Jake," she said, "have a drink and relax. We're not enemies."

"I'll just stick with this."

"You're not a teetotaler?"

"Nothing that bad. I'm alcoholic, and I'm trying to stay sober." When they hear that line, most people either shut up because they don't know what to say or rattle on about how brave you are to be fighting your addiction. In Erika's case, it shut her up. And that was the first honest reaction she'd shown since I met her. It almost made me feel good about her.

"I still haven't found your documents," I said, "but I did find out some things you ought to know."

"OK," she said, nodding her head, her long blond hair shifting slightly back and forth as she nodded. She had just enough makeup to accent her flawless Scandinavian features, and she wore a low-cut dress with a very attractive cleavage that caught my attention.

"Jake, I said OK," she repeated.

"Sorry, I got distracted."

She smiled, knowing full well it was her cleavage that had distracted me. Sometime I would like to spend a day strolling around in the body of a beautiful woman just to see what it is like to have people stumble and fawn in your presence. Sort of like I was doing now.

With effort, I brought myself back to my task. "There's been some strange things going on, Erika. My office and Lars' home were broken into, and Sonia's being stalked."

"What does all that have to do with me?"

"I'm not sure what it has to do with you, except that your boss has an inordinate interest in Sonia, and I wouldn't be surprised if he had a hand in these things."

"What makes you think that?"

"I'll tell you what I know. Don't ask me how I found it out. But if I were you, I'd get a new job. In California or some place as far away from Moneybags as possible. Maybe even Mexico."

"Why would I do that? I get paid very well."

"Before Lars was murdered, he had some very suspicious cash transactions with Moneybags that will draw the attention of the IRS, if they ever find out. And with the police pouring over his financial records, some of it is bound to get passed on to the IRS. Maybe Lars was blackmailing Moneybags over this and the evidence supporting that blackmail is what Moneybags is so eager to get back."

"I've never heard of anything about blackmail. However, Lars and Mr. Radezewell did have a falling out barely a month ago."

"So I ask myself, what were Lars and Moneybags up to? You told me Radezewell's looking for respectability. But why is he so suddenly anxious to get respectability now when he didn't care about it before? How is he making his money now, and what did Lars have to do with it?"

"He buys distressed companies, breaks them into pieces, and

sells off the pieces. If he does it right, the whole process generates enough cash to pay off the money he borrowed for the buyout and give him a nice profit. Then he contracts with someone like you to get him a decent return on the cash until the next buyout opportunity comes along."

"How did Lars fit into all of that?"

"He was a genius at spotting the opportunities and analyzing whether the pieces were worth more than the whole. Mr. Radezewell would contract with Lars to oversee the analysis."

"If Lars was doing that, then why did he need to keep working as a college professor and run a string of laundromats?"

"The buyouts do not take place often enough that Lars could count on full time work from Mr. Radezewell. Besides, he didn't really want to work full-time at it. He didn't have the personality to be a desk-bound bean-counter."

"What's he working on now?"

"Mr. Radezewell?"

"Yes."

"Something totally different. He bought up a lot of lakeshore property in the Boundary Waters Canoe Area and plans to build a world class resort where wealthy people can go for conferences, retreats, vacations, yachting, or hunting trips into Canada. He's already bought a pontoon plane he's been using to ferry potential investors back and forth."

She sipped from her black Russian and continued.

"You've heard of the Bohemian Grove in California where important bigwigs go for retreats. This is going to be Bohemian Grove North."

"It'll never work. Why would anybody go freeze their ass at a Bohemian Grove in the Boundary Waters instead of going to the real thing in California?"

"There's a ten year waiting list to join the Bohemian Club in California. So there's a lot of people in the Midwest and elsewhere who'd jump at the chance for something like this."

"Even if they did, it still wouldn't work. Motor traffic in the Boundary Waters is tightly restricted. They'll never be able to use those yachts and planes you were telling me about."

"His property is on the edge of the Boundary Waters. All he needs are flyover rights and a few variances, and he spends a lot of time in Washington lobbying Congress for that. Think of it, Jake. This is the last pristine area in the continental U. S. A lot of rich people would like to see it, but they aren't thrilled about driving all the way up there and rubbing shoulders with a bunch of outdoors men from middle America. Mr. Radezewell will fly them in, give them a yacht to fish from, let them sleep in a luxury hotel, and give them a forum where they can get to know each other in private without a bunch of newspaper reporters snooping around. Lobbying Congress for the right to do this is perfectly legal."

"If it's all legal, why is he strong arming Sonia and me?"

She shrugged. "I don't know that it's him. Maybe it's somebody else. But I can tell you that she should have been a little more restrained at that banquet. Mr. Radezewell does not react easily to insults."

"Another thing I'm curious about: you're a lot more forthcoming here than you were in your home. What gives"

"Well, nothing that I've told you is secret. You just haven't read about it yet because we haven't started the public relations campaign. But none of it is secret."

She stopped talking and I asked, "Anything else?"

"I shouldn't tell you this, Jake. But I think my apartment might be bugged. So I'm careful of what I say there."

"Why would you think your apartment is bugged?"

"Because my office at work is bugged."

"Does Moneybags know you know this?"

"No. I discovered it by accident."

"So you and I were taped?"

"Possibly."

"And are you going to send those tapes to Sonia?"

"I'm not. I don't even know if any tapes exist."

"But knowing we might have been recorded, wasn't it a little unnerving for you to have sex with me?"

She looked at me like I was a shiny faced boy scout. "It's my job, Jake. I work the soft side of the business. And when I'm dealing with an attractive man like you, it is a very pleasant job. Some of the clients aren't much fun to entertain, though." She took a sip of the black Russian.

I must have looked shocked, because she laughed at me. "It's a tough world out there, Jake. Some of us aren't brilliant money managers. And we've got to make do with the assets we've got." She signaled the waitress for another black Russian, her third. She leaned forward to push her empty glass toward the end of the table, giving me a wonderful view of her assets. She was not wearing a bra and it was a very warming sight. "Don't judge me, Jake. If you're going to stare down my dress like that, don't judge me."

"I'm not judging you. I take the world as it is. In fact I'm beginning to like you and your new openness. I don't know why I'm beginning to like you, since it's probably your boss who is making my life a nightmare. But I'll tell you this. If you're smart, you'll get out. Get out while you can. Moneybags is skating on thin ice, and when the ice cracks, there's no telling how many people are going to fall through with him."

"I'm beginning to like you, too, Jake." She lifted her glass to me. "And I do have one other piece of information for you."

I pushed my jaw forward slightly, signaling for her to continue.

"What you asked me about. Mr. Radezewell didn't see anybody that day. He wasn't even in town. He'd just come back from Washington."

"Washington? What was he doing there?"

"I don't know. At first I thought he was lobbying Congress on the Boundary Waters. But that doesn't make sense, because he didn't stay in town at the Hay Adams where he usually stays. He stayed way in the hell out in McLean. When he got back on the twenty-fourth, he took Lars up north to visit the U. S. Hockey Hall of Fame."

I was so stunned I dropped my fork and it landed on my plate with a loud clink. A woman at the table next to us looked over.

"Jake, what's so shocking about that?"

She hadn't pieced together the significance of McLean, the date, and the location of the U. S. Hockey Hall of Fame. I didn't see any point in giving her clues. "Nothing," I lied. "I just got a sharp pain in my tooth. I think I might have cracked it." I clearly don't have the imagination to be a good liar. How could anybody crack his tooth munching on au gratin potatoes?

"Jake, there's something else you should know." She took a long sip from the black Russian, half emptying it, before she put her elbows on the table, and tapped the glass lightly with her fingertips.

"What?"

"It's probably not Mr. Radezewell who did the stalking and burglary you told me about. But if he is the one who behind it, then you and your girl friend should be very careful. He hates you both. I've known him once or twice to hire people who are very mean to get people to tow the line."

"I appreciate the warning. But why are you telling me this?"

She twirled her black Russian glass on the table cloth and bent her head down before looking at me from out of the corner of her eye. "I'm betting that you're not the type to run back to Mr. Radezewell with anything I've told you. If what you told me about the IRS is true, Radezewell Enterprises might not be as fun to work in as it has been. Besides, I know too much. I am the only one in the organization who knows all these connections between you, Lars, your girlfriend, the Boundary Waters, the income tax evasion, and these strong-arm tactics you say are being used on you. Other people might know pieces, but I'm the only one who knows it all. If things start falling apart, I'd like to have a few well-placed friends outside of the organization."

"I might not be much help to you. I'm just a money manager, not a tycoon with big connections. But as I said before, if I were you, I'd get as far away from that son-of-a-bitch as I could. Mexico might not even be far enough. Go to Australia. At least you won't have to learn a new language there."

We ate mostly in silence after that. She ordered a fourth black Russian. "Are you driving?" I asked.

"I took a cab," she said. "But I could use a ride home."

XVIII

At Sonia's church the next morning, people were milling by the front entrance where the priest was standing, shaking hands, and chatting with those who passed by, half of whom appeared to be African-American. This made her easy to spot, because her complexion, which always struck me as dark—almost cinnamon colored—made her look pale in comparison to most of the people around her. She had the silver chain with the feega around her throat, and she wore a demure looking multi-colored dress with very feminine ruffles on the cuffs of the sleeves. She was talking to another woman, and Rodrigo was at her side sipping from a cup of juice. Given the tenseness of our previous conversation about Erika, I felt anxious about what to say to her. But she introduced me to her friends as though there were no tension whatever between us. "Jake, this is my friend Dora and her husband Pedro."

Dora smiled as she extended her hand to me, then turned to Sonia and let loose with a string of words in Portuguese.

"What?" I asked.

They both laughed and replied together, "Nothing." Dora's husband shook his head in bemusement.

I looked down at Rodrigo. "She said you are a charming jewel."

Sonia blushed slightly at Rodrigo's translation, and I pulled her aside to tell her about my dinner with Erika, hoping it wasn't going to become a sore point. "Sonia, I've got to assure you that nothing happened."

She lifted her right hand and waved her index finger back and forth a couple of times. "Wait, Jake. I have no questions about last night. True, I didn't like your meeting that woman, but I went down the path of jealousy once before with my ex, and I'm not going there again with you. Just tell me if what you found out was worth the anxiety you put me through? Is it going to help us out?"

"Yes. But you'd better hold on to your hat while I tell you."

"I don't need to know the details right now, Amor. You can tell me tonight."

She led me by the hand to introduce me to the priest, a huge, bruiser of an Irishman with an infectious, welcoming grin, who looked like he also had the hots for Sonia. Then we went back to her friend Dora.

"So I can take Rodrigo to the Mall of America?"

"Oh, I wish you had never mentioned it, Jake. He's so excited that I can't disappoint him. But I'm afraid to let him out of my sight. I'm going to go with you. I already called in sick at the gallery. We will drop off my car at my apartment and then I will ride with you."

Rodrigo climbed into my BMW, we picked up Sonia at her duplex, and then we headed for the amusement park at the Mall of America. I hadn't felt so giddy in years. I was falling head over heels for a woman whom I had yet to see naked. It violated all logic. But I hadn't felt this exhilarated since I was a teenager. Sonia rolled down her window and let her long, black hair blow in the cold October breeze. When we got up to freeway speed, she rolled up the window, turned, and smiled at me

We caught up with Bob Vukovich at the Sears entrance to

the Mall of America and parked our cars together in the small lot across from Sears. The three boys whom Bob had brought noted Rodrigo's slightly asymmetrical face and all-too-eager grin, and they stayed back from him. His face lit up as the amusement rides came into view, but he clamped his hands over his ears at the noise as we entered the area. "He's very sensitive to noise," Sonia reminded me, "and it'll take him a moment to adjust."

When they got to the first ride, the other boys jumped into one car together, and Rodrigo had to ride alone. He looked hurt by the snub, and Sonia's face screwed up like she was about to cry. But Rodrigo smiled once the ride started moving. He got disoriented getting off the ride, and a look of panic crossed his face until Sonia shouted over to him, telling him how to get to the exit.

As the boys moved from ride to ride, Bob, Sonia, and I did not have much to do other than keep an eye on them. After a few moments, I got bored, but Sonia looked anything but bored. She was anguished each time the other three boys tried to avoid sitting next to Rodrigo on a ride. Then when the ride was over and it was time to move to a new ride, she hovered over him with the intensity of a mother bear watching a cub.

Bob went off to get a coffee while I sat alone with Sonia on a bench, watching the boys zoom around on the roller coaster. Rodrigo laughed in delight as his roller coaster car paused at the top of a hill and then plunged toward the dip that was right in front of where Sonia and I were sitting. "When it comes to heights, that kid is fearless," I said loudly to Sonia. I had to talk loudly to be heard over the noise of the amusement park. I was smiling at her in appreciation of Rodrigo's fearlessness.

"Jake," she said, nodding her head toward Bob walking back toward us with a coffee in his hand, "I don't trust him."

"Why not?"

"I don't know why. It is just a feeling. I want to get Rodrigo out of here right now, and you should arrange to pick up your shoe boxes of money from Bob."

When I weighed her vague feelings against five years of experience with an old friend, I had to trust the history of experience. But if she wanted to get Rodrigo out of there, that is what we had to do. "After this ride, we'll steer them to the Legos area, then we'll get them an ice cream and leave."

"What about the shoe boxes?" she said.

"What'll I do with them? I can't just stick them in my hall closet. The police can search my place any time they want."

"Stash it with your lawyer like you originally planned."

"I changed my mind about that."

She gave me a look of extreme disappointment and said, "You should come to your senses, Jake, and give that money to your lawyer. But until you do, I will show you how to hide it. I learned a lot about hiding things from Lars. And remember, he was the Michelangelo of hiding things."

We walked to the Lego display where there were thousands of green, red, yellow, blue, and black tiles, and you could take as long as you wanted to build whatever you fancied. "What should we make?" I asked Rodrigo.

"An airplane!" he said.

For me, playing with the Legos was the best part of the outing. It wasn't much of a plane that we put together, but it did have wings, a fuselage, and a tail. I found a Lego propellor, but Rodrigo said, that it was a jet plane. He picked it up and began flying it through the air, quietly humming a song as he did so.

I edged over to Bob and asked when I could come by to pick up the shoe boxes.

"I'll be home tonight," he said.

I glanced at Sonia who looked so tense watching Rodrigo that I wasn't sure she would want to be left alone.

"Tomorrow would be better. How about eight o'clock?"

As we headed back toward the exit, Rodrigo spotted the glass elevator moving down from the top of the four story atrium.

"I want to ride the elevator, Momma. Let's ride the elevator."

Sonia looked up at the glass enclosed cage and said, "There is no way I will get inside that thing."

"Please, Momma!" said Rodrigo.

"Let me take him," I said. "You can wait down here with Bob, while I just take him up and back down."

"I told you I don't trust Bob."

"You don't have to trust him. You're surrounded by a thousand people here. He couldn't harm you if he wanted to."

"Please, Momma!" said Rodrigo.

She grabbed the boy's hand, pulled him toward the elevator door, and said to me. "Take his other hand, Jake. I'm going to keep my eyes closed the whole trip."

As we stepped on to the elevator, she grabbed my hand. She was so tense from her fear of heights that her grip was crushing my fingers. I stood stretched out between Sonia, who was pushing against the only non-glass wall of the elevator, and Rodrigo, who was trying to pull himself away from my hand so he could press against the glass side of the elevator and watch the people on the bottom floor shrink smaller and smaller as the elevator rose.

"Are you still holding his hand?" she asked, her voice cracking.

"Yes," I said.

She turned slightly to the left and opened an eye to see if I was telling the truth, then squeezed it shut when she looked out the glass wall and saw how high we had risen. Beads of sweat were breaking out on the side of her neck. The other passengers looked amused. When the elevator reached bottom and she could finally open her eyes again, she noted the smiles on their faces.

"Oh, Jake, I am so ashamed," she said. "I'm such a coward when it comes to heights."

"You're no coward," I said as I flexed my fingers, trying to uncramp them. "What you did for Rodrigo took a lot of guts."

We got ice cream cones for the boys and headed for the exit.

I was watching Rodrigo lick his ice cream cone as we came out of Sears and crossed into the parking lot when, from out of nowhere, a man in a black, leather jacket rammed me with a body block and knocked me over. A second man, also in a black leather jacket, scooped up Rodrigo, and the two of them ran toward a red SUV with the engine running and doors open, waiting for them.

XIX

I scrambled to my feet, dove at the legs of the man running off with Rodrigo, and brought him down with a desperate tackle. Rodrigo squirmed free as he and the man hit the pavement. Then, just as I got up to grab Rodrigo, the first man raised his arm and smashed something down hard on my forehead. I fell back to the pavement and felt blood trickling over my left eye. Sonia was screaming in the background. From the corner of the other eye, I saw Bob Vukovich roar up and snatch Rodrigo. At the sight of Bob, who is built like an NFL linebacker, the two kidnappers ran back to their red SUV and sped out of the parking lot into the traffic on 24th Avenue. I tried to read their license number but couldn't see around Bob, who was standing in the way.

Rodrigo was crying in terror and there were scrapes on his cheek where he had hit the pavement. Sonia snatched him from Bob's arms and began murmuring Portuguese into his ear in a soft, soothing voice. Using my left hand to press a handkerchief against the blood flowing out of the cut in my forehead, I pulled my cellphone from my pocket with the other hand and punched 911.

The local police and the Mall security guards arrived at almost the same time. They put salve on Rodrigo's scraped cheek and a bandage over the cut in my forehead, suggesting that I head to an emergency room to have it checked. It only took a few moments for them to take our statements, because we didn't really know very much to tell them.

Sonia huddled with Rodrigo in the back seat of my BMW. "I should have followed my instincts," she said. "I never should have let Rodrigo come here."

Then she was silent for the entire ride home. She kept Rodrigo clasped tightly against her side as we came into her apartment. She forgot about the security alarm system, and the telephone rang within minutes of our arrival. She punched her security code into the key pad and finally turned to me.

"Jake, I wish I had never let you bring him there. But you did save him, and that is what counts."

"No, Bob saved him. I got knocked on my ass. If it hadn't been for Bob, I don't know what would have happened."

"I have to do something about this," She said, bending over to talk with Rodrigo in Portuguese. When he shook his head no, she got down on one knee, forced a smile, and held his hands as she talked in a soothing voice, making it sound like something very nice was going to happen to him, and he finally nodded yes. I had no idea what they were saying and felt a little annoyed to be left out of the conversation. Finally, she turned to me and said, "Rodrigo agreed to take a short vacation in Rio."

She pulled out her cell phone, called her father in Rio de Janeiro, talked for a few moments, then disconnected the phone and turned to Rodrigo. "Vovoh . . .," she said, then turned to me and added, "That is his grandfather." She turned back to Rodrigo and continued in English so I could understand as well. "Vovoh said they would be delighted to have you stay with them for a few days until Jake and I catch the men who tried to kidnap you. You can go to the beach and the zoo and the Emperor's palace. You can ride the trolley up to the Corcovado and look down on the whole city from a thousand feet up in the air. You can have lunch on the Sugar Loaf. Maybe even visit a samba school to watch the dancers rehearse for Carnaval." She said this as though he were just going away for a long weekend, and it sounded so appealing I wanted to go myself.

She turned to me. "My father will make the arrangements and call me back. He wants to fly to Miami and meet Rodrigo there." It was only then that she reacted to the bloody cut that was throbbing on my forehead. She pulled off the bandage. "Oh Jake. You are going to need stitches. Take a look at yourself." She pulled a mirror from her purse and held it up for me to see. It looked messy.

"But I cannot take you to the emergency room right now. I have to wait for my father to call back."

"You don't have to take me to the emergency room. I can go myself."

"Oh, Jake. Don't leave us alone here. After what happened, you have to stay with us tonight. Does he not, Rodrigo?" Rodrigo nodded yes.

She sat me at the kitchen table and used paper towels to wash out my wound. "All we need to do is pull the edges of this cut together with a butterfly bandage," she said. "I have some left over from the time that Rodrigo fell down the stairs. Remember that Rodrigo?" She smiled at him as though that tumble down the stairs must have been one of the most heart-warming moments in his young life. He smiled back in recollection. She was doing a masterful job of making him feel relaxed and safe after the ordeal he'd been through that afternoon. She flooded my wound with some kind of burning antiseptic that made me jump. "Hold still," she commanded as she put on the bandage. I felt the adhesive stick to the skin and then felt her draw the two sides of the cut together as she pulled the bandage tight and smoothed it against my forehead. "That closed it. You might not even need stitches." She was still smoothing her hands over my forehead, and I didn't want her to stop. The ruffle from the cuff of her dress brushed against my cheek.

Just then her father called. She wrote notes on a pad of paper. Rodrigo would fly nonstop from Minneapolis to Miami, leaving at 10:30 am, and arriving in Miami in mid-afternoon. The grandfather would fly from Rio to Miami and, thanks to the time difference, would arrive there with plenty of time to spare before Rodrigo's plane came in. The airline guaranteed that Rodrigo would be watched over from the moment he boarded the plane until the moment he was picked up in Miami. No one but the grandfather could pick him up.

When she hung up, she let out a long sigh and her shoulders relaxed for the first time since we had come through the door. She handed me the flight confirmation number her father had given her over the phone. "Jake, while I pack Rodrigo's things, would you use my computer to print out a boarding pass?"

Rodrigo suddenly blurted out, "Momma, they knocked my ice cream on the ground." He was pouting as though he was about to start crying again.

I reminded her. "He was eating an ice cream cone when this happened."

"I have just the thing for you," she beamed. "Come with me." She led him into the kitchen, while I logged onto the Internet.

I was pulling the boarding pass out of the printer when Rodrigo came out of the kitchen carrying two bowls of rocky road ice cream with chocolate sauce. "Here's one for you," he said. We took the bowls to the living room, where I surfed the TV channels. Rodrigo was so exhausted that he slumped over and fell asleep. Sonia pulled his luggage over to the front door. She smiled down at Rodrigo asleep on the couch. "Jake, would you carry him to his bed? He is getting too heavy for me to lift anymore." She put pajamas on him and we went back to the couch in the living room.

"I could use a drink," she said.

"Sonia, I hope I never have to ask you this again. But please don't get a drink right now. After what happened, and after I let you down the way I did, I need a drink in the worst way. It's like I'm gasping for air and your liquor cabinet is an oxygen tank."

She didn't say anything for several minutes or even touch me. Then she asked, "How did you let me down?"

"I never should have suggested going to the mall in the first place. And I was totally unprepared for those two goons coming out of the blue. Even after I tackled the one, I couldn't get Rodrigo back." I shuddered at the thought of what had almost happened.

"Nobody would have been prepared for those goons. And if you hadn't tackled that one guy, Rodrigo would be gone." She shivered. "You didn't let me down. You were a hero."

I was about to say that no, Bob was the hero, but I didn't. If someone thinks you're a hero, why disabuse them? Besides there was something suspicious about the incident that I couldn't put my finger on.

She shuddered again and said. "I do not like this business of Rodrigo flying alone. I want to double check with the airline what my father said about their procedure for handling unaccompanied children." She got up to use the phone on the desk by her computer. Even in the billowing, non-form fitting dress she was wearing, her hips swayed in a sensuous rhythm as she stepped across the room. Yes, she could accompany the boy through the security gate. Yes, somebody would watch over the child for the entire flight. Yes, the grandfather was the only person to whom the child would be released. Yes, they had procedures in case the grandfather was delayed. Yes, they would call her if there were any problems. Yes, they had an emergency number she could call.

She didn't look relieved when she rejoined me on the sofa, but at least she had taken every precaution she could think of. She said, "I don't know how I am going to get through the next twelve hours, and it's hard to think of anything else, but you never told me what you found out from that woman."

She spat out the words "that woman" like Erika was a disgusting toad or something.

"Three things," I said. "But she had no idea of their significance when she told me. First, remember what Moneybags called Wellstone?"

"I will never forget," she snarled. "A little chicken shit."

"No. He called him a tree-hugging little chicken shit."

"Don't play word games, Jake, especially right now."

"It's not a word game, and you'll know why when I tell you the second thing." I paused. It's a natural reaction for a person who makes his livelihood selling dreams. You make a suggestion, then pause until people ask you to fill in the gaps you've left.

"Well, tell me," she finally said.

"Moneybags is lobbying Congress to open up the Boundary Waters to more motor traffic and a luxury resort he intends to build." I filled her in on Radezewell's plan to build a Bohemian Grove North.

She snapped upright. "He killed Wellstone, because Paul would never vote for such a crazy thing."

"Let's not jump to conclusions," I said. "Up to this point, nobody has voted to open up the Boundary Waters."

"You're wonderful person, Amor. But sometimes you are so naive. When the time comes and Moneybags makes a big enough offer, support for keeping the Boundary Waters off limits will melt just like that ice cream in Rodrigo's dish." She pointed to the goop in Rodrigo's bowl sitting on the coffee table.

"You can't say that," I protested. "There are many honest people in Congress, and you at least have to give them the benefit of the doubt until they do something."

She rolled her eyes, like I'd just said somebody should have given Al Capone the benefit of the doubt. "But you have to admit one thing, Jake."

"What?"

"We now know what the motive was for killing Wellstone."

"Not really. We have a suspicious circumstance that we don't understand yet, but calling it a motive is premature. We don't know for a fact that anyone killed Wellstone. Besides there is another suspicious circumstance that isn't consistent with this one."

"What is that?"

"Just before the plane crash, Moneybags spent several days at a motel in McLean, Virginia. And on the day of the crash, he and Lars were touring the U. S. Hockey Hall of Fame."

"And?"

"McLean is just a stone's throw from Langley, Virginia."

"So?"

"Langley is the headquarters of the CIA. And the Hockey Hall of Fame is in Eveleth. Wellstone's plane crashed just outside the Eveleth Airport."

She gasped and brought her hands up to her face. "Oh, that pehDAHsso de bosta!" She repeated it three times.

"You ever going to tell me what that means?"

She ignored me. "Let me make sure I've got this. He might have killed Paul in order to get the Boundary Waters opened up."

"Possible, but not likely."

"Or, the CIA might have engaged his help to kill Paul to keep him from galvanizing opposition to the war."

"That is also possible," I said, "But also unlikely."

"Why?"

"There is no known instance of the CIA murdering a U. S. official. This would be a first."

"The CIA has murdered lots of people," she said.

"But no Americans that we know of."

"What a wonderful sense of ethics," she sneered. "Hundreds of murders, but no Americans."

We sat quiet for a second. Then she said softly and slowly. "He killed him, Jake. He killed him with Lars' help. And then he had Lars killed. Why would Lars get involved in such a thing? It's not like him. Why would he do it?"

"Sonia, the only thing we know for sure is that we've found a string of coincidences. And remember, these hypothetical motives are inconsistent with each other."

"Why?"

"Moneybags wouldn't have killed Wellstone over the war. He didn't care about the war one way or the other. All he cared about was making another fortune from his crazy Bohemian Grove North scheme. And the CIA wouldn't have killed him to open up the Boundary Waters. They wouldn't care about that."

"Unless they wanted a facility up there for some reason. Face it, if you wanted an unobtrusive place for debriefing people or moving them in and out of the country, that would be the perfect spot. You just fly them into and out of Canada."

"Farfetched. Everything north of the Boundary Waters is Canadian wilderness. The logistics would be terrible."

She frowned.

"So what are we going to do?"

"I don't know. Jim Anderson went up to visit Lars' brother in Eveleth to see if he knew what the killers were after. Let's see what he finds out."

"There is one other possibility," she said.

"What?"

"Those shoe boxes. Did you look through them all?"

"No. I counted the money in the first box and multiplied by six. The other boxes I just glanced at. Why?"

"Maybe Lars stuffed some clue in one of the other boxes that we haven't seen yet. When you get them back tomorrow, maybe we should take a look at them."

We sat in silence after that. She flicked on the TV, but neither of us could concentrate. Her eyelids kept closing and her chin kept slipping down to her chest. Finally, after her head dropped so low she almost fell off the couch, she said, "Jake, I have to get some sleep." She paused before adding, "You can join me."

"Oh God, there's nothing I want more. But what if Rodrigo wakes up at midnight with a nightmare about being kidnaped? He's going to need you."

She brought me a pillow and blankets and poked her fingers inside my shirt collar until she found the chain with the Saint Jude medal and tugged it out. She planted a kiss on my forehead right next the bandage. "You're a very noble man, Jake."

Of course, my willingness to stay out of her bed had nothing to do with nobility. You don't need a doctorate in family therapy to know that the quickest way to get on a woman's bad side is to get between her and her child during a moment of trauma. What had never occurred to me was that the opposite could be true. Facilitate her getting close to her child and she will think you are noble. Very noble in fact. And a hero to boot. I was basking in this new image of myself as I lay under the blankets listening to the sounds of Sonia shifting around trying to get comfortable on that small, crowded bed she was sharing with Rodrigo in the next room. But something vague still nagged me about the sequence of events that afternoon. I dropped off to sleep and the next thing I heard was an alarm clock going off in Rodrigo's bedroom.

XX

I pulled the covers over my head as Sonia stumbled out of Rodrigo's bedroom, tripped over something on her way to the kitchen, and started the coffee maker before heading to the bathroom. The smell of the coffee seeped through the covers, but I paid no attention. My mind was fixed on a vision of her in the shower, her body lathered with soap, and the hot water streaming down on her.

I finally dug out from under the covers, pulled on my pants, and headed for the kitchen where she had set out two bowls of sugar-frosted flakes for Rodrigo and me. I dumped one into the garbage and poured some milk into the bottom of the bowl so it would look like I had eaten the cereal. No point in making her think I failed to appreciate the breakfast she'd set out. Then I put some rye bread into the toaster, smeared it with jam after it popped up, and took the toast, along with the coffee back to the living room couch where I used the remote control to check out the business headlines on CNBC. After that, I ate the toast and sipped the coffee while flipping back and forth between CNN and the network morning shows.

The water turned off in the shower, and moments later Sonia appeared with a white terrycloth robe wrapped tightly about her. She gave me a brief kiss and said, "You can use the shower now, Jake, while I get Rodrigo up and fed."

"I don't have a change of clothes. I'll shower later when I go home to change after we come back from the airport."

"You can change clothes later, but you need a shower now. Your hair is a mess. It has clumps of blood, and you need a shave. There is a razor in the medicine cabinet." With that she went into her bedroom and closed the door so she could dress without me watching.

When I got out of the shower, Rodrigo was sitting at the kitchen table, eating his bowl of frosted flakes. "I went down to the porch and got the newspaper for you, Jake." He motioned to the *St. Paul Pioneer Press* sitting on the table. As I picked it up to glance at the headlines, he said, "You'd better fold up those blankets before Momma sees them, Jake. She doesn't like things thrown around."

Sonia came in at that moment, wearing a pair of blue jeans and a contrasting white blouse. "You embarrass me, Rodrigo." She smiled at me. "He exaggerates."

"But you do like things neat?"

"That's the way I am, Amor. You will just have to get used to it."

"Oooh, oooh, oooh," said Rodrigo with a big, teasing grin. "You called Jake Amor!"

"He *is* an amor," smiled Sonia, swirling her hips like a teenager. "You will see a lot of him around here when you get back from your vacation in Rio."

She turned her back to me and I saw the top buttons on her blouse were open. "Would you button these for me, Jake?"

The trip to the airport was tense, with both Sonia and I constantly turning our heads to see if we were being followed. I parked on the top level of the ramp and was nervous rushing Rodrigo and Sonia toward the elevator. There was no one else walking around that we could call to for help if we got jumped. I breathed easier when the elevator reached the underground level where several people were milling about, waiting for the shuttle tram that would take us to the main terminal.

The airline did not want to give me a pass to accompany Rodrigo and Sonia through the security check point, but Sonia pulled Rodrigo forward so the clerk could see his asymmetrical face and hear him humming his song as he stared out in space. The clerk took one look at the boy and relented. When we got to the waiting area by the gate, Sonia couldn't sit still. She double checked one more time on the airline's procedures for handling unaccompanied children. Then she came back and sat down between Rodrigo and me and forced herself to look at ease. But her leg was pressed against mine, and I could feel her toe tapping a nervous beat on the floor.

Rodrigo bent forward to see around his mother and said to me, "Jake, come over here. I want to show you something." He pulled me out of earshot of Sonia, gave me a twisted, just swallowed-the-canary grin, and said, "Piece of shit."

"What?" I was startled. I'm not used to eight-year-old boys dragging me into a corner to say things like that.

"Piece of shit," he repeated. "That's what you said."

"Rodrigo, what are you talking about? I didn't say that." I was trying to look stern, like I had some authority over him and could force him to clean up his language.

"Yes, you did. That day in your car."

"PehDAHsso de bosta?"

"Don't say that," he cautioned. "We don't want to upset my mother. Don't tell her I told you."

"It's our little secret," I said, tousling his hair and heading him back to his mother.

"What are you two grinning about?" she asked.

"Nothing," we both said.

She dropped to one knee and gave Rodrigo a long hug before

turning him over to the airline attendant who led him by the hand down the gateway toward the plane. We hung out at the gate, staring out the plate glass window at the plane as it was pushed onto the tarmac so it could taxi toward the runway.

Sonia didn't say a word during the drive back to the duplex. She just looked out the windshield with a blank stare, lost in her worries. When we reached her place, she sank, exhausted, onto the sofa, and I sat tentatively next to her. She stared at the dark TV screen across the room. A tear trickled from her eye. Then another. Then her shoulders began to sag. She fell toward me, sobbing and shaking and shuddering. This went on for several minutes. I put my arm around her shoulders, but it did no good. She just kept sobbing until she exhausted herself and the sobbing slowly abated. She finally sat straight up.

"Amor, please get me a paper towel."

She wiped her eyes and blew her nose in a loud, messy honk that was most unfeminine. Then she handed the snot soaked towel to me. What she expected me to do with it, I didn't know. I set it on the end table.

"Oh, I am so frightened for him. I am so frightened. I am so frightened."

"Sonia, he's safely on the plane. In three hours, he'll . . ."

"Amor," she said. "Call me Amor."

"Amor." I felt funny saying it. "In two more hours he'll be safe with your father. This is the best thing you could have done."

"I know that. It's not just his safety right now I'm afraid for. When he got on that plane, it came back to me like it always does. It is so hard raising a child who is never fully accepted by the people around him. His grandfather will not be here forever. I cannot protect him forever. What will become of him?"

I had no idea what to say to make her feel better. We just sat in silence. Finally, she took my hand and gave me a weak smile. "Thank you, Amor."

"For what?"

"For not saying anything. For just letting me cry. A lot of men would not be smart enough to do that."

Of course, it had nothing to do with smartness. Sometimes, you just have no idea what to say.

She said. "Jake, I need to be alone for while."

I was relieved to hear that, because I had some things to do myself and didn't know how to break away from her. "I have an appointment at one thirty and some other errands to do," I said. "But I still need to go up to Center City tonight and I don't want to leave you here alone. Will you go with me?"

"Yes," she said.

"I need one other thing from you before I go. Can we take a head and shoulders picture of you and one of me on your digital camera.

"Of course," she said. We snapped photos of each other posing in front of a blank space on her dining room wall, and then she handed me the memory card from the camera. "Just take this to any print store and they can make the photos for you."

I stuffed it into my pocket and said, "Promise me you won't leave the apartment until I get back."

She agreed, but she didn't make any move to guide me to the door. "There has been something bothering me ever since that attack on Rodrigo. I couldn't put my finger on it. But it finally came to me."

"Yes?"

"How did the kidnappers know that you and Rodrigo were going to be at the Mall of America? Were you followed?"

"I don't think so."

"And neither of us told anybody. The only person who knew about it was Bob."

"Bob? Tip them off? He wouldn't do that."

"The day I was being followed, what was the license number of the car that was tailing me?"

"RET 873. Why?"

"Jake, you have a great deal of trouble staying focused on things, and yet you were alert enough to get that number and two days later you still remember it. You tried to get the license number of the kidnappers, but Bob blocked your vision. And when you asked him if he got the number, he said he never saw it. There is something fishy here."

"But, if he tipped them off, why did he save Rodrigo?

"He never expected you to tackle that guy. Once you did that, the game was over. He had to do something to make us think he was on our side."

"But Sonia, Bob is the oldest friend I have in Minnesota. He would not do anything like that. I must have been followed."

She looked at me as though I'd said the earth is flat.

Just as we moved toward the front door, her doorbell rang, startling both of us. "Who is it?" she called through the intercom.

"Sergeant Olson with the St. Paul Police."

XXI

"You two have some very unpleasant acquaintances," he quipped, looking seedy in dark slacks and a rumpled sports coat, when he reached the top of the stairs. "What can you tell me?"

Sonia led us to the living room where she directed him to an easy chair, then sat with me on the sofa. We recounted the car chase on Friday and the attempt to kidnap Rodrigo on Sunday.

"Where is the boy now?"

"On a plane headed to Brazil," she said.

"Brazil?"

"His grandparents live there. My parents. I had to get him someplace safe."

"Well, it makes sense," he said. "But why didn't you go with him? You would be a lot safer there, too."

"I have a business to run," she said, "and commitments to people. We've installed a lot of security equipment here, and I'm in a second-floor apartment, so this place should be safe."

She pointed out the electronic keypad and mentioned the motion detectors and glass breakage detectors and the security light on the back steps.

"What is your parents' phone number? Just in case we need to reach them."

She said the number slowly, as though she had to pause to think up each individual number.

"And an address?"

She rattled off the address, but he couldn't follow the names of the streets as she said them in Portuguese, so she walked to her desk in the dining room to write the address and phone number on a piece of paper. Detective Olson's eyes followed the sway of her hips until she reached the desk, then he shook his head sharply, like a boxer trying to clear out the cobwebs from his brain. For the first time, I found myself wishing that she did not have such a sensuous walk. She handed him the slip of paper.

I had never seen her handwriting before, and I noted a little horizontal mark she'd put through the number seven, just like Europeans do.

"If we have to phone them, will your parents be able to speak English with us?"

"It all depends," she said. "If he thinks you're protecting me, my father will speak English as well as I do. But if he thinks you are investigating me, he will not understand a word you say."

Officer Olson grinned. "That will be very helpful information to have in case we need to phone. Thank you Ms. Lindquist. I wish your friend, Mr. Morgan, were half as cooperative."

"Officer Olson, I just want to get my son back to safety and get those goons out of my life," she replied. "I will cooperate in any way I can."

"What will you do about school?" he asked. "Sometimes it takes awhile to crack these cases. So there's no way to know how long your boy will be out of school."

"What does that have to do with the investigation?" I said.

"Nothing," Sergeant Olson admitted, suddenly becoming the friendliest guy in the world. "I'm just trying to imagine what it would be like if I had to take one of my kids out of school and send him to a foreign country for an extended stay."

"We'll put him in the English language school in Rio."

"He doesn't speak the local language?" asked the cop. He obviously didn't know what language Brazilians speak any more than I had known before she had told me.

"Oh, he speaks perfectly," said Sonia. "But his school work is in the English part of his brain, sort of the way that telephone number I gave you a moment ago was in the Portuguese part of my brain, and it took me a second to translate it into English. If we can keep Rodrigo's studies in English, it will be easier for him to make the transition both going there and coming back here."

Officer Olson pursed his lips and nodded, as though he had worlds of experience in the intricacies of bilingualism.

"Oh, God, he is not even there yet, and already I miss him," she said, bringing the palms of her hands up to her cheeks. "Like I said, I want to do whatever I can to help you solve this. And I want to do it before I have to tell my ex that I sent Rodrigo to Rio. He is going to hit the ceiling when he finds that out."

"Hit the ceiling?" Officer Olson looked puzzled.

"She means hit the roof," I said, and I must have been smiling, because she shot me a dirty look to tell me that this was no time to make fun of her English.

"Well," said the cop, handing her his business card, "I can't help you with that. But if he has any doubt about the danger the boy was in, have him call me, and I will confirm that sending your son to Brazil was the second smartest thing you could have done."

"The second smartest thing?"

"The smartest thing would have been to get on that plane with him and stay there until we get this case settled. You, on the other hand," he said to me. "I want to stay in Minnesota."

"You think I'm the one stalking Sonia?"

"No. But we're still pouring over Johanson's finances, and at some point we're going to have a lot of questions for you," he said. "In the meantime, I need to know why the two of you are being stalked."

"At first they were after Jake because they thought Lars had given him something that they wanted. Now they think I have it."

"What is it?" asked the detective.

"We don't know what it is. However, I have a pretty good idea where it is, because I know Lars' secret hiding places. And the killers somehow found out about my knowing that."

"And where is this secret hiding place?"

"The most likely one is under his bathtub. He would open up that panel that lets you get to the pipes and then use his fireplace tongs to put things back out of sight. When he wanted to retrieve them, he would use the tongs to pull them out."

She was about to add something when Olson snapped and turned to me, with a tinge of anger in his voice, "Why didn't you tell me that when I talked with you last week?"

"He didn't know it then," said Sonia before I could answer. "I never told him about the hiding places, and we only found out that the killers had turned their attention to me when Erika Bergstrom called Jake and tried to get him to pump me for that information."

"Who is Erika Bergstrom?"

"She's administrative aide for Oscar Radezewell, the owner of Radezewell Enterprises."

"The philanthropist?" he said in disbelief.

"Look at the sequence of events," said Sonia, her voice rising a notch above its normal, husky level. She was starting to talk faster and seemed irritated at the cop's skepticism.

"The killers lose interest in Jake as soon as Radezewell's aide tries to recruit him to spy on me. Then when he refuses to do that, the killers begin to stalk me. You question Oscar Radezewell and you will have this case solved." She fixed a hard, piercing stare on Olson.

"This is the guy who just announced a multi-million dollar gift to Northland College. If you want me to make an accusation

against a person like that, you'll have to give me a lot more than
this sequence of events to go on."

As she picked up on Olson's skepticism, she grew more ani-
mated. She began waving her arms about, and I feared she was
going to start jabbing her finger into the cop's face liked she'd
done at Moneybags' face the night of the banquet.

"You want more?" she blurted out. "There is more! He also
killed Wellstone!"

He rolled his eyes toward the ceiling then shot a questioning
glance at me as if to ask where I'd found this scatterbrain. Sonia
saw the look, and she made an angry grimace. Olson looked as
though he thought both Sonia and I were floating in outer space,
but he must have felt duty bound to ask.

"And what makes you think Radezewell killed Wellstone?"

"He said so," she said, "At the Northland College banquet
two weeks ago."

The cop looked at me again. Since I wanted to stay in Sonia's
good graces, I probably should have kept quiet, but we had to get
this conversation away from Wellstone and back toward the killers who were on Sonia's tail.

"He said something very inflammatory at the banquet," I
said, "But we're not agreed on what it was. Sonia heard him say
that he got rid of Wellstone and I heard him say he was glad that
Wellstone had died. I don't know what other people heard."

"You want me to risk my career accusing the most generous
businessman in Minnesota of killing your friend, stalking you,
and assassinating Wellstone?" he scoffed, shaking his head and
pausing long enough for us to absorb his sarcasm. Then he stood
up as a signal that he was ready to leave.

"But somebody is after you, and you're not safe here," he
said to Sonia. "We've got a patrol car running through here several times every night, and we're giving the highest priority to
any calls from this address. But we can't be with you every minute. Your security system could probably be disarmed just by cut-

ting the phone line. You're in even greater danger when you're on the street, going to your car, or even being in a public place. The guys after you are very resourceful, as you can tell from what's happened so far. Once they follow you for a few days and find out what your habits are, they will pick you off with no trouble."

Sonia grew pale.

"Go to a woman's shelter. Or a friend's house. Or live out of hotels for awhile. Or better yet, join your son in Rio."

After he left, Sonia turned to me and said, "Jake, he blew us off. He thinks I'm nuts. He didn't even give me a chance to tell him about the other hiding places that Lars had."

I tried to sooth her. "Sonia, give him a day to calm down, and then we can call him about that. In the meantime, I have some appointments to keep, but I'm afraid to leave you here alone. How about coming to my office for the afternoon? After I'm free we can decide what to do."

"Jake, at your office I would either be in your way or Li Vang's way, and from the way you've described her I don't think she is the kind of person who would like me being in her way. I'll be safe here for the time being. Just get back as soon as possible, and we can drive up to Center City. Then let us go up north for a couple nights to get a break from this tension. Could we do that?"

She was waiting for me when I got back to her duplex just after five. She picked up a huge purse with a long strap, slung the strap over her shoulder, and grabbed a small overnight case with her other hand.

"Let me drive, Jake. I am so loaded with nervous energy that I'd go nuts sitting in the passenger seat."

I tossed my gym bag with my overnight stuff into the back seat of her Escort, and she slipped behind the steering wheel. Taking the strap of her purse off her shoulder, she lifted it over to me. "Please take this, Amor."

"This thing is a little heavy. What do you have in here?"

She turned on the ignition. "Open it and see."

I gasped. Sitting right on top of her wallet was a small revolver. "I hope you have a permit for this."

"Nope."

"Oh, Jesus."

"Don't be critical, Jake. This neighborhood is not safe, and I got the gun a long time ago to protect myself and Rodrigo."

"Do you know how to use it?"

"It's been a long time since I took the instructions. I was hoping you might know how."

"Me? I don't know anything about guns. I told you what happened the last time I used one. I don't like them. They're dangerous."

"So is getting my fingers cut off. Your fingers are not all that safe either, Jake. Maybe you should get a gun, too."

I gave her a blank stare at that idea, then set the purse on the front floor by my feet and said, "Head out I-694 to the Paul Bunyan Steakhouse in Brooklyn Center so we can get a bite to eat before we go out to Bob's."

"Brooklyn Center? That's not on the way to Center City."

"I want to show you something there. We'll double back afterwards."

We reached the steakhouse and parked under one of the bright overhead lights in the parking lot. She focused immediately on the short, young, round-faced male host who was picking up menus and guiding people to their tables. She watched every gesture and noted every word as he led us to a table by the fireplace. I let Sonia take the side looking at the fire.

"That is what you wanted to show me?" she asked.

"After you told me about your fears for Rodrigo, I had to show you. This young man clearly has Down syndrome which is much more debilitating than Williams syndrome. Yet he does a perfectly good job of hosting. He's probably not totally independent, but he holds down a demanding job. If he can do it, think what Rodrigo might be capable of with his bilingual abilities, his music, and his charm."

"How did you know he would be here?"

"I just took a chance on that. But I've seen him before. I volunteer at a youth treatment center not far from here and sometimes I stop here on the way."

"Leave a big tip, Amor."

It was dusk when we left the restaurant and eight o'clock when we reached Bob's house.

He said, "I don't understand why anybody would want to kidnap your son. He is such a charming boy."

"Do you think it could have been for ransom?" she asked, scrutinizing every feature on his craggy face as he shrugged his massive shoulders, causing an up-and-down motion in the flannel woodsman's jacket he was wearing. She extended her hand as we stood up to leave. "Bob, I cannot tell you how grateful I am to you for saving my son. I don't know what I would do if you had not been there and he had been taken. You really saved the day."

She was laying it on a little thick and I was getting annoyed. What about my tackling the son of a bitch? I hadn't exactly just sat on the pavement sucking my thumb. But she just kept heaping all this praise on Bob who, just a few hours earlier she had blamed for tipping off the kidnappers.

As we left his porch and walked to her car, there was no moon shining on the lake in front of his house. All that could be seen was a blackness beyond the immediate trees. Having been a city boy surrounded by lights, I've never been comfortable with the blackness of nights out in the woods. She slipped into the passenger side of the car, pushed the seat back into its recline position, held out the ignition keys for me, and closed her eyes.

You drive, Jake, " she said. "I'm going to take a nap."

"Nap?"

She turned her head slightly toward me, opened one eye, and grinned. "I am thinking that you will want me fully rested when you get us wherever we will spend the night."

With no objection, I shifted into gear, headed back Highway Eight to the interstate and turned north. It was past eleven when we reached the crest of the hill overlooking Duluth. I nudged her shoulder.

"Wake up, Amor. You'll want to see this."

She rubbed her eyes with her fists, then set the seat into its upright position.

"It probably doesn't compare to your view of Rio at night back home in Ipanema, but it's still worth seeing."

"Rio, of course, is spectacular, especially at night," she said. "I can't deny that, although you don't get to see much of it from our place. It's on the beach facing the ocean, so the only thing we see at night is the dark water. But this is nothing to apologize for, Jake. It is beautiful."

She stared silently out the windshield at the lights of the harbor twinkling in the dark as we drove down the hill into town to look for a hotel on the waterfront.

XXII

When we reached our room, Sonia set her big purse on the night stand next to the bed, stood in front of me, and looped her hands around my neck. She fished under my collar with her fingers and pulled out the chain with the St. Jude medal, gave me a weak smile, and sat down on the edge of the bed.

"Could we put the gun out of reach?" I asked.

"What if we're attacked?"

"Sonia, nobody knows where we are, and there are hundreds of people milling around. We're safe. And having that gun nearby makes me uneasy."

She set the purse on the floor, got up from the bed, turned her back to me, and pointed to the base of her neck.

"The buttons or the necklace?"

"The buttons."

That night is seared in my memory. What I remember most is what happened afterward, when I was nodding off. She poked me in the ribs.

"Wake up, Amor," she said. "We need to talk."

So we talked. And talked. And talked. And talked.

"Jake," she said. She was lying on her side, facing me, her

head propped on her hand, the covers above her waist, and the wooden feega lying between her small breasts. "We are starting a journey, and I don't want us to drive off a cliff like we both did in our marriages. What do we do to avoid that?"

"Do we have to figure this out right now?"

"Yes."

"You don't have to do anything. Just keep being the way you are. Keep doing what you've been doing."

She smiled and said softly, "You don't have to worry about that, Amor. I will be good to you. Very good. Just understand that there will be some moments when I can't accommodate you. But other than that, I will be good to you. I promise that."

She went on without waiting for me to reply. "I need you to be caring, Jake, like you were at the orchard with Rodrigo and like you were when you showed me the Down boy tonight. I don't want you to be macho. I've have had my fill of macho men."

"This is leading up to something," I said. "What?"

"Remember when we were at the Lexington?"

"Yes."

"I shouldn't have had that champagne that night. I send you a mixed message when I drink in front of you."

"Sonia, I told you then and I'm telling you now. You can't stop me from drinking if I relapse. And you can't drive me into a relapse by having a drink yourself. It's my problem, not yours."

"I just want you to understand, Jake, that I will never again live with an alcoholic who drinks."

She shifted position in the bed until she was sitting up straight. She pulled the covers up to her neck so I couldn't see her breasts and she put a serious look on her face.

"If you ever start drinking, Jake, I will leave. It's a terrible thing to say to you right now, but you have to know it."

"Sonia, all I can promise you is that I won't drink for the rest of the day. Tomorrow you'll have to ask me to promise all over again. And the day after that the same thing. That is the only way I've stayed sober the last five years. To do anything else is to set myself up to fail. That's why I took you to that restaurant, the Day by Day. That's the only way I can do it: day by day. All I can promise you is that I won't have a drink before midnight."

"That idea scares me, Jake."

"Sometimes it scares me, too. But one day at a time is the only way I can do it. Sometimes it's one hour at a time. Last night in your apartment it felt like one minute at a time. I can promise you this; when you wake up in the morning I will be sober. And when you go to sleep tomorrow night, I will be sober. After that I can only promise you one day at a time."

She didn't look happy about what I'd said, but she didn't object. She reached over to finger the St. Jude medal that was still hanging from my neck. She smiled, then lay down on her back, her long black hair spread out on the white pillow case. And she stared at the ceiling.

We must have fallen asleep after that, because the next thing I knew the room was pitch black, except for the red numbers on the clock which read, 3:30. I was lying on my back when I woke up, and Sonia was on her side, her arm draped over my chest, her leg laying across me, her thigh resting on top of my groin, the nipple from her breast touching my arm. I didn't want her to move, so I lay as still as I could to keep from disturbing her. "This is all I want out of life," I told myself. I felt so good about her that I wanted to wake her up and promise that I would never again touch a drop of alcohol for the rest of my life. But the mere thought of making such a pledge got me so anxious that my fingers began to drum on the bed sheet. The only thing I knew for sure was that I could make it till midnight without a drink. I'm not a religious man, but I fell asleep praying to St. Jude that she would be able to live with me like that.

XXIII

She was still asleep when I woke up in the morning. I put on the coffee maker, shaved, showered, and came back to the room with a towel around my waist. I was starting to pick up the shoe boxes when she called out.

"Jake, what are you doing?"

"Checking out the shoe boxes."

"Look over here."

She was sitting straight up, her breasts pointed out at me, her head cocked to one side, a big, happy smile on her face. "You can check the boxes tomorrow. Today is our holiday and I want a break from our troubles. Please bring me some of that coffee you made, Amor, while I call Rodrigo. And drop the towel."

Due to the time difference, she explained to me, eight-thirty in Duluth would be the perfect time to phone Rio. Rodrigo and her mother would be back from the beach by then and their morning chores would be finished. She jabbered in Portuguese, then handed me the phone and said, "He wants to talk to you."

"Hello, Rodrigo," I said.

"It is spring here, Jake. I went to the beach this morning. I've got Legos here and I made an airplane."

After we hung up, I asked Sonia, "Weren't you a little uneasy having me talk to Rodrigo and letting your mother know you had a man here at this time in the morning?"

She chuckled and twisted toward me to plant a kiss on my lips.

"Oh, my poor, little, inhibited Jake!" she teased. "Helping you loosen up is going to be the pleasure of my life."

We propped the pillows against the head board and sipped from our coffee cups, the bed covers pulled up to our chests, our bare shoulders touching.

Not having to look out for stalkers made her more relaxed than I'd seen her since those first few moments before Moneybags had called Wellstone a chicken shit. She happily visited any place I suggested. I probably should have skipped the train museum, because she has no interest in machinery. Nevertheless, she ambled willingly through the huge collection of steam engines, Pullman cars, cabooses, club cars, one after another, all jammed into an enormous shed.

"Rodrigo would like this," I said. But she didn't comment, and I had a second thought. Who was I kidding? A kid who had flown on the Concorde wasn't going to be impressed with a bunch of old steam engines.

More interesting was our visit to the Split Rock lighthouse several miles up the north shore of Lake Superior. She forced herself to climb the staircase to the top where we looked out at an iron ore freighter plowing its way through the lake. Drops of sweat beaded on her forehead when she looked down the stairs and realized she had to climb back down them. Pressing against the wall, she turned backwards, closed her eyes, and crawled down the steps, pushing each foot slowly and tentatively down to the next tread, calling in a frightened voice for me to get closer so she could feel my body next to hers. When we reached the bottom, she turned around and sat for a moment on the last step. Her face and neck were drenched with sweat.

"It was exhilarating, Jake. And terrifying. I must have been out of my mind to let you take me up there."

At Gooseberry Falls on the way back to town, she insisted on climbing over the rocks. She slipped off her shoes and began to untie my shoe laces.

"Sonia, it's barely forty degrees out here. That water's going to be ice cold."

She laughed. "If I can climb the lighthouse, you can get your tootsies frozen."

"That's freeze your tootsies, not get your tootsies frozen."

"Whatever," she said, pulling off my socks and tugging me out onto the rocks. She squealed as her foot went into the frigid water, but continued pulling me further out. It was so cold it felt like my toes would fall off. Then her foot slid off of a rock, she lost her balance, and pulled us both into the freezing water. We got soaked up to our chests. I'd never felt anything so cold, and it's a wonder we didn't each have a cardiac arrest.

Of course we had no dry clothes in the car, so we had to sit shivering in our seats with the heater turned up full blast trying to warm ourselves. When her teeth finally stopped chattering, she started to laugh, then her laugher infected me and in seconds we broke into an uncontrollable giggling fit, much like the time when she'd misbuttoned her blouse that night in her duplex.

We ate dinner at Grandma's Delicatessen, a tourist fixture on the site of a brothel that had served the sailors on the lake freighters a hundred years earlier. She craned her head looking at the antique ornaments dotting the walls. "What was it like getting your tootsies frozen?" she joked, flashing her impish smile.

"You pulled me into that water on purpose, just to get even with me for what I said about tootsies."

"I wouldn't do anything like that," she said, laughing. "But you really should not mock me just because I mangle one of your colloquialisms."

On the walk along the dock back to the hotel, she put her

arms around me and lifted her face for a kiss. She made the kiss linger when I started to pull away. We took hands again and continued walking along the dock.

It was check-out time the next morning when we left the room and went down to the car. Parked next to us was a black Lincoln Continental with a bumper sticker that read, "Wellstone's Dead -- Get Over It." I rushed Sonia past the car so she wouldn't see the sticker. I put the shopping bags between my feet in the front seat. As she drove out of the parking lot, I pulled out the first shoe box and examined it. The duck tape had been cut and another piece wrapped around it, but the edges of the new tape didn't match perfectly with the old tape.

"It's been opened," I said, then examined each of the other five boxes. "Same thing."

"Anything missing?":

"It's hard to tell, but it looks like he took about $20,000."

Taking my cell phone out of my pocket, I called Li Vang to let her know I would not be in that day. She was annoyed at the news, and there was a long pause on the other end of the line when I told her I was with Sonia. But she gave me the names of people she said I absolutely had to call. I wrote their phone numbers on one of the shopping bags and began calling them. The last person I phoned was Jim Anderson who picked up his phone on the first ring.

"I can barely hear you," he said. "Where the hell are you?"

"In Sonia's car. We're in Duluth. What did you find out from Lars' brother?"

"Meet me for lunch tomorrow, and I'll tell you about it then. You sound so chipper right now that I don't want to spoil your day."

We agreed on a place to meet, and I added, "One other thing. I need a favor."

"What?"

"You got all kinds of connections. Can you get me a gun?"

Sonia almost jerked the car into a ditch when she heard that.

"Go to a sports store. They got any gun you could want."

"I want a pistol with a silencer. And I don't want there to be any record of it."

"That's beyond me. I'm a reporter, not a Teamster. Maybe you should just tell the cops about the stalkers."

"We tried, but they weren't very helpful."

"I'd like to help you Jake. But I wouldn't even know who to call. What are you going to do?"

"I don't know. Maybe I'll try the Teamsters like you suggested."

I clicked the phone shut and took a glance at the speedometer. Eighty. I slumped down in the seat and shut my eyes.

"I thought you didn't want a gun."

"I changed my mind."

"And you're going to arrange it through your father?" she asked.

"How'd you figure that out?"

"He is the only Teamster I know."

We rode in silence as we drove the next few miles through the grey countryside. The leaves on the trees had totally changed color from green to brown, and a wind was blowing them off the trees. The sky was overcast.

"What's your plan for the money?" I asked.

"You could just put it in a safety deposit box."

"If the police ever get serious about investigating me for money laundering, that's one of the first places they'll look. And I'd have a lot of explaining to do about sitting on a million dollars cash."

"You could toss it in the Mississippi and pretend it never existed."

I didn't respond to that. I just gave her a dumbfounded look.

How could she possibly think that a man who's entire career was built around the accumulation of money could just throw away a million dollars? She saw the look on my face.

"I was just checking," she said. "You don't have to raise your eyebrow. But this money was ill-gotten by Lars, and you are going to end up regretting that you didn't get rid of it."

"Sonia, it was a gift from an old friend, an inheritance practically. You saw the note. I just have to keep it out of sight until after I get out from under this suspicion of money laundering."

"OK," she said. But she didn't look persuaded. "We just have to hide it in places that are not likely to be searched by the police. Let me know if you see a shopping mall along the way."

She pulled into a mall and ran into an office supply store. While she did that, I dropped the shopping bags of money into the trunk and went into an electronics store, where I bought two prepaid cell phones. She came out of the store pushing a shopping cart, pulled the shopping bags out of the trunk, dropped them at my feet, and handed me two items from the bag of stuff she'd bought at the store, a box of small, white envelopes and a plastic container with two drawers for storing checks, a relic from the days when banks used to return the customers' canceled checks.

"How many of those $50 bills will fit into the check box?" she asked.

I crammed as many bills as possible into the two drawers and then made an estimate. "I would guess six thousand."

"Wrap the check box in that duck tape I bought and we will look for a secluded spot at the Veterans' Home where we can bury it when we visit your father."

The logistics looked impossible to me. "How are we going to do that? We can't just carry this box into the Veterans' Home and walk out empty handed. Besides we'll need a shovel to dig a hole, and I can't very well walk around with a spade over my shoulder."

She picked up her big purse and methodically began emptying it into the back seat. She lined each item up along the back of the seat with the same meticulous care that Rodrigo had shown the day he had emptied the pots from my kitchen cabinet onto the floor. Then she carefully lowered the check box into her purse, looked up, and beamed me a grin. She went to the trunk of her car and came back to the driver's side with an old, folded-up Army trench shovel, her big ear to ear grin lighting up her face.

"My ex gave it to me. He said it would be good to have in an emergency. After all these years I have finally found some use for it. You can hide it by sticking the handle under your belt and zipping your jacket around the blade. No one will see it."

As I began the task of wrapping the check box in duck tape, she handed me one of the white envelopes she'd bought and said, "We got six thousand bills into the check box, so we have fourteen thousand left. How many will fit into one of these envelopes and not be more than half an inch thick?"

"About a hundred," I said after counting them out. "What's your plan?"

"Most paintings have a small space between the canvas and the cloth or paper that covers the back. We will cram as many envelopes as possible into there and replace the backing. Then we will hang them someplace other than in your condo or your office. One possibility would be that picture in your father's room of four dogs playing poker. Would he let us borrow that overnight without asking too many questions?"

"I don't see why not."

"We can probably get twenty-five or thirty envelopes behind that one, and we can probably get an equal amount behind that reproduction of Monet's garden in Giverny in your living room which we can give him."

"That'll never work. He hates it. Use the Thomas Kincaid that's hanging across from my couch. It has sentimental value."

"How could a Kincaid have sentimental value? They are mass produced by the hundreds."

"That sounded snobbish," I complained. "That Kincaid is a jigsaw puzzle that he and I put together when he first got here, and it has sentimental value because it is the only thing in our entire lives that the two of us have ever completed together. That was why I had it mounted and framed."

She took her right hand off the steering wheel and lay it on my shoulder. "Amor, I am so sorry for what I just said. Please forget I said it."

I began the task of slipping money into the envelopes, licking the flaps to seal them, and dropping them into the first shopping bag. By the time we reached the cities, I had done barely half the envelopes. I rubbed my mouth on my sleeve. "That stuff tastes like shit," I said.

She laughed. "Why do you think I insisted on driving?"

"Well, I have to take a break. Let's go visit my Teamster. Take 35-W into Minneapolis, then go out Hiawatha Avenue."

XXIV

She got off at Hiawatha Avenue as I instructed and headed south, parallel to the Light Rail tracks. She drummed her fingertips on the steering wheel each time we stopped for a red light. One of the sleek, yellow and gray light rail trains glided past us as we were stalled at the 46th Street station, waiting to turn east into Minnehaha Park and the Veterans' Home. Before going inside the building, we walked around the grounds, keeping an eye on her car and anybody who pulled into the parking lot. When it became clear that nobody suspicious was on our tail, I pulled open the main door so Sonia could enter before me. The weight of all those fifty dollar bills in her purse pulled down on her shoulder, and the trench shovel tucked under my belt felt awkward, but nobody paid us any attention.

Pop was in the day room watching "Jeopardy" on the television set when we arrived. He looked up as we came into view, smiled when he saw Sonia, then frowned. "Where's Rodrigo?"

"It's a long story," I said. "Is there someplace where we can talk in private?"

I must have had a very sobering look on my face, because he didn't even ask why. He simply directed us back to his room to pick up a jacket and then led us out to the picnic table. Sonia and

I filled him in on everything except the $980,000 dollars in cash that we were toting around.

"You should call the police," he said.

"We did. They blew us off when we told them Radezewell was behind the kidnapping attempts. And their eyes started rolling when Sonia told them it had something to do with Wellstone's death."

"It figures," he said.

"Wellstone's murder," she corrected me.

Pop stared up at her for a second, but it was impossible to tell from his look whether he agreed with her conspiracy theory about Wellstone's death or whether he thought it was as off the wall as the cops had thought.

"What I need," I said, "is an unregistered gun with a silencer so we can protect ourselves. But I don't know how to get one. You're the only person I know who's got any experience at all dealing with people who know how these things work."

"Forget the gun. Your experience with guns hasn't been very good."

Neither Sonia nor I said anything in response, and after staring at us for a few seconds, he said, "That cop was right. Sonia should go to Rio, and you should tag along."

"After last Sunday, we have to think about it, Jake," she said. "Come with me."

"Go to Rio?" I was stunned. "What about your business? What about Rodrigo and his father?"

"Remember the jaytoo I told you about? The way to get around things? There is always a jaytoo. I'll find one. You can too. Let's do it, Jake. It's only for a few months until this stuff with Moneybags blows over."

"It's impossible. This is one of my busiest times of the year coming up, what with the annual appreciation dinner I hold for my clients, and getting Li Vang launched at financial planning."

She shook her head slightly in apparent annoyance at my

concern for Li Vang and looked over to my father for support. But he didn't say anything.

"Sonia, it is a good idea for you to go, if you can work it out with Rodrigo's father and with the gallery. You'd be safe. But for me it's out of the question. I've spent five years getting my business to the take-off point. If I left town right now, I'd be set back by three years, and it would be a terrible thing to do to Li Vang, who really needs some mentoring to get licensed and get started. Besides, I wouldn't give the bastards the satisfaction of knowing they'd run me out of town."

"I didn't think so," said Pop, as he shook his head back and forth. "You're just as pigheaded now as you were as a kid. Let me use your cell phone and see if I can find someone to talk to about getting a gun."

"Use this one," I said, handing him one of the prepaid cell phones. "It will be harder to trace than my regular cell phone. I've programmed a number into the speed dial so you can reach me whenever you need to."

To give him some privacy for making his calls, Sonia and I headed to the chain-link fence overlooking the lock and dam. We walked along the fence to the edge of the property where an evergreen hedge hid us from anybody's view. It only took a few minutes to hack out a hole with the trench shovel and bury the money that she had been carrying in her purse. I stomped on the mound of dirt, kicked dead oak leaves over the top of it, stuffed the handle of the trench shovel into my belt, and then zipped my jacket shut over it.

We ambled along the fence, keeping a good two paces away from it so she wouldn't have to look down the precipitous drop off. She held my hand, made an occasional bump of her shoulder against me as we walked, and gazed vacantly at the water pouring over the dam, the arches of the old bridge in the background, and the tower of my condo jutting out over the treetops on the other side of the river. She stopped walking and pulled on my hand for me to face her.

"I'm not going to Rio, Amor. We will find a jaytoo here to get us out of our situation. And we will find it together. Are you still wearing that St. Jude medal I gave you?"

I used my finger to pull the chain out from inside my collar for her to see, still astounded that she somehow seemed to think that St. Jude, who had died two thousand years ago, was going to get us out of our desperate situation today.

She smiled, then put her hand on the nape of my neck to pull my head forward and gave me a peck of a kiss on the lip.

"Ti amo, Jake."

"Ti amo, Sonia."

She looked surprised. "You understood what I said."

"Not really. But you told me once before that the words can mean whatever we want them to mean."

A cryptic smile emerged on her face, but she didn't say anything. Logically, we should have been buying plane tickets to Rio. Instead, we were holding hands, trusting that St. Jude would find us a jaytoo, and saying "Ti amo" like a couple of teen-agers in the cold October air by the chain-link fence overlooking the dinghy barges going through the concrete lock on the Mississippi.

Pop brought me out of my reverie by shouting at us and waving for us to join him. "This'll take a few days, and it won't be cheap," he said, putting a frown on his grizzled face.

"Whatever it costs, it's cheaper than getting killed."

"I'll need two thousand dollars now to mail to a guy who's going to contact a guy in the Bronx. One thousand for him and another grand for the other guy. When they get somebody lined up in Minneapolis, he'll have to be paid, too. All in cash."

"No problem," I said. "I've two thousand in the car, which I'll get for you right now. That way you can mail out the envelopes and I won't even have to know where they're going."

Pop smiled for the first time since I'd brought up the subject of a gun. "You're learning, Jake." He shifted his smile to Sonia, but she didn't smile back.

"As soon as we can arrange a delivery, I'll leave a message for you to call me."

"When you call," I said, "make sure you use that prepaid cell phone I just gave you. And use the number that I programmed into the speed dial. Just in case anybody's eavesdropping on me I don't want to take any calls of this sort on my regular phones, and we don't want any calls traced to the switchboard here."

We brought him the money from the trunk of her car. When Sonia asked to borrow his picture of the dogs playing poker, he put a skeptical look on his face. And who could blame him? The idea that an art historian would have any true interest in that picture was fishy on the face of it, but he gave it to us without asking any questions.

As we started to leave, he said, "Jake, give me a moment alone with Sonia."

I walked to the front entrance and waited for her to emerge. When she did, she smiled warmly, grabbed my biceps with both hands, and pulled us close together as we walked out the door into the cold air. "That's quite a reaction," I said. "What did he say to you."

"I can't tell you. It was a private conversation." Then she handed me the keys to her car. "You drive, Jake. I don't like driving over that bridge." She nodded toward the Ford Parkway bridge, towering on its graceful arches over the Mississippi. She closed her eyes the moment we reached the entrance ramp just as she had the previous time we'd driven over the bridge.

When we reached the other side, she opened her eyes and asked, "Were your parents happy together?"

"I never thought much about it. He refused to go to the Broadway musicals she loved. Said it was unreasonable to ask a man to watch a bunch of other men prancing around like sissies.

Sonia, in the last few years I was too busy loading up on alcohol to notice whether anybody else was happy. But they seldom fought. And when they did, they always found a way to work things out. As long as he didn't have to go to any musicals, he'd do anything she asked of him. I guess they were happy. Why?"

"No reason. Just wondering."

XXV

It took two trips up to my twelfth-floor condo to carry up all stuff she'd bought. She laid Pop's picture face down in the living room and sank to a kneeling position to work on it. I bent over her, put my hands on her shoulders, then slid them down to her breasts. She let me rest them there for a second, then shrugged her shoulders, "Later, Jake," she said, adding with a warm smile, "I won't forget you."

While she packed the money behind the pictures and replaced the backings, I finished working on the envelopes. Then I brewed us each a cup of tea, and we leaned back on my couch to survey our work. The pictures were sitting on the floor across from us, leaning against the wall. She pointed to the lower right corner of the Kincaid.

"Jake, there is a piece missing from your puzzle."

"'It's not missing. It's right here." I took out my wallet and extracted a small piece of the puzzle. She looked baffled.

"In AA, the first thing you learn is that your addiction is a craziness. And the second thing is that a power greater than yourself can restore you to sanity. When Pop and I completed this puzzle, it was the first anniversary of my sobriety. I kept a piece of the puzzle as a sign that I really do have a higher power."

A slight smile began to form on her lips.

"Don't laugh. I'm serious."

"I'm not laughing, Jake. I'm pleased. There is a spiritual side to you that you never showed me before."

She squeezed my hand, then abruptly changed the subject.

"We still have fifty envelopes to go, but I have no idea where to put them to get them out of your condo."

"How about if we put them in those two abstract paintings you have at your duplex?"

She looked startled. "Jake, that is a quarter of a million dollars. You trust me with that?"

"Why not?" I shrugged my shoulders. "A person who just an hour ago suggested tossing the money in the Mississippi is hardly going to run off with it."

"But Jake, after the cops search your place, the next place they will search is mine. Could I store the paintings at the gallery?"

"You are going to leave a quarter of a million dollars lying around the gallery?"

"The paintings will be locked up, and I will have a receipt. So if they are stolen, the gallery will have to pay for them."

"Pay for the paintings, yes, but that won't get back the cash."

"True, but since no one knows they contain cash, they will be safe. They will be safer there than at home. They will be safer there than here, in fact."

We packed our stuff to go over to her duplex and hide the remaining bills behind her paintings.

"Jake," she said. "I don't feel safe staying alone in my place right now. Would you be willing to stay with me for a few nights until I get used to being alone?"

It seemed like a small sacrifice on my part to assure her piece of mind, so I said OK.

"There is one thing, though," she said. We were standing, facing each other, and she wasn't smiling.

"Yes?"

"Jake, I can't live in a clutter like this." She swept her hand toward the hallway where my jacket was lying on the floor and toward the living room where my couch was littered with newspapers, a dirty tee shirt, and a few empty cola cans. She pointed at the mess that Rodrigo and I had made in kitchen three days earlier. "What you do here in your place is your business, but I am telling you that I cannot live in a mess like this. While you are staying in my place, we have to work out a division of the chores, and you have to pick up after yourself. If not, you will drive me crazy, and we will never get along." She paused, then smiled and added, "Amor."

Astounding! She was being stalked by killers, and yet her most immediate worry seemed to be getting me to pick up after myself.

"No discussion?"

She gave me a soft smile. "We can discuss it as much as you want. I am committed to making this relationship work, and I promise that I am going to be very good to you. Just understand that it will be easier for me to keep that promise if I also get what I need from you. And one of the things I'm going to need is for you to be a little neater when you're in my place."

"You mean good to me like last night?"

She laughed. "Among other things."

It sounded liked a good deal to me. And to get it, all I had to do was break the habit of a lifetime.

I filled a suitcase with items I'd need, and we headed down to the garage. We left my car parked in the garage and drove to the duplex in her Escort.

XXVI

Despite the killers on our trail, we tried to carry on the normal routines of our lives. I got up the first morning, made coffee, showered, picked up the newspaper from her porch, brought two cups of coffee back to the bedroom, scanned the paper while she showered, and then watched her get ready for the day. Wearing a bra and underpants, she stood in front of her bedroom mirror to blow dry and brush her hair, grabbing my complete attention in the process.

When she caught my eye in the mirror and saw that I was watching, she smiled and gave a wiggle of her hips. She put on a skirt and a splashy, multi-colored sweater. Then she made her telephone call to Rodrigo, and afterwards we sat facing each other across the kitchen table as we ate breakfast. I took her to work and drove her Escort to my office.

Li Vang was upset about the amount of time I'd spent out of the office recently, and she turned up her nose when she found out that I'd spent the last few days with Sonia. She had a mountain of correspondence piled on my desk.

At midmorning, Sergeant Olson called.

"What the hell kind of a goose chase were you two sending us on?"

"What goose chase?"

"That one about Johanson's hiding place. We tore out the entire ceiling under that bathtub and didn't find a thing."

"She told you it was the most likely hiding place. She was trying to tell you about the others when you blew her off."

"Well, where are they?"

"I don't know. She's the one that knows. You'll have to ask her."

"That woman's a fruitcake. Send her back to Brazil before she gets hurt."

I met Jim Anderson for lunch at Figlio's in Calhoun Square in Uptown and paid him what I owed for his trip up north.

"Lars' brother was killed," said Jim. "Shot through the chest, with fingers of both hands cut off."

"Jesus," I shuddered. "Any leads?"

"I didn't wait to find out. A Twin Cities reporter poking his nose into an Eveleth murder is going to draw attention that you don't want."

At five o'clock I picked up Sonia at the gallery. She wedged her purse containing the pistol between the two front seats, and we sat for a moment parked on the street, looking out over the gray presence of Loring Park.

"Did Sergeant Olson call you?"

"No. Why?"

"He's pissed about not finding anything under Lars' bathtub. Says we sent him on a wild goose chase."

"Tough. He should have let me finish telling him about the other hiding places."

I told her about Lars' brother, and the color drained from her face as she stared vacantly out the window at the park. There were no longer any leaves on the trees, the sky was overcast, and the air was turning cold. It was that dreary part of the year between the golden colors of early October and the snows that come by Thanksgiving.

Eventually she said, "Jake, everything is too dreary. The news is too dreary. The sky is too dreary." She leaned forward and pointed out the windshield at the sky. "Everything is too dreary. We need some color." She had me drive to the flower conservatory at Como Park, an elegant glass dome nearly a hundred years old. The fragrance and color of the gardens lifted her mood. She sat on a bench overlooking the fish pond and pulled me down by the arm.

"Jake, you need a new suit."

"What brought that on?"

"You need more color. Look at all these wonderful colors in here." She swept her arm around at the red and green and yellow vegetation. "And how dreary all those conservative pinstripes are in contrast." She scowled at my suit coat.

"I'm a conservative businessman. That's what businessmen wear."

"You need something more playful for the opening of my art show at the gallery next month. Maybe one of those suck seer suits men wear in the summer."

"It's seersucker."

"Whatever."

She didn't even warn me not to correct her English. She just kept talking, anything to avoid thinking about what we'd gotten into. "Or maybe one of those silver tinted-linen suits you could wear without a tie and show off that beautiful neck of yours." She touched the tip of her index finger to my neck and drew it up to my chin. She gave me a coy smile. "When I get my check for the sale of that painting, I want to buy you a new suit. Can I do that?"

"Sure," I said. Why let style stand in the way of a woman's happiness?

The next afternoon, when we returned to her duplex, I pulled on a pair of jogging pants and bent over to tie my shoes.

"Where are you going?" she asked.

"Jogging. I always jog at this time of day."

She didn't say anything, which was an eloquent way to let me know she disliked the idea.

"Amor, it's been part of my routine ever since I got out of treatment. It helps me stay sober."

She still didn't say anything, just fixed a disbelieving stare on me.

"Exercise is healthy," I protested defensively. "Wellstone was a great believer in it. He worked out regularly."

"How do you so much about Paul's habits?"

"One group of my clients pointed to them as something positive, and another group complained that his spending time at that was an abuse of taxpayer's money."

She wasn't amused. "If you go wandering around out there, they will get you."

"How are they going to do that? I run seven minute miles. If anybody shows up, I'll just outrun them."

"You can't outrun a bullet, Jake. Don't be macho. If you need exercise, join a gym."

I took off the jogging shoes and headed to the bedroom to change back to regular clothes when she stepped in front of me, smiled, and gave me a kiss. "But keep the jogging pants on, Amor. They make you look rugged."

Rugged, good. Macho, bad. The difference escaped me.

We had barely sat down for dinner in her small kitchen when my prepaid cell phone rang.

"You can pick it up tomorrow."

"Where?"

"Stop by to see me before lunch. I'll tell you then. And bring your friend. I've arranged lessons for the two of you."

At the Veterans' Home the next morning, it only took Pop a moment to tell us where to pick up the gun and get our lessons.

"You're getting a Glock nine," he said.

Of course, I didn't know a Glock nine from a Colt forty-five, and it must have showed on my face, because he grimmaced.

"That's a nine millimeter pistol made by Glock. I'd feel a little better about this if you at least knew what things are called." He paused, then added, "Sonia, give me a second with Jake."

"Jake," he said after she stepped out of the room. "Take that woman to Brazil before she gets killed. She is a warm and caring woman, maybe the warmest you are ever going to find. But she's not going to be any good to you if she's dead."

"I'd send her right now if she'd go. But she won't."

"Well, at the very least, get out of your apartments and live out of hotels for awhile. She cares much more for you than is good for her. When this is over, show your gratitude by doing any reasonable thing she asks of you. That worked between me and your mother. But right now get her someplace safe, whether she likes it or not."

"What did he say to you?" asked Sonia as we clasped hands and walked back to her car.

"I should do any reasonable thing you ask of me."

She grinned. "I like that."

"Did he also tell you to do any reasonable thing I ask of you."

"Not exactly," she said. "He said if I treat you right and keep you sober, I can have you in the palm of my hand."

"Well, you can't keep me sober. I'm the only one who can do that. And forget about holding me in the palm of your hand."

She smiled. "It's a very tender palm, Amor. But if you object, that's OK. I'll settle for you doing any reasonable thing I ask."

I added, "He also said I should force you to go to Rio before you get killed."

"I'm not going to Rio. Even if I went, I couldn't stay there forever. I have no right to deprive Rodrigo of his father, and I would be sick with anxiety every time I sent him back here alone. At some point, I would have to return here, and then we would confront the same problem at that time. We have to deal with the problem now. That's what Wellstone would do. Trust me, Jake. Trust in St. Jude. There is a jaytoo and we will find it. We will find it together."

When we arrived at the gun club in suburban Oakdale, our contact person looked nothing like the Mafioso stereotype that was in my mind. He was tall, thin, blond, blue-eyed, extremely pleasant, and he answered to the name of Olaf. Good choice of an alias. There must be a thousand Olafs in the Minneapolis phone book.

Olaf showed us how to disassemble the gun for cleaning. I was hoping our mess would be over and we would be able to get rid of the gun long before it needed cleaning. He showed us how to attach the silencer, but instructed us to leave it off while he gave us our lessons in firing the gun. A silenced gun on the firing range would drawn unwanted suspicions. Sonia jerked the trigger the first time she fired the pistol, and it almost flew out of her hands from the kickback and the shock of the loud noise it made.

"Squeeze the trigger, Sonia," he said. "Don't jerk it." Even after an hour's practice, she still hit the target less than half the time. I was almost as bad as she was. We should have ordered one of those guns with the laser spotting device, but it was too late for that. I stuffed the pistol into my cloth briefcase, and, with the silencer attached, it took up the entire space.

After dropping Sonia at the gallery and making sure she got inside safely, I drove out to a deserted corner of the apple orchard where I had taken her and Rodrigo in what seemed like a million years ago. I set up ten pumpkins in a row and practiced firing my nine millimeter pistol. With the silencer attached, the gun only made a poof sound that attracted no attention. It took several shots before I finally hit a pumpkin, splattering it apart. After the last pumpkin was shattered, I put the gun back in my briefcase, tossed it in the trunk of the car, and headed back to my office.

I pulled Sonia's Escort into the alley behind my building and drew up next to a panel delivery truck that was sitting next to my parking spot. No sooner did I step out of the car and slam the door shut, than a huge, powerful goon emerged from behind the panel truck and grabbed my left arm. Another one appeared in front of me and grabbed the other arm. They were so powerful that their grips felt like vise clamps on my arms. Even though I was struggling, one of them managed to slap a piece of duck tape across my mouth. They lifted me off my feet and, in a matter of only seconds, dragged me into the back of the panel truck and pulled the doors shut.

XXVII

They pinned me to the floor while they wrapped duck tape around my wrists and ankles. They sped onto the freeway, and, from what little I could make out through the windows on the rear doors, they appeared to get off the freeway after crossing the Mississippi and head out Hiawatha Avenue to south Minneapolis. They stopped in a weed strewn parking lot by a deserted factory, cut the tape from my ankles and forced me to walk to the building where they shoved me into a closet, slammed the door shut, and disappeared. I heard their footsteps recede and an outer door slam shut. Then everything was silent.

I cursed myself for being so stupid. Blind-sided twice in a single week. First at the Mall of America, and now here. My eyes adjusted slowly to the dark closet. Only a faint glimmer of light came through the opening at the bottom of the door. I tried slamming my shoulder against the door, but it wouldn't budge. With my wrists bound behind me, I turned my back toward the door in order to grope around for a doorknob, but the door was locked. I jumped when my fingers sliced against a piece of sheet metal jutting out from the door panel. Then I rubbed the duck tape against the edge of sheet metal to see if I could cut through the tape. It was very slow work. The action made my arms ache and I had to rest every few minutes. For what seemed like a long time, I made no progress cutting through the tape.

Finally, there was a slight give in the tape when I pushed outwards with my forearms. This was the first bit of hope I'd had since being thrown into the panel truck. I switched back and forth between slicing the tape against the sheet metal edge, pushing outward against the tape with my forearms, and resting when the pain in my arms got to be too much. Between the slicing action and the pressure from my forearms, the tape finally started to tear. I was on the verge of breaking free when someone came through the outer door and flicked a switch that send a sliver of light under the closet door. Heels clicked on the concrete floor as someone seemed to be coming in my direction.

The closet door burst open, and the sudden flash of bright light blinded me for an instant. One of the goons grabbed me by the shoulders and pushed me out of the closet, down a hallway, and into a room where I spotted Sonia sitting on a straight-backed chair in front of a small table. Her wrists and ankles were bound just as mine had been, and a roll of duck tape sat on the table in front of her. She also had a strip of the grey tape across her mouth, and there was a look of terror in her eyes. The goon pushed me into a hard-backed chair directly across from her.

The larger of the two goons came over to the edge of the table. He was bigger than Bob Vukovich, and he looked like he spent a lot of time pumping iron. His face was pock marked and carried a scowl. He didn't look like he'd spent much time in sensitivity classes. He slammed two quart-sized bottles of Jack Daniels on the table. From his hip pocket he pulled a pair of pruning shears, which he waved in front of us before setting them on the table next to the whisky bottles. Sonia's eyes opened wide at the sight of the shears and she made a slight jump in her chair.

Pockface glowered at me, then at Sonia, then back at me. He picked up her purse and dumped it on the table, her small pistol ending up under the pile of stuff that was crammed inside the purse. He picked up the pistol between his thumb and forefinger, sneering like it was a piece of used toilet paper, and dropped it on the floor.

"We're tired of fucking around with you two. You are going to answer every question I ask, and you are not going to pull any shit. You are not going to scream or do anything except answer my questions. Is that clear?"

We nodded our heads. I jumped as Pockface pulled the duck tape off my mouth, ripping out a good bit of my facial hair in the process. Sonia gasped. I moved my jaw back and forth to work out the kinks from being gagged.

"How did they get you?" I blurted.

"I got a phone call that you had an accident. A woman with an Asian voice offered to drive me to you, and I thought it was Li Vang. But as soon as I got into the car they taped me up and took me here."

"Shut up!" roared Pockface. We both jumped at the ferocity in his voice. "The only one you talk to is me. Where's the boy?"

Neither of us said anything.

He looked at Sonia and changed his ominous tone to a soothing one. "We're not going to harm your son. We just need him to make sure you cooperate and don't send us on any wild goose chases. As soon as we get what we want you can all leave. No one will be hurt and everyone will be happy." He lifted the pruning shears from the table. "Or you can watch us cut off Morgan's fingers one by one. And he will have to watch us have a little fun with you. After that we will pour this whiskey down your throats and arrange a fiery car accident that will burn your bodies so bad nobody will notice the missing fingers. They'll need your DNA or something to identify you. Morgan here, being a drunk, everybody will think he went back on the booze."

Sonia turned white, and I guess I did, too.

He looked back and forth between us. "It's your choice," he said, shrugging his shoulders. He turned his head and grinned at the other goon who was standing behind him, a revolver stuck in a shoulder holster by his chest. Then he turned back to Sonia. "Frankly, I hope you choose the hard way, because I would like to get some of that beautiful little ass of yours. But my orders are not to harm you as long as you cooperate."

He paused to let his words sink in, shifting his eyes back and forth between us.

"So what is it? The easy way or the hard way? Where did you put Johanson's photos?"

"What photos?" she asked.

He leaned over until his face was just inches away from hers, smiled, and said in a calm, quiet voice, "I guess we have to do it the hard way. Where is the boy?"

She spat in his face, and he slapped her so hard she fell half-way out of the chair.

"I told you not to fuck around with me."

My whole body tensed as I watched, and the pressure from my forearms finally broke through the duck tape. But I kept my arms behind my back so neither of the goons could see that my hands were free.

"Maybe a little lubrication will get you two relaxed enough to talk," said Pockface. He opened one of the bottles of Jack Daniels, pulled my head back by the hair, pointed the lip of the bottle toward my mouth and said, "Drink!"

I clenched my teeth. He punched me in the stomach with the hand holding the whiskey bottle, spilling quite a bit of it on my lap. When my mouth popped open from the punch, he jam-med the bottle between my teeth. I tried to shake my head free, but the smell and taste of the bourbon were more than I could resist. Sonia scowled in horror as she watched. Finally the bottle came out, but I must have swallowed half of it, and I wanted more. He bent over and pushed his jaw toward me like he had toward Sonia and snarled,

"Where's the boy?"

I spat in his face, just as Sonia had. He belted me across the face with the whiskey bottle, knocking me out of the chair, and spilling the rest of the bourbon over my shirt. As I fell from the chair, I pulled my hands from behind my back and reached out for Sonia's pistol that was still lying on the floor where Pockface had dropped it. I pointed it directly at his chest, then swung it toward the other goon before he could reach into his shoulder holster.

"Hands up!" I screamed.

They raised their hands tentatively, but obediently. What else could they do with an angry drunk pointing a pistol at their chests?

"Lie down!"

They sat on the floor.

"On your stomachs! Hands stretched out, palms down!"

They did that.

"If either of you even twitches, I will shoot you." With my left hand pointing the pistol at them, I used my right hand to unwrap the tape from Sonia's wrists. Without a knife and with only one hand, it wasn't easy, but it worked. She bent over and undid the tape from her ankles. I grabbed the roll of duck tape from the table and pushed the pistol toward her.

"I am going to tape them up while you aim the pistol at them. If either of them resists in any way, shoot him. Even if he just tries to scratch his nose. Do you understand?"

She gave a weak nod with her head.

"Can you do that? Can you shoot them? If you can't, they will kill us. You have to be able to shoot them. And you have to do it the minute they move a muscle. Can you do that?"

She hesitated, looking pleadingly at me.

"Can you do that?"

She gave a weak nod of her head.

"Say it out loud so they can hear you. They have to know you will shoot them. Say it out loud. If you don't say it, they will kill you and me, and Rodrigo will be an orphan!"

"Yes!" she said in a voice so harsh that it startled even me. "I will kill them both!"

XXVIII

They offered no resistance as I wound inches and inches of tape around their ankles, their wrists, their mouths, their foreheads, any part of their bodies I could think of that might enable them to squirm free. I even stuck a big piece of tape on the nape of Pockface's neck. Then I yanked it off. I was starting to get that reckless buzz that comes when the liquor first takes effect.

"See what it's like to have your hair ripped out!" I screamed. "Maybe I should just shoot you bastards right now." I reached over to Sonia for the pistol. But she pulled it back and stuffed it into her purse along with her other belongings that she was retrieving from the table. I plucked the unopened bottle of whiskey off the table and was trying to unscrew the cap when she grabbed my hand and pulled me toward the door.

She ran across Hiawatha Avenue toward the Light Rail station at 38th Street. I couldn't keep up with her, and I fell down, stumbling off the curb. She came back, snatched my hand, and pulled me up. For the first time, she saw the bottle of Jack Daniels clutched in my hand. She tried to take it from me, but I wouldn't let go. She took her purse by the strap, swung it in a huge arc, and brought it down on my wrists, knocking the bottle from my hands and smashing it on the pavement where it shattered into pieces. With surprising strength, she grabbed my arm and pulled me toward the station. I kept looking back at the bottle as she tugged me along. We were in the middle of the road, and at least two drivers had to slam on their brakes and swerve to avoid us. Several horns were honking. At the platform, she pulled some bills from her purse, stuck them into the fare machine, and got us our tickets just as the train pulled into the station. I almost didn't make it through the doors, but she tugged on my arm and pulled me toward a seat. I bumped into a bicycle that was standing on its rear wheel, wedged into the bicycle rack in the middle of the car, and the owner gave me a dirty look. With me stumbling down the aisle and reeking of whiskey, several passengers moved to the other end of the car. Sonia heaved a sigh of relief as the train pulled out of the station, but even as drunk as I was I could see that her hands were shaking as she sat in the seat and leaned against me.

"Jake, we can't go back to my duplex. It's not safe. They will get us there."

I looked out the window at the scenery passing by, and in my mind I was a boy again riding the train back in Queens and it was my cousin beside me.

"Jake, I am talking to you. Do you hear me? Look at me."

I looked over and had trouble focusing. I couldn't remember my cousin ever looking so fuzzy.

"Jake, where can we go. We cannot go to my apartment."

"My condo," I mumbled, realizing she wasn't my cousin. "Go to my condo. The bottle, Sonia. Why did you break the bottle? I need a drink."

"Oh, Jake, Jake, Jake, Jake, Jake, Jake," she sobbed. She buried her face into the space between my neck and shoulder. "What have they done to us, Jake?"

Three passengers at the end of the car were staring at us, disgusted looks on their faces. I waved my hand for them to go away.

The next thing I remember was Sonia pulling me off the train in downtown Minneapolis and hailing a taxi. It was dark out. I couldn't figure out how it got dark so fast. By the time we got to my condo, Sonia was looking much less fuzzy, and I was no longer stumbling as we got out of the taxi. My mind was clear enough that I was able to push the key into the door lock on the first try. But I wanted another drink so badly that it felt like I was suffocating.

"Sonia, I'm starving, but there's nothing to eat here. I'll go get us some take-out and bring it back."

She saw through me. "Jake, you can order it by phone."

"I have to get some fresh air."

"Jake, no."

I headed for the elevator. She slammed the door shut and followed me. I walked toward the Highland Village mall. She followed. It had started to drizzle, and we walked through the rain. The fresh air had sobered me up, and I was walking so fast she had trouble keeping up with my pace. I turned toward a sports bar on Ford Parkway. She grabbed my arm.

"Jake, do not go in there!" She had a hard look in her eyes and a twisted look on her face. "I will not let you. I will not let you."

"Sonia, I told you before. If I need a drink, you can't stop me." I opened the door and stepped inside. One television set was blaring a football game at full volume, another a hockey game, and a third a basketball game. The Timberwolves were winning. I went to the bar and ordered a glass of Jack Daniels. The bartender poured a double shot, and I motioned for him to fill the glass. She followed me to the bar, pulled on my arm for me to face her. "If you are going to drink it, Jake, you will have to do it in front of me. You cannot slink off in a corner feeling sorry for yourself." She looked mean and angry.

I picked up my glass and walked to a booth. She sat down opposite me, staring at me with her jaw jutting out in my direction. The bourbon smelled good. As I lifted the glass, she put her hand on my wrist. "If you drink that, Jake, I will walk out of here and you will never see me again. You have already lost one woman because of your drinking, and you will lose me. Oh, God. I do not want to lose you, Jake, but I will not live with a drunk."

She was getting on my nerves and I wanted her to go away. All I wanted was to feel the bourbon burning down my throat again. I raised the glass to my lips.

"Please, Jake. One more day. You said you could make it one day at a time. You owe me that, Jake, and that is all I am asking. Is there anything you ever asked of me that I have not given you? You owe me one more day. If you drink that glass, you will drive me away right now. All I am asking for is one more day."

The tears were flowing from her eyes now, streaming down her cheeks. "Put it down, Jake, or I am going back to my duplex."

"They'll get you if you do that."

"I do not care anymore, Jake. I will not live with a drunk. And neither will Rodrigo."

I wanted her to go away and leave me alone. But when she mentioned Rodrigo and stood up to step out of the booth, she startled me. I don't know why, but I set down the glass. Before I could reconsider, she grabbed my hand and pulled me from the booth. All I really wanted was that bourbon sitting on the table top, but I let her pull me through the door. The rain had stopped, but the sidewalks gleamed from the moisture. She grabbed my arm and hurried us down the sidewalk. "Oh, Jake, I am so proud of you."

I stopped and screamed, "Shut up! Shut up!"

She looked stunned. I sat down on the curb and put my head in my hands. She waited an instant and then I felt her sit down on the curb beside me. She didn't touch me. The enormity of what I had almost done began to sink in. If I drove her away and she was left on her own, she was sure to get picked up again. So was I. Our only safety lay in sticking together. I lifted my head and looked at her.

"Sonia, I am sorry. I did not mean that. I will never say that again."

"Jake, it has been a very tough day. You saved my life." She spread out the fingers of her hand, palm down and looked at them. "I'm grateful just to be in one piece and not to have to walk out on you. Right now, you can say whatever you want."

"I don't want to say that. I am sorry."

We sat for a moment and I said, "My ass is getting wet."

"So is mine."

"Let's go home." She grabbed my hand as we walked back to the condo. I woke up once in the middle of the night, and her leg was lying across me, just as it had that night in the Duluth hotel. But I didn't really want her leg across me. What I really wanted was that glass of bourbon I'd left on the table in the bar. I rolled away from her and lay on my side.

In the morning, I woke up first, as usual, put on the coffee, then brought two cups back to the bedroom. My head wasn't too bad, considering all the booze I'd swallowed. She leaned over and kissed me. Her breath was terrible, as I suppose mine was, since our toothbrushes were in her duplex. She propped her pillow up against the headboard and leaned back, leaving her small breasts deliberately exposed so I couldn't help but see them. She smiled. "Jake, you made it through the night."

I didn't smile back. "Sonia, you have no idea what it's like. I wanted that bourbon more than anything else in the world. I still do. And I will tomorrow and everyday for the rest of my life."

She pulled the covers up to her throat so I could no longer see her breasts, and she said softly, "I have no idea what it is like? I know that, Jake. But . . ." She paused before going on. "Do you have any idea what it is like to raise a disabled child who is repeatedly rejected by the people around him? Do you have any idea what it is like to have your child hunted down by killers who want to cut off his fingers? Do you have any idea what it is like to love a man who rolls away from you in the middle of the night because he wants a glass of whiskey more than he wants you?"

She gave me a hard stare.

"Jake, I lay awake half the night thinking about this. You are not going to like it, but it has to be said. I feel like I am living with two men. One man is resourceful and gutsy and saved my life last night. Given all that whiskey he swallowed, I don't know how he did it, but he did. Thank God, he did. The other day when I had to put Rodrigo on the airplane, that man was the most tender and caring companion I could have asked for."

"Why would I not want to hear that?"

"It's the other man you won't want to hear about. The other man tells me I cannot count on him for the rest of my life. I can only have him one day at a time. He wants his whiskey more than he wants me, and just a moment ago he was whining in self pity because he has an affliction with alcohol. Everybody feels sorry for themselves now and then, Jake, and after your gutsy action yesterday, maybe you earned the right to a moment of self-pity. But it has to end now."

Her voice was starting to crack, and her eyes were filling with tears. "For the first time, Jake, for the first time, I truly understand what you meant when you said you live one day at a time. To be honest with you, I don't like it. I don't like not being able to count on you for anything more than one day at a time."

She blinked the tears from her eyes and gave me another hard stare. It was clear that she really didn't understand what I had told her, so I tried to explain.

"Sonia, it's not that I lack a plan to stay sober. I do have a plan. You just have to understand how powerful the urge can be sometimes. The only way I can fight it is one day at a time. That's all I'm telling you."

I still don't think she understood, because the hard look in her eye did not soften in the least.

"I have committed myself to you Jake, just as long as you

don't drink. But I realized last night that I am now living under a
cloud of uncertainty, because I can never know for sure that you
will still be sober next year or next month or even next week. I do
not like living that way any more than I like Rodrigo being disabled. But I cannot change it, so, as you say in your serenity
prayer, I have to accept it. I can even accept getting angry about
it now and then."

"But you and I have to save ourselves from those goons, and
we can't do that if we wallow in self pity. I have to raise Rodrigo,
and self-pity will not help me do that either. So I don't want to
hear any more whining about your affliction with alcohol. And for
my part I will try not to whine about only getting to have you one
day at a time."

She still didn't understand. I said, "So what do you want me
to do? Do you want me to lie to you and promise I'll never drink
again? Alcoholics are good at that. I'll bet your ex-father-in law
promised that to his wife a hundred times. What do you want me
to do different than I'm doing?"

"Just keep being that first man I told you about. I accept you
as you are, Jake. But that first man I told you about is the one I
want you to be. And give me one more thing." She paused and
stared me in the eye. "Promise another twenty-four hours. One
more day. Can I have you sober until tomorrow morning?"

"Are you going to ask me that everyday?"

"Every time I need reassurance."

"I will do the best I can."

"Right now I'm going to shower, and then I want us to go out
someplace that the killers don't know about. Let the bastards
know that they cannot destroy our spirits. Then let's check into a
motel where we will be safe and try to figure out what to do."

XXIX

We went first to retrieve her Escort, which was still parked in the alley behind my office. She held her pistol in her hand while I pulled my briefcase containing the gun and silencer from her trunk where I had put them the day before. We stopped by her duplex to pick up enough clothes to last us for the weekend. I slung my briefcase strap over my shoulder and gripped my fingers around the pistol inside the briefcase as we walked up the stairs to her duplex. Nobody was there. I parked her Escort in the garage, and we drove off in my BMW.

She pointed out that the date was October 25th, the anniversary of Wellstone's death, and said she wanted to visit his grave site. There was little chance that Moneybags would look for us there. We picked up two roses from the flower section of a supermarket. "One for Paul and one for Sheila," she said. Then we drove to the Lakeview Cemetery in south Minneapolis where the gravesite overlooked Lake Calhoun. There were two small headstones and a large marble boulder behind the headstones. Several other flowers were already on the grave by the time we got there. She laid the two roses by the headstones and stood silently before the grave. I knew she was praying, because I could see her lips move.

We tried checking into a hotel in downtown Minneapolis but were told that the room would not be ready until three o'clock.

To pass the time, she dragged me to the Minneapolis Institute of Arts and made a stab at improving my mind. Anything to distract us from the mess we were in. I slung the briefcase strap over my shoulder and kept it there as we roamed.

She would enter a room, stop in front of object or painting, and study it for several minutes. At first, she would grab my arm, pull me over to what she was looking at, and point out her observations to me, but she eventually gave that up when she discovered how hard it was for me to stay interested. We ended up at the coffee kiosk where we sat sipping from paper cups as we looked out a huge picture window at the vista of downtown Minneapolis rising in back of a park, where small children were chasing each other, playing tag.

We sat in silence watching the children. With the killers never totally out of our minds, it was getting hard to keep up the act of two lovers enjoying a leisurely weekend. Suddenly, out of the blue, she broke the silence.

"Tell me about your wife, Jake."

"My ex-wife," I corrected. "And I already told you about her."

"You told me about terrorizing her into thinking you had blown out your brains, but you did not tell me what she was like. Was she blonde with big boobs or was she dark haired and flat chested like me?"

"You're not flat chested. You're perfect chested."

"Was she American or an immigrant like me?"

"American and blonde. But that was years ago. What difference does it make?"

"It makes a difference because you might be one of those men who is always looking for something exotic. Face it, Jake, none of the women in your life today are Anglos. Your assistant is Hmong and I'm Brazilian. Why?"

"I don't known why. I've always been attracted to people who were just a little bit different. Maybe it's just the alcoholic's craving for excitement. When cultures mix, you get excitement and creativity."

"So that is what I am to you, some exotic clash of cultures?" But she smiled as she asked that and leaned closer to me. I could tell she was not offended. She was teasing.

"Well, you are exotic. But how are you any different from me? You went halfway around the world to marry a man you barely knew. Then when you got here, you joined a black church and started wearing Afro-Brazilian symbols. And now you're an art dealer who has taken up with a businessman whose suits are too dreary. Maybe we're both looking for the exotic. But I'll tell you something The world needs people like us."

"Why?" She looked amused at my overstatement.

"Would the art lovers of Minneapolis be any better off if you'd never shown up with all that Latin American art you've brought in?"

"Somebody else would have brought it in."

"Would my clients be any better off if I'd never downshifted and shown up to set their financial houses in order?"

"Somebody else would have done it."

"Marco Polo went to China and came back with the compass and I don't know what else. Would the world have been better off if he'd just stayed home and never made the trip?"

"So now you're Marco Polo?" She was starting to laugh.

"Yes. And so are you. Just remember, when cultures mix, exciting things happen."

"Well, maybe we both feel exotic together. But that feeling will wear off some day. What happens then? What happens when everything becomes mundane?"

"God gave us a gift. Let's just enjoy it while we've got it and trust that we will also enjoy whatever comes next."

She laid her fingers on the back of my hand and said with a grin, "For a pragmatic businessman, Mr. J. P. Morgan, you are surprisingly refreshing. I think St. Jude has been looking out for you all along."

We looked out again at the children playing in the park, and I pulled an envelope from my pocket.

"The other day, after we took the photos of each other, I used the pictures to get fake driver's licenses for us. I want to use these when we check into the hotel, just to make it harder for anybody to trace us."

She looked at the plastic cards. "Nellie Forbush? And Emile de Becque? How did you come up with those names?"

"They were the stars in *South Pacific*."

She laughed. "Jake, you lead the strangest fantasy life of any person I've ever known."

On Sunday she brought me to church, the same African-American Catholic Church where I had picked up Rodrigo the previous week. I was the only man there with a briefcase slung over his shoulder. Although I am not a churchgoer, I found the service enjoyable. It almost seemed Baptist, what with its gospel choir, highlighted by a female vocalist. Sonia introduced me again to her friend Dora and prodded Dora to speak English so I would know what they were saying.

After church she insisted on going to a book store where she bought a set of instructional Portuguese language tapes. "I'll try not speak Portuguese in front of you Jake, because you look uncomfortable when I do that. But it is not natural for me to talk English when I'm with other Brazilians, and I insist on talking Portuguese with my son. Please use these tapes so that when we go to pick up Rodrigo in Rio you will at least be able to say hello to people."

Even as she handed the package to me I knew I was living in a dream world. But it was the best dream I'd ever had and I didn't want it to end. If studying Portuguese would keep the dream going, that's what I would do. That's how captivated she had me. I would have studied astro-physics if that's what she had wanted. Compared to that, Portuguese would be a pleasure. Anything to keep the dream from ending.

Wherever we went in public we repeatedly looked over our shoulders for possible threats, and I was growing tired of the task. We spent Sunday afternoon hiding in the hotel room. I read the weekend business news, while she sat in the middle of the floor and sorted one more time through the photographs of her upcoming art show at the gallery. That used up barely an hour of the time on our hands, and we turned on the television set. But I had no interest in the art documentary she wanted to watch, and she looked annoyed when I turned on a football game. We settled on a movie that held little interest for either of us, and I found myself pacing around the room. She didn't object to my doing that, but the expression on her face told me that my constant motion was irritating. So I sat next to her on the couch and tried to focus on the television while my fingertips beat a rhythm on the couch's pillow. She put her hand in mine, a gesture designed more to stop the irksome tapping of my fingers than to show affection. The movie ground to an end, and I said, "Let's go eat."

Since Moneybags had no way of knowing where we were, we were probably safe, but I was in no mood to take chances and brought the briefcase with pistol down to the restaurant.

"Jake, this constantly being on the lookout for the killers is making me a nervous wreck. We have to do something before I go nuts."

"You could call Detective Olson and tell him about Lars' secret hiding places."

"He doesn't believe anything I say. He botched things when he tore out the ceiling under Lars' bathtub, and then he botched his attempt to capture the killers that time at Lars' house. We should go search Lars' secret hiding places ourselves. At least we know what to look for now. Right before he slapped me, that goon said they were looking for a photo."

"Sonia, there were hundreds of photos scattered on the floor in Lars' study. We'd need storage boxes to cart them all out."

"We don't need to sort through those photos, Jake. They've already been picked over. We are going to look in Lars' secret hiding places."

"You realize that we can be prosecuted if we get caught?" I asked. "I don't know if they could revoke your citizenship for committing a crime, but I'd almost certainly lose my license."

"At this point, Jake, what difference does it make? We're amateurs at this hide-and-seek game, and the killers will eventually find us, just like that cop said."

I didn't respond.

"Please, Jake. We have to take the risk. I love you, and I know I told you I wouldn't go to Rio. But if we don't get ourselves out from under this threat of being killed, I'm going to have to go to Rio anyway."

"We'll take a look tomorrow morning while the neighbors are at work and there will be less chance of our being spotted."

The next morning we drove to my condo to pick up the key I had pilfered from Lars' garage. Then we drove around his block twice. Seeing nothing unusual, I parked on a cross street and we snuck up the alley to the back of the house. As soon as we entered the house, she led us to the basement and pointed toward a sump pump that was set into a well in a corner.

"You cannot tell by looking at it," she said, "but the liner of that well can be twisted loose and pulled off."

It wasn't easy pulling out the well liner. I had to twist it back and forth until it released a notch. With her lifting one side and me the other, we slid the liner out of the well.

She grinned and pointed to a metal cash box sitting in a

concrete niche that Lars had dug into the wall of the sump pump well. "Bingo," she said.

"Do you recognize it?"

"No," she said. "Just grab it and go. We can examine it later."

I reached into the hole and pulled out the box. We wrestled the liner back into the hole, twisted it into its locked position, and headed upstairs.

"Those photographs I told you about that are in Lars' study upstairs. Several of them were of you. As long as we are here, do you want to look through them?"

"No," she said. "Lars had his faults, but he wasn't kinky. When it came to sex, he only wanted one thing, and he wanted it as fast as possible. There won't be anything embarrassing up there."

I felt a little awkward for having suggested there might be.

"I just want to get out of here before somebody sees us. But we need something to pry open that cash box."

She took a sturdy butcher knife from the kitchen and looked a little conspicuous clutching it in her hand pointed down as we hurried through the alley behind Lars' house toward my car. But nobody spotted us, and as I drove off, she sat in the passenger seat prying open the cash box.

I was on I-94 in the middle of the bridge crossing the Mississippi when the top finally popped open. She pulled out a digital camera. "This is a surprise," she said, holding it up. "Lars always scorned my digital camera. No matter how good they were, he claimed they could never match the quality of his 35 millimeter camera. Now it turns out he had one all along."

She touched the power switch and looked surprised when the camera turned on. "And he's used it recently. The batteries still work."

"What's there?" I asked as she began clicking through the pictures.

"They're documents of some sort. Financial papers it looks like. We're going to have to make prints so that you'll be able to read them and figure out what they are."

She bent forward to get the viewer out of the sunlight and continued clicking through the images. I almost swerved into the guard railing when she suddenly screamed, "Oh, meu Deus! Jake, pull off. You have to see this."

XXX

I maneuvered onto the Riverside Avenue exit and pulled into a fast food restaurant parking lot. Using her thumb to point at the image, she passed the camera to me. Somebody was aiming a pistol at somebody else who looked like he was falling over. The man with the pistol was Moneybags, and we didn't recognize the victim. We both sat in shock for several minutes.

I said, "We need someplace private to look this stuff over and decide what to do. Let's use the printer in your duplex to make prints."

"No," she said. "There is something fishy going on there. Do you realize how odd it is that nobody has bothered us there in the last several days?"

"They can't get past your security system," I said.

"Maybe. Or maybe they have somehow bugged the phone line. If they eavesdrop on us, they know every place we go and they don't need to break in."

We went to a print shop near the University of Minnesota and used its equipment to print copies of the images on the digital camera. After that we went into Sergeant Preston's, a popular hangout at the University's West Bank campus, took a secluded table in the rear, and ordered a late breakfast while we spread the photographs on the table. I put the gunshot photo at the bottom of the pile so we wouldn't have to see it and began to examine the documents that Lars had photographed.

"Oh, Jesus!" I said. "I was right about Bob Vukovich."

She looked down at the document I was holding, then back up at me, waiting for me to continue.

"Do you remember the story he told me about his job pulling the electric cables through the muck in the iron mines and saying that it was no wonder he'd become a drunk?"

"He has gone on the wagon?"

I almost chuckled at her misusing the phrase off the wagon, but I stifled the urge. "Sort of. He's not drinking, but I should have picked this up from all the time he spends at the casinos. He's become a gambling addict and is deeply in debt to Moneybags."

"Jake, that doesn't make sense. Why would a hard nosed businessman like Moneybags lend cash to a hopeless gambling addict?"

"Control. He was using Bob as a bagman for delivering cash to congressmen and federal officials he would need to get the variances for the Bohemia Grove North he wanted to build in the Boundary Waters."

I handed her another document that listed several names and a dollar amount by each name. Some of the dollar amounts exceeded the legal limit for campaign contributions.

"It still doesn't make sense," she said. "Why would Moneybags give away all this cash up front when all he needed to do was give them a little piece of the action once the place became profitable?"

"There could be a lot of reasons. Maybe they needed the cash immediately. Maybe he was expecting profits so huge that it would be cheaper in the long run to give away the cash up front. Maybe he just didn't want to share the ownership. Who knows what his motives were?"

The waitress brought our breakfasts then, and I turned the materials face down so she couldn't see them.

"Jake, we have to give this to Sergeant Olson."

"We've got to think that over. He'll want to know how we got it, and as I said before, you and I will be in deep trouble if the police find that we broke into Lars' house."

"We can just mail it to them anonymously."

But that option also had drawbacks. No matter how the police got the information, once they started to investigate it, we would be sucked into the investigation, along with just about everybody we'd talked to, possibly including both my father and Jim Anderson. Coordinating all of our stories would be impossible. They'd find out about the money stuffed behind the pictures, the telephone calls to the mafiosos in New York, and the guns we were carrying around without a permit. I'd end up losing my license, and her budding career as an art dealer would come crashing to a halt as her potential clients began avoiding her. We'd be lucky to avoid prosecution. And if Olaf, who'd given us our gun lessons, got drawn into the investigation, he probably wouldn't be any more pleasant to deal with than Moneybags was.

"That is still better than getting killed," she said.

From my viewpoint, however, we not only needed to stay alive, we needed to avoid all these other outcomes. She frowned, unconvinced. Our choices were limited. We could put the camera back in Lars' hiding spot and pretend we'd never seen it. But that wouldn't get Moneybags off our backs, and returning to Lars' house would put us at an enormous risk of getting caught in the act of breaking and entering. We could slip the documents to Jim Anderson and hope that whatever he wrote about it in his newspaper column didn't pull us into the police investigation that was sure to follow. We could negotiate with Moneybags, offering to give him the camera if he would get his goons off our back. But then Lars' murder would go unpunished, and we had no way to know if Moneybags would keep his word. There were no good choices. And the only other choice I could think of was so horrible I didn't even mention it to her. We could get rid of Moneybags.

We were sitting in the booth across from each other, the photos spread out between the plates on the table between us. We'd been there a while, and the stale odor from the coffee cups drifted into our nostrils.

"Sonia, my father was right and so was Sergeant Olson. Go to Rio until this is over. Once you are gone, Moneybags will lose interest in me. That will give me time to get Li Vang set up and to figure out how to run my business remotely. Then I'll join you in Rio, get licensed in Brazil, build a clientele among the Americans living there, and you can teach me Portuguese, which is what you've been trying to do all along anyway."

"That is not a plan. It's a fantasy. And it also means keeping Rodrigo from his father during the part of the year he is in Rio and keeping him from me during the part of the year he is up here. I am not going to turn him into a ping pong ball bouncing back and forth between us."

"So what do you want, then?'"

"I really want to turn this stuff over to the police."

"If that's what you really want, there is nothing I can do to stop you. The camera's in your purse and all you have to do is take a taxi to the nearest police station."

"You are big enough and strong enough to stop me from doing that anytime you want."

"Sonia, I'm not a monster. I will never use force on you."

She smiled for the first time that day. "I was hoping you would say something like that, Amor. And for my part, I don't want to take any one-sided decisions about something that affects us both. I am willing to work on any reasonable plan you can come up with. But if you can't come up with a plan, Jake, we have to give this stuff to the police. Can we agree on that?"

"Just give me some time to think it over."

She frowned. "If you need time to think it over, let's at least go someplace safe while you do that. This constant looking over our shoulders for the goons is getting to me. Let's pick up my car and get out of town until you think of a plan."

"Why your car?"

"Because I want to drive so I can work off some of this nervous energy, and I'll be more comfortable driving my own car than I will driving yours."

"Where do you want to go?"

"Rochester?"

"Why Rochester?"

"It's out of town, and the killers won't know where we are. I've got some paintings placed on consignment in a couple of galleries there, and I could check in on them. I could also stop at the library at the Mayo Clinic and see if they have any new information on Williams syndrome."

"Couldn't you look it up over the Internet?"

She tilted her head downward and fixed a serious stare on me.

"Don't make problems, Jake. Just humor me. I want to turn this stuff over to the police right now, and the only reason I'm holding off is to give you time to come up with a better idea. While you're doing that, let's just get someplace safe where I'll feel comfortable and have something to do."

Watching carefully to make sure that no one was on our tail, we picked up her car at the duplex and headed south on Highway 55 in the direction of Rochester.

XXXI

She drove very fast, and an hour later, we got off Highway 55 at the Rochester exit and headed downtown.

"That's the Gonda Building," she said, pointing at a sleek, new, stone facade on her left. "If I remember right, the library is on the fifth floor. Give me a couple of hours and then come to get me there. Have you got that?"

"Don't you want to check into a hotel first?"

"I'm too nervous to hang around a desk clerk while you try to get by with our phony IDs. I've got to start moving around before I go nuts, and this will be a safe place." Then she reached her right hand in front of me and pointed out the passenger window. "That's the Kahler Hotel. They have a parking ramp around the corner. Check us in and then come up to get me. Do you know where?"

"Gonda Building. Library. Fifth Floor."

"Yes. Show up in two hours."

She pushed the car door open and started walking toward the Gonda Building entrance. I lifted myself over the gearshift, settled into the driver's seat, and edged the car forward. When I reached the stop sign at the end of the street, something caught my eye. Parked in front of the Methodist Hospital at the end of my street was a red SUV that looked just like the one that had been waiting at the Mall of America during the attempted kidnap of Rodrigo two weeks ago. My pulse must have doubled in ten seconds, I was so startled. It was hard to get a clear view of the driver, but he seemed to be wearing the same type of black jacket that Moneybags' goons had worn when they had tried to kidnap Rodrigo.

A horn honked behind me, urging me to turn. I drove past the hotel parking ramp. If that indeed was one of Moneybags' goons, I did not want to tip him off that we were staying in the Kahler Hotel. I drove several blocks, but saw no sign that the SUV was tailing me. Looking for a place to pause and collect my bearings, I pulled into a public parking ramp and parked on the second level. Looking out over the wall, I spotted the red SUV sitting near the exit waiting for me to come out.

How did they know that we were in Rochester? Maybe they had snuck into Sonia's garage and put a tracking device on her car. I crawled under the car and there it was. Attached to the rear axle with duck tape was one of those GPS devices that parents use to keep track of where their teen-agers are driving. Brilliant. They didn't even have to stay in sight of her. All they had to do was wait for her to get someplace and they would know exactly where to show up.

For a moment, I didn't know what to do. It didn't make sense to check into a Rochester motel if the goons knew we were in town. On the other hand, it also didn't make sense to leave Lars' camera and our stuff in the back seat of her car while I spent two hours searching for her. I decided to check into the hotel, so I'd have a place to park our stuff until we decided what to do. The worst that could happen would be that we'd leave immediately and pay for a night in a hotel room that we wouldn't use.

I slung the briefcase strap over my right shoulder, placing my hand inside the briefcase pocket and keeping my fingers wrapped around the handle of the nine-millimeter pistol, the silencer fastened to its barrel. With my left hand I pulled the suitcase toward a pedestrian exit the opposite side of the ramp from where the SUV was waiting. The exit led to a system of skyways and underground walkways called the subway. The skyway and subway network linked the Rochester downtown with most of the buildings in the Mayo Clinic complex. Nobody took notice of a forty-year-old man pulling a suitcase on rollers and toting a brief case over his shoulder. Of course, nobody knew that my fingers were clenched around the handle of a deadly pistol.

The skyway-subway system was well marked, and I had no trouble making my way to the Kahler Hotel. The lobby had old-fashioned decor reminiscent of the 1920s. I registered us as Mr. Emile de Becque and Mrs. Nellie Forbush. The desk clerk didn't bat an eye at my fake driver's license, but he insisted on a $300 deposit when I told him I wanted to pay with cash rather than use a credit card.

I set the bag in our room and went across the street to the Gonda Building, my briefcase slung over my shoulder, my hand inside the briefcase clutching the nine-millimeter pistol. The first thing I noticed was a sign on the door: Mayo Clinic bans guns in these premises.

I got off the elevator at the fifth floor and stepped into the most luxurious waiting room I had ever seen. Floor to ceiling windows looked out on downtown Rochester, including the carillon atop the original Mayo building. Visitors sat in easy chairs looking out the window at the vista, some of them with their feet on the footstools that were provided. I'd never before seen a waiting room with footstools. Patients sat in rows of comfortable chairs facing the reception desk waiting to be called to their appointments. Three or four tables held partially completed jigsaw puzzles that visitors could work on while they waited for their relatives or friends to emerge from the examining rooms. Some people sat at computer terminals connected to the Mayo Clinic library. The reception desk and the door jambs were set off by elegant wood moldings. The walls and building support columns were lined with a shiny stone facade.

But no library was in sight. A sweet-voiced, twenty year-old Scandinavian goddess at the reception desk told me that I was in the wrong building. The library was in the subway near the cafeteria. But I was free to use the computer terminals in the reception area that were connected to the library. She pointed at the bank of computers. It was still almost two hours before I could find Sonia, so I sunk into one of the easy chairs by the window, put my feet up on a footstool, pulled out my cell phone and called Li Vang.

"I can't come in the next couple days, Li."

"Mr. Morgan, our business is starting to slip. What am I going to do about all the appointments you have?"

"Leave me a list on the answering machine and I'll call them with an apology. In the meantime, if anybody needs me, give them my cell phone number. But it can't be helped. There is an emergency with Sonia."

She didn't sound like she cared a great deal about Sonia's emergency. Of course, I'm not sure that Sonia cared a great deal about Li Vang, either. The two most important women in my life at the moment and they disliked each other, even though they'd never met. It was a mystery to me.

Two hours finally passed, and I found the library. Sonia was hunched over a computer terminal reading something. She jotted some information on a piece of scrap paper, brought it to the reference desk, and the librarian printed out several pages of information which she handed over to Sonia. As we walked to our room at the Kahler Hotel, I kept a constant lookout for anybody in a black leather jacket, but no one materialized. She dropped herself into the easy chair, kicked off her shoes, and propped her feet up on one of the beds.

"Jake, could I have a little more time alone? Could you go

window shopping or something for a couple of hours before we go to dinner?"

"We can do whatever you want, but first we're going to have to make a change of plans."

"Why?"

I told her about Moneybags' goons stalking us.

"Oh no," she said. "Not now. We've got to get out of here."

"It's going to take some maneuvering. We can't go anywhere until I cut that GPS device off your rear axle. Then I'll move your car someplace else. While I'm doing that, don't leave this room. OK?"

She nodded her head.

"And don't open the door to anybody. Nobody! Not even the maid or room service. We can stop and get something to eat later on the way out of town."

"Knock first, when you come back, Jake. Don't startle me. I am going to keep my gun next to me all the time, and I don't want to shoot you."

"Lock the deadbolt. That way nobody can come in unless you unlock it. And one other thing," I said. "If anybody phones, we're registered under our fake names."

The first thing I needed was a pair of scissors to cut through the duck tape holding the GPS device to Sonia's rear axle. There were several of them at the hotel gift shop, and after buying a pair, I headed out to the parking ramp. The SUV was gone, but her Escort was still there. After cutting the duck tape I put the GPS device on the pavement under the front bumper of the car next to the Escort. Then I drove out of the ramp, leaving the goons to think that the car was still parked up there with the GPS device that was beeping away or doing whatever it did to send its signals to outer space and back to our stalkers. I drove straight for the Kahler Hotel parking ramp and found a spot across from the second floor ramp entrance to the hotel.

All I had to do now was to pick her up from our room, take the hotel elevator down to the second floor, walk through the hallways to the parking ramp, and get out of Rochester before the goons knew what was happening. We wouldn't even have to check out of the hotel, since we were prepaid and registered as the non-existent Emile de Becque and Nellie Forbush.

Pleased with myself for being so clever, I decided to pick up some pastries and coffee, since there was no way to know how long it would be before we could eat, and we hadn't eaten anything since our late breakfast at Sergeant Preston's in Minneapolis. I found a coffee kiosk next to the cafeteria in the subway, picked out a Danish for myself, a cinnamon roll for her, and a large coffee that we could share. Stuffing the pastries in my briefcase and holding the large coffee cup in my free hand, I stepped away from the kiosk and toward a marble lined pillar where my eye caught sight of a striking bronze sculpture. I paused for a moment to look at it, a Rodin, according to the placard. I had never before seen a health clinic with original Rodin sculptures. I suppose there are such places, but this is the first one I'd ever seen. I should point it out to Sonia. Just then, I was suddenly bumped against the marble pillar. I felt a jab in my back and heard a sharp voice, "Don't move a muscle, Morgan, or I'll push this knife through your kidney. Where is she?" At the same time, he grabbed my jacket with his free hand so I couldn't run off.

I turned my head to look and saw that it was the same pock-faced goon who'd planned to kill us the previous week. He jabbed the knife deeper into my skin. "I said, don't move. Just do exactly what I say. We're going to find a place with a little more privacy, and you're going to give me the hotel and room number where she's staying." He jabbed the knife in a little deeper to make his point and left me with no doubt that the knife would plunge all the way into me as soon as he got what he wanted. "Start walking slow, back toward that corridor." He jabbed me again.

"Now turn right."

The subway was extremely crowded at that time of afternoon with patients, visitors, and health care workers all headed in different directions as they finished their day. Nobody took notice of the man cuddled up to my back, holding on to my jacket. Maybe they thought we were lovers. I was still carrying my coffee cup in my left hand and my right hand was still wrapped around the pistol in the briefcase. Pockface had never told me to take my hand out of the briefcase or to drop the coffee on the floor.

As we started to enter the main corridor, a volunteer pushed a wheelchair right in front of me and I had to stop. The knife jabbed deeper into my back. Then a young man stepped back from an information booth and bumped into Pockface, pushing him to his left, and slashing his knife across my back. In reaction to the knife slicing my skin, my left arm shot up and back, dumping the hot coffee into the goon's face. He let go of my jacket, and I took off as fast as I could. The coffee splash in his face gave me a ten yard head start, and unless he, too, was a trained runner, he would never be able to catch me in an open field.

But I didn't have an open field. I had to push through a mob of people. The briefcase was pulling me off balance, and I was slowed down by the pain from the slash across my back. People shouted as I shoved them out of the way. I tore to the left, down a corridor leading back to the Kahler Hotel. When I turned I got a quick glimpse behind me and saw that the thug had pulled out a gun. Just before I made another turn, I heard a deafening explosion behind me, and the glass shattered in a store window. The noise of the shot cleared my path as people pushed themselves against the wall or dropped to the floor. Only those stuck in wheelchairs were left out in the open. One volunteer was down on his knees hiding behind the patient in the wheelchair he was supposed to be pushing. Another shot rang out just as I entered the spot where the subway makes several sharp turns around the basement of the Kahler Hotel and the Methodist Hospital. I came into an old, stark, tile-lined tunnel with no shops or people.

The tunnel had several sharp turns that slowed me down but also kept the gunman from shooting. One final left turn and I came into a big corridor so wide that I would be an easy target. On the right side of the corridor were doors to a ballroom where dozens of people milled, apparently at the conclusion of a conference. In the midst of them was a large, black, grand piano, and a pianist dressed in a tuxedo. He was playing music for the people winding up their conference in the ballroom. With a man shooting at me from behind, I shouldn't have noticed the song, but I did. "The Party's Over."

The thug followed me into the open corridor and fired a wild shot. The piano stopped. I turned hard left in front of a barber shop, just as a bullet whizzed by me and shattered the barber shop's glass window. Ducking behind a ledge for a stairway, I rested my right forearm on the ledge, and pointed my pistol at the thug's chest. I recalled Olaf instructing Sonia, "Squeeze the trigger, Sonia. Don't jerk it." The squeeze seemed to take an hour. Pockface was coming straight at me, raising his gun again. My gun went poof, and he ran into the bullet.

The corridor exploded in bedlam with people screaming, doctors from the conference room rushing over to the man I'd shot, and patrons in the barber shop dropping to the floor. I sped up the stairs, which took me to street level where no one had heard the commotion below. And nobody below was foolish enough to chase a man who had just fired a pistol that had a silencer.

I forced myself to slow down to a brisk walk, jammed the gun barrel inside my belt, and covered it with my jacket. I walked as normally as possible past the restaurant at the top of the stairs. Dozens of people were coming and going, and I walked through them until I found a door that led to the parking ramp I had just left moments before. Police sirens were blaring, and they seemed to be getting closer by the second. It sounded like there were a million of them.

I walked up the ramp to the second floor entrance to the hotel and forced myself to walk as nonchalantly as possible. But it's hard to be nonchalant when you've just escaped death, your heart is beating two hundred times a minute, your back is burning with pain, and your shirt is getting bloodier by the minute. I tried to bunch up the tail of my jacket and press it against the knife wound to hold back the bleeding so I wouldn't leave a trail of blood to our room. I didn't want to take the elevator for fear of being spotted, so I walked up to our fifth floor room and rapped on the door for Sonia to open it.

XXXII

Her mouth gaped open when she saw me. I went straight for the bathtub, stripped myself naked, bunched the clothing together, and lay down against the bundle, hoping I could press tight enough against it to stop the bleeding. My back was throbbing too much from the pain of the cut for me to worry much about the guy I'd shot, but a lot of thoughts ran through my mind, including a disturbing sense of accomplishment that I had fought off the killer so well.

She ordered me to roll to my side so she could examine the wound. "The bleeding has stopped. You did a good job of that. It looks like there's a puncture wound, so you might need a tetanus shot. But the cut is only skin deep. If we had some butterfly bandages, we could hold it closed. I'll go get some right now."

"We can't wait. If the police start looking for me, an out of town guy who registered without a credit card is going to draw attention."

"Why would the police be looking for you?"

"I'll tell you in the car. Throw my bloody clothes into the suitcase. Then press something against the cut as tight as you can and find something to hold it in place long enough for me to get down to your car. Then rinse all that blood in the bathtub down the drain and hope that the cops aren't very thorough if they inspect this room."

With the bleeding stopped, I stepped out of the tub. She turned on the shower to rinse the blood down the drain and left it running while she pressed the least bloody of my clothes against the cut. "Hold this tight while I look for something to tie it with," she commanded.

She came back with a pair of her light slacks, wound them around my waist and tied the legs together in a square knot. It wasn't much of a bandage, but it would hold the makeshift dressing in place as long as I kept my hand pressing against it. We stuffed everything into the suitcase, she turned off the water in the bathtub, picked up her purse and my briefcase, and grabbed the handle to pull the suitcase toward the elevator.

"Take the stairs," I said. "We'll be spotted on the elevator."

"Can you walk down three flights of stairs?

"There's no choice. I'll have to."

The clerk at the parking ramp gave Sonia change for her ten dollar bill without batting an eye, and she headed us back toward Highway 55.

"What do we do, Jake?" she said as she roared onto the highway.

"The first thing is to drive within the speed limit and come to a complete stop at all the stop signs so we don't draw attention."

She shot me a dirty look, but she did ease up on the gas pedal and our speed dropped to fifty-five.

"Then find us another hotel, preferably one that's not on the straight line from Rochester to Minneapolis."

"We can't do that, Jake. If the cops start asking around at the hotels for guests registering without a credit card, they are sure to discover our names and send out an alert to all the hotels in the area."

I bent forward as far as the pain in my back would permit and retrieved a small envelope from my briefcase. Opening the envelope, I pulled out two drivers' licenses. "We're going to cut up the old licenses and throw them out and use these instead. I was afraid something like this might happen, so I got three sets of fake licenses."

That should have brought a smile to her face, but it didn't. She just said, "And who are we this time?"

"Edie Doyle, that's you. And I'm Terry Malloy."

"And they're from?"

On the Waterfront, I announced proudly.

She finally smiled. "Jake, I was wrong when I said you lead the strangest fantasy life of any man I know. You lead the strangest fantasy life of any man alive."

"It's one of my character flaws. Just get us some place, Sonia. That cut is really throbbing."

She turned east at the first major highway and half an hour later pulled into Red Wing, a Mississippi River town. She picked up a bagful of bandages and antiseptics from a drug store and then drove to the St. James Hotel. For $200 cash, the clerk allowed her to register as Edie Doyle without showing a credit card. She lay me in the bathtub as she had before to work on my wound without leaving any traces of blood on the bed or carpet. "The bleeding has stopped nicely, Jake. We just need to clean out the cut."

Then she poured the bottle of peroxide over my wound.

"Aoww!" I screamed. "Take it easy!"

"Don't be a baby. You have a puncture wound that we have to clean. You need a tetanus shot. But if the cops are after you like you say, you can't just go to an emergency room. So for the time being we have to clean it out as best we can." She dipped a cotton swab into the peroxide and began pushing it into the puncture.

"I don't need a tetanus shot. I had one five years ago."

"Nobody knows off the top of their head when they had a shot."

"It was about five years ago. Just stop poking at that cut."

She made one last jab of the cotton swab into the puncture wound and used my last clean tee shirt to pat the wound dry. She used the butterfly bandages to pull the slash edges together and taped gauze pads on top of the butterfly bandages. "I think you'll be able to walk, Jake. Just don't make any sudden moves. Do you think you could make it to the restaurant? I'm starving."

She looked at her watch. It was seven o'clock, and we hadn't eaten since ten that morning.

"I don't think so. Could we do room service?"

"I'm too antsy to sit up here, Jake. I've got to move around. I'll go down by myself and bring something back for you. What do you want?"

"A couple of burgers and a milk shake or something. And keep your hand on your gun."

After she left, I used my prepaid cell phone to call Bob Vukovich.

"Bob," I said. "Sonia and I need to get away for a few days. Would you have any interest in going hunting with us up by that shack you have up north?"

"I thought you weren't a hunter."

"I wasn't. But as long as I'm living in this state, I figured it was about time I got with the program and did what everybody else does."

"What about Sonia? She strikes me as even less likely to be a hunter than you do."

"I don't know if she'll actually hunt. But she wants to go up north. She'd at least tramp through the woods, and she'd probably cook for us."

"How about Monday? Get your licenses and come up. Do your remember how to find the shack?"

"Yes. We'll meet you there at eight-thirty Monday morning."

Then I called Jim Anderson. "I think I can get you a scoop on Moneybags and the Wellstone plane crash." We talked for forty-five minutes, solidifying my plan. The more we talked the more excited he got. When we finished, he said, "You got balls, Jake. I told you once that you and I had the basis for a good partnership. But I never dreamed of this. You got balls, man."

Sonia came back with my burgers, kicked off her shoes and lay down next to me on the bed. I rolled onto my side, moving slowly so I wouldn't pull the butterfly bandages loose. I faced her and laid the palm of my hand on her cheek. I left my hand there for a moment, then withdrew it and said, "I've got a plan."

She turned her head toward me.

"If you reject it, we can drop it and take our chances going to the police. But hear me out first. We'll hide out in a hotel for a few days to recuperate. Then we go hunting."

"Hunting? You'll bleed like a stuck pig if you start moving around. And you want to go hunting?"

"I have a week to get better before the hunting." I explained my plan to lure Moneybags to Bob Vukovich's hunting shack and strike a deal. She agreed immediately, and that surprised me. I was expecting a long argument. Maybe she was as sick of being stalked as I was. Probably sicker. After all, she's the one who had to send her son five thousand miles away just to keep him safe.

"Just one question, Jake."

"What?"

"You seem awfully certain that Moneybags will come to the hunting shack. What makes you so sure?"

"He has tried three times to kidnap us. And now we're offering ourselves to him on a silver platter. He won't pass that up."

"Bob was your oldest friend. What makes you so sure that he will betray you?"

"Amor, I'm alcoholic and I would have betrayed my Mother

for a drink if I needed it. The only difference with Bob is that his addiction is gambling. It's put him up to his eyeballs in debt to Moneybags. He'll do anything to stay on that guy's good side."

"And if he doesn't betray you? Or Moneybags fails to show up?"

"Then we'll just have to pry as much information as we can from Bob and get him to propose a deal to Moneybags for us. We have a lot of leverage we can use on him. He wouldn't want the police or his employer finding out that he was involved in the attempt to kidnap Rodrigo. He also knows we have a lot of cash that he might think he could tap into if he cooperated."

She gave me a disgusted look at the idea of using these pressure tactics.

"He might even be glad for any chance to get out from under Moneybag's thumb," I said. "There's also another part to the plan. Will your friend Dora help you out without asking too many questions?"

"I am sure she will. But we cannot put her in danger, or have her do anything illegal."

"Just in case we have to deny that we're meeting with Moneybags on Monday morning, we need to establish that we were someplace else at that time. Let Dora and her husband use your credit card and driver's license to enjoy a romantic stay at the Nicollet Inn. It's on a picturesque island in the Mississippi just across from downtown Minneapolis."

"They are going to pretend to be us?"

"Exactly. She's about your size and she's got dark hair. Make sure she's the one who does the check in and the ordering of breakfast so that everyone will pick up on the Brazilian accent. And since her husband is supposed to be me, warn him not to speak Portuguese any place where he can be overheard. In fact, unless his English is perfect, it might be better if he didn't speak at all."

She laughed at me. "Jake, expecting two Brazilians to have

a romantic dinner and not carry on a conversation is impossible. Besides, how am I going to explain all this to Dora without making her suspicious."

"I don't know. Improvise. Tell her you'll explain later."

She punched Dora's number into her cell phone, but I made her disconnect.

"We don't want any calls going from your phone to Dora. Calls from your cell phone can be traced. Use my prepaid phone instead."

She reached Dora and they spent half an hour talking it over. The act of talking with someone else in her native tongue seemed to have a calming effect on Sonia, and she smiled as she clicked the phone shut. "All set," she said, raising her hands, palms up. "We can drop off the license and credit card when we return to town tomorrow."

At nine o'clock we turned on the TV news, and the coverage of the shootout in Rochester looked gruesome. One man, with no identification, shot to death in one of the world's premier health clinics. Store windows shot out. A patient knocked out of a wheelchair during the chase. Yellow police tape stretching for hundreds of yards through the subway. And a second man, bleeding from an apparent wound, gone from sight. No leads as to what caused it all or where the wounded man went.

Sonia had a strange look when the camera panned on the dead body being wheeled away on the litter.

"What was it like for you, Jake?"

"What was what like?"

She paused as though it was hard to say. "Killing someone. Please don't tell me you liked it."

"No. I didn't like it. I was scared to death. I was trapped in this corridor and he was shooting at me. I had no choice but to shoot back. But no, I did not like it. I hated it."

"Keep hating it, Jake. Please keep hating it." We were lying in the bed, our heads propped up on pillows so we could see the

TV screen. "Look at me, Jake." I turned my head and we were looking into each other's eyes. "Don't turn macho on me, Jake. Whatever happens, don't turn macho. I have told you that before. I want a tender man. I don't want a macho man. Tell me you won't turn macho."

I just looked at her. I'd never thought of myself as macho. I didn't even know exactly what it meant.

"Tell me, Jake. Tell me."

"I won't turn macho. I promise." But a small part of me deep inside was not nearly as repelled by what I'd done as I was letting on to Sonia.

She kept her gaze on me, looking like she was reading my mind, then raised herself up on her elbow, leaned over, and gave me a long kiss on the lips. "Do not break that promise, Jake. Whatever you do, don't break that promise." She reached up to turn out her light and rolled over on her side to face away from me, leaving a big gap of space to separate our bodies.

Something was happening between us, and I didn't know what. I feared that it wasn't good. It was a long time before I fell asleep.

XXXIII

We spent less than an hour at her duplex trading the Escort for my car and packing the things we'd need through Monday. We stopped at a sporting goods store and bought everything the salesman recommended for a weekend hunting trip up north. I cut holes in the right hand pockets of the hunting jackets, so we would each be able to conceal our pistols there. I located a store that sold security equipment and bought three kevlar vests. Then we headed to a bed and breakfast in the river town of Stillwater where we planned to hide for the rest of the week.

Before I filled out the registration card, Sonia warned me, "Don't use our fake drivers licenses, Jake. Pick out a fake last name, but use our real first names."

"Why?"

"I'll never be able to get through a week calling you a fake name, and we don't want them to have any suspicions about us."

"What if they demand to see our driver's licenses?"

"Then we'll just go someplace else."

We registered as Jake and Sonia Smith, and the innkeeper showed us to a spacious room with a four poster bed. The house was located on top of the hill overlooking downtown Stillwater. At dusk, we could see the lights twinkling along the streets and on the old, steel, lift bridge. We walked to the top of the stairway that would take us downtown where we could get something to eat. But given my shaky physical condition, we would never be able to climb back up those steps. There must be a hundred and fifty of them. We went back to the B&B, picked up my car, and drove downtown to a small, Italian restaurant where I had a veal marsala and she ordered a chicken cacciatore.

Back in our room at the B&B, she asked, "Jake, are you still wearing the Saint Jude medal?"

I pulled it out of my collar for her to see.

"Good. Don't lose it."

In the morning, she changed the bandages on my back and put the dirty bandages in a bag that I tossed into a public trash can where the innkeeper would not see them. "This is coming along nicely," she said, admiring her work. "If you just don't do any sharp twists, your cut should be well closed by Sunday."

At breakfast I got the first genuine smile from Sonia that I'd seen in two days. The innkeeper heard us talking at the breakfast table, and she asked, "Where are you from?"

"La Crosse," said Sonia. "We work at the University there."

"I mean originally," said the innkeeper.

"Spain," said Sonia.

"Oye, that's why you have that accent," she said with a plastic smile. Neither of us said anything. "It must be very nice for you to be able to come here where everything is modern." Then she went back to the kitchen.

I grinned at Sonia and said, "I see now what you were trying to say when you told me about your in laws looking down on you. If you hadn't told me that I never would have picked up on that little bit of smugness. Do I sound like that?"

"No, Jake. You never sound like that. I get mad at you sometimes, but you have never sounded like that. I love the way you sound." That was when she smiled. It wasn't her big, ear to ear smile. But it was genuine, and it made me feel good.

"Do you want to go down and take a look at the galleries?"

"Not yet. I'd like to go back to the room and relax for awhile. We can look at the galleries this afternoon when it is warmer."

While she propped herself up in bed and opened her book, I went down to the car, drove back to the deserted part of the apple orchard, and once more lined up some pumpkins for target practice. By the time I finished, I could hit my target more than half the time from a distance of about twenty-five feet.

I drove to the Veterans' Home in south Minneapolis and brought my father out to the picnic bench where we could talk. I outlined my entire plan and how he fit into it. He looked skeptical.

"Jake, this is madness. Send that woman to Brazil before you both get killed."

"She won't go. I even offered to go with her and transfer my whole business to Rio, and she still wouldn't go."

He just gave me that skeptical, gaunt look.

"All I'm trying to do is strike a deal with Moneybags, and, as I explained to you, there are several backups planned in case anything goes wrong. You're a critical part of the backups. They won't work without you. Will you do it?"

"If this fails, Jake, it's going to be on my conscience for the rest of my life."

"It's not going to fail. Just remember, as soon as this is over, destroy that cell phone I gave you and get rid of it."

It was a lazy week that Sonia and I spent at the bed and breakfast. We read books and magazines. We browsed more galleries, antique stores, and dress shops than I ever want to see again in such a short time period. The innkeeper turned out to be quite pleasant, but I couldn't warm up to her after what she'd said.

Sonia said, "Don't be a snob in reverse, Jake."

"After what she said, you're calling me the snob?"

"You're the one who tells me you accept people as they come. I'm just following your example. It's what Wellstone would want."

She called Rodrigo each morning, and I tried to pretend that we were reliving the delight of our earlier visit to Duluth a short time ago. But it didn't work. Knowing what we had to do at the end of the week kept us both on edge. I had several conversations with Jim Anderson to fine-tune our plan. I visited the apple orchard once again to practice shooting pumpkins. By Saturday my back was feeling better. We tested our strength by walking down the stairway into town for lunch, browsing the shops for a couple hours, and climbing back up the stairs again. Then on Sunday morning I paid our bill and we headed up north to go hunting.

Jim Anderson met us for lunch at Brainerd. He showed up with an unexpected second person, a muscular Hispanic who had the hard look of a man who did dangerous things for a living.

"This is Chico," said Jim. "He doesn't speak English."

"Why is he here?" I asked, irritated. Jim hadn't mentioned another person in any of our conversations.

"We need a backup, just in case anything goes wrong. And we need a backup who is not going to understand anything that you and Moneybags talk about once you get inside that shack."

"How do you expect to communicate with him if he doesn't speak English?" I said.

Jim rattled off a string of Spanish. The only word I caught was gringo. Chico laughed.

"Where'd you learn Spanish?" I asked, impressed.

"I'm from California."

"A lot of people are from California, but they don't speak Spanish."

"They do if they grow up where I did."

We spent the afternoon casing out the area near the shack where we were to meet Bob Vukovich the following morning. The deer hunters were out in force, and rifles went off intermittently.

Jim had an extra shot gun in his trunk. He put it in a waterproof case and hid it under some leaves next to the road. "Just another backup in case we need it," he said. He also brought a very expensive video camera and scoured the outside of Bob's shack until he found a sizeable hole in the wall where he wedged the camera so that it was out of sight. He turned the videocam on and off with a remote control that had been customized for the task. Then he pulled the machine out of the hole where he'd put it previously and pushed the playback button. "Perfect," he boomed.

We determined where to park our cars, where Chico was to stand, when he was supposed to follow us into the shack, how to get to our escape routes if necessary, and where to rendezvous in case we got separated. I used a GPS device we had purchased at the sporting goods store to get the exact latitude and longitude of the shack's location.

I phoned my father on the prepaid cell phone and gave him the latitude and longitude coordinates. Sonia would call him every half hour starting at eight o'clock Monday morning. If she missed a call by more than two minutes, he was to tell both 911 and the local sheriff's office that a murder was about to take place precisely at those coordinates. "If you have to make those calls," I reminded him, "destroy that cell phone afterwards and get rid of it immediately."

We had done everything we could think of, and there was no more to do. We went back to the café in Brainerd where I bought dinner for the four of us. Sonia had the grilled walleye pike filet, and I ordered the prime rib. I pulled Jim aside to gave him the third kevlar vest. I didn't have one for Chico, since I had no way to know he'd be there. We agreed to meet at seven the following morning, and then we parted for our hotel rooms.

XXXIV

Sonia looked so tense the next morning I feared she might shatter if I so much as touched her. I gave her as much space as possible in that small motel room and stepped outside as soon as I got my clothes on. She finally came out all dressed, looking bulky with the kevlar vest under her hunting jacket.

Jim and I drove separately. We backed his car into an opening a quarter mile from the shack, hiding the car from sight. He and Chico walked through the trees parallel to the road so they could keep an eye out for any of Moneybags' goons who might be lurking about. The only vehicle in sight when I pulled up to the shack was Bob's truck. I drove around it, through a mud puddle, and parked with the front of my car pointed away from the shack for a quick getaway.

Following our plan, I went into the shack first, with my fingers clenched around the nine millimeter pistol tucked into the space where my jacket pocket had been cut open for it. Sonia kept five paces behind me, covering my back, her hand around the pistol in the cut out pocket of her hunting jacket. Despite the kevlar vest, I felt naked, not knowing whether I was going to get blasted from the front by one of Moneybags' goons or shot from behind if Sonia's aim was bad. I stepped to the right as I came through the door, and she stepped to the left.

"Come in," growled Moneybags, standing by a bare wooden table where he and Bob had been waiting for us. On the floor in back of them was a propane heater that was burning away, taking the chill out of the cabin. Next to the heater was a set of pruning shears, and Sonia gasped when she saw it. Sitting on the table was a gun I couldn't recognize, but I thought it looked like an Uzi. Standing up, Moneybags looked huge, much bigger than he had looked at the banquet a month earlier. He was taller than Bob and just as muscular.

"What's that gun for?" I demanded. "It doesn't look like a hunting rifle."

"Just a last resort in case you and your friend try anything rash." He moved his hand toward the gun.

I pulled the nine millimeter pistol from my pocket. "Sit down. Put the palms of your hands on the table and leave them there."

"What's going on?" demanded Bob, a startled look on his face.

"Just do what I say." I nodded to Moneybags. "What is it you're after that you think we have? What do you want from us?"

He didn't answer my question. Instead, he complained with a scowl, "You have caused me an enormous amount of expense, Mr. Morgan." He was not in the least flustered by the pistol pointed at his chest.

"I have caused you expense," I screamed. "You damned near killed Sonia and me. And you think I've caused you expense. Get on the floor."

They didn't move. His hand moved almost imperceptibly toward the gun on the table. I aimed the pistol at the space between them and squeezed the trigger. The silenced gun went poof and a bullet shot through the wooden table, sending splinters in several directions. They dropped to the floor.

"Against that wall!" I motioned to the far wall. "Put your backs against the wall and spread your feet apart." Bob moved to the right of the propane heater and Moneybags to the right of Bob. A look of terror covered Bob's face, but Moneybags simply looked back at us with a sneer. "Put the palms of your hands flat on the floor and keep them there."

They did that.

"What did you want from us? And why did you kill Lars?"

"Your dear friend Lars turned out to be a turncoat."

"So you killed him and set it up to look like just another drug deal gone bad?"

"You don't play the game, you pay the price," said Moneybags. The coolness with which he said this and his lack of concern that I might report him to the police was unnerving.

"I have to know what you're after," I said. "We found something, but unless I know if it's what you want, it's totally useless. What are you after?"

He said nothing. I squeezed the trigger again and a bullet dug into the floor boards between his legs.

"Show me what you've got and I'll tell you if it's what I'm after," he snarled.

I pulled the trigger once more and another bullet landed between his legs.

"What did Lars take that was so threatening to you?" I lifted the pistol and pointed the barrel at his stomach.

"The negatives," he said. "The ones he passed to you or your girl-friend."

"What negatives? Lars was a photographer. He had thousands of negatives."

"Don't be cute. You know what I'm talking about."

"Did these involve the transceivers he bought for you?" Of course, I knew that the photos on the digital camera had nothing to do with the transceivers, but I was fishing to find out what he had used the transceivers for.

"You know so much about me, you figure it out," he sneered.

"You and Lars set up the transceivers in the woods to pull Wellstone's plane off course, and he took photographs of you doing that."

"Wellstone's plane? You're crazy. I was glad that the little bastard got what he deserved. But I didn't do it. That would be stupid."

When he said bastard, I feared that Sonia might shoot him on the spot, but she didn't move a muscle. She was following our plan perfectly, letting me try to find out who it was in the photo she had printed from Lars' digital camera, and letting me try to find out what this had to do with Wellstone.

"Then why were you talking to the CIA? You spent a week with them in Langley just before Wellstone's death. What was that about?"

"CIA? You think I was talking to the CIA? It was people working on one of our projects, investors, PR people, and lobbyists."

"Bohemian Grove North?"

"You seem to know an awful lot about my business."

"Why would the CIA buy into that?"

"The CIA buy into my resort? What the hell could they do for me, except bring me trouble?" He shifted his eyes toward Sonia. "You've let that little cunt addle your brains."

I pulled the trigger again, shooting another hole in the floorboards just inches from his crotch. I shifted my aim over to Bob's crotch, and his face turned white.

"Lars helped Mr. Radezewell set up the transceivers."

"Shut up, you fool!" screamed Moneybags.

I shot another bullet into the floor between Moneybags' legs. He pushed back against the wall, fear finally showing in his face, as though he'd just realized for the first time that he'd lost control of the situation to a madman. I shifted the pistol back to Bob. He stared at it without saying a word.

"What were the transceivers for?"

Bob said nothing. He just stared at the pistol.

"Bob, I want to know what the transceivers were for. If you don't tell me, I will have to shoot you. But you're an old friend, so I'll give you a choice. You can take it in the kneecap or you can take it in the balls. Which do you want?"

Bob's pale expression turned even paler.

"They had nothing to do with the Wellstone or the CIA. We needed them to communicate with a plane that we'd bought. Mr. Radezewell wanted me to take a suitcase with two million dollars in small bills to Washington. And we used our private plane so there wouldn't be any record of me flying the commercial airlines. The pilot landed on an old gravel road that nobody uses anymore. As soon as I got on board with the suitcase, he was supposed to take off. The trouble was, the pilot had no idea how sensitive his mission was, and he brought along a passenger who had somehow conned him into going along for the ride. Mr. Radezewell was enraged. He thought the passenger was an informer for the Treasury Department."

"Shut up, you fucking fool," Moneybags shouted. Bob hesitated and I raised the pistol until it was pointed squarely at his crotch. His eyes widened. "I threw the suitcase with the money into the plane, but before I could climb in myself, I heard a gun go off behind me. Mr Radezewell had shot the passenger, and we sank his body in a nearby lake."

"So was he a Treasury agent?"

"Apparently not, because nobody came around investigating. Apparently he was just a hitchhiker who took a ride to the wrong place."

"Why did you wait until now to go after Lars?"

"It wasn't until Lars tried to blackmail us that we found out he had taken a photo. You and Sonia were the only other people who could know where he put it. Even his brother didn't know."

"You knew about Lars' brother?"

"Not until you told me."

Sonia gasped, the first sound she'd made since she'd spotted the pruning shears on the floor when we entered the shack. She had told me about Lars' brother and I'd told Bob. Both she and I were instrumental in the brother's death.

"This had nothing to do with Wellstone?"

"We didn't even know he was flying in. His plane crash happened the same day, almost at the same time. In the confusion, our pilot took off. I guess he figured he might get shot as well as the hitchhiker. He took off with the money I'd put into the plane, and he disappeared. Wellstone cost us two million dollars."

I pulled the trigger and the bullet went into the floor an inch from Bob's left knee. He jerked his leg away from where the bullet hit the floor.

"Why did you do this?" I said to Bob, so agitated that I was almost shouting it "You were my best friend and you set me up. You were a great CD counselor. You didn't need the money. Your retirement fund has tripled."

"Ah," said Moneybags. "It turns out that Bob here likes the casinos a little too much and he is deeply in debt.

"You just traded one addiction for another," I said to Bob. "Why didn't you just take out more cash from Lars' million dollars I stashed in your kitchen? That'd be better than stalking us and kidnaping us."

"Million dollars!" roared Moneybags. "You got your hands on that money the pilot flew off with." He stared me in the eyes with the most spiteful look I'd ever seen.

Nobody said anything for a moment. I looked at Sonia. Neither of us knew exactly what to do next. Our expectation that Moneybags had killed Wellstone had fallen apart. The money they'd collected to bribe Congress had disappeared before any bribery could take place. Nearly half of that money, I now realized, was sitting in the hiding places where Sonia and I had tucked it. The video recorder we had set up so carefully was use-

less. Worse than useless. With its images of me shooting my unli-
censed, concealed gun left and right, I'd have to destroy the camera just to protect myself.

As I was pondering that, Moneybags' face relaxed and a
nasty smirk spread on his lips. "Don't move a muscle, Morgan. I
want you alive for awhile. Just drop your gun."

"You're not paying attention," I said. "My pistol is aimed at
your heart, not the other way around."

"Don't move a muscle. One of my men is pointing an M-16
rifle at your back. Both of you just turn your heads slowly to see
and then drop your guns."

Sonia and I both twisted our heads and saw the gunman
standing just inside the doorway, swinging his automatic rifle
back and forth in an arc between Sonia and me. It was the second of the two goons who had kidnaped us the previous week.
We dropped our guns to the floor.

Moneybags leapt up in a rage, kicked me in the stomach,
and slapped Sonia across the face with the back of his hand. We
each sagged to the floor. He bent and picked up Sonia's pistol just
as Chico burst into the doorway. The rifleman started to turn. A
flash and a loud bang exploded from Chico's gun, and the man
with the rifle crumpled to the floor from a bullet that Chico had
put through his back. Moneybags shot Chico in the chest. Just
then Jim Anderson loomed in the doorway, toting the shotgun he
had hidden by the road the day before. Moneybags fired and hit
Jim in the chest. The bullet was stopped by the kevlar vest, but
the force of the shot threw Jim back against the door jamb. Re-
flexively, he pulled the trigger, but it was a wild shot, hitting no
one. It smashed, instead, into the propane heater that was just
inches away from Bob who was standing between the heater and
Moneybags. The propane exploded, and Bob caught the full force
of the blast, which drove him forward into Moneybags, knocking
them both to the floor. The two of them shielded Sonia and me
from the brunt of the explosion, but the heat was tremendous,

and the back wall of the shack was already on fire. Bob screamed in pain as he rolled on the floor trying to put out the fire that was eating through his clothes.

I scrambled forward, grabbed my nine-millimeter pistol from the floor, and shot Moneybags in the stomach just as he got back on his feet and fired a shot that fell between Sonia and me. He dropped her pistol. I picked it up and shoved her toward the door, shouting, "Move!"

She scooted past Jim Anderson and out the door. I helped him to his feet, shoved the shotgun into his arms, and pushed him toward Sonia. We ran fifty feet, then turned to look. The entire shack was ablaze. I spotted Moneybags stumbling toward the doorway. He'd picked up Chico's pistol and was pointing it toward Jim, Sonia, and me. I raised my gun, aimed it at Moneybags' chest, and squeezed the trigger. He fell back into the fire from the force of the bullet.

Then Bob crawled forward and lay across Moneybags' body. He'd picked up the M-16 and was trying to aim it in our direction. His face was badly burned from the flames, and he must have been in terrible pain. I didn't know how he was able even to lift the rifle, much less aim it. But he didn't really have to aim it. All he had to do was hold the trigger and sweep the bullets across us. The rifle looked like a Howitzer as it swung in our direction. I lifted my pistol until Bob's nose appeared right on top of the sight. At that moment Bob seemed to lose strength, because the muzzle of his rifle dipped toward the ground. I squeezed the trigger, and his face splattered like one of those pumpkins I'd practiced on two days earlier.

I ran over to where Jim had stuffed the video camera into the wall opening. The wall was so burned out that only the two-by-four studs were left standing, and the heat was so intense I had to cover my face with my arm. The videocam had fallen on the ground and was lying under a blazing piece of siding. I was able to kick the siding away and reach the camera. All that remained was a melted blob of plastic, but I did not want to take a chance that the recording of Sonia and me in the shack could have survived. It was too hot to pick up, so I kicked it several times like a soccer ball back to where Jim and Sonia were standing. Then I scooped it up with the sleeves of my hunting jacket. The three of us stared in shock as the ceiling of the shack collapsed on the four people inside.

XXXV

When nobody else tried crawling from the ashes, Jim and I scrambled toward our cars. Sonia just stared at the rubble, a stunned look on her face, her shoulders slumped forward.

"Sonia, let's go," I shouted.

But she didn't move. I tossed the guns and molten videocam on the floor under the steering wheel, then ran back for Sonia, grabbing her by the shoulders, and pushing her back to the BMW. She stared vacantly out the windshield and made no effort to buckle her seat belt. I snapped it for her, got behind the steering wheel and headed out of the woods toward the highway and south toward the Twin Cities. Sonia continued staring out the windshield, not saying a word.

We had barely reached the highway when I heard a siren coming toward us. Jesus! Sonia must have missed her last call to my father, and he must have called 911. Luckily, I found a trail that crossed the ditch beside the road and I pulled in behind some trees until the sheriff's car sped past us, siren blaring and red lights flashing. "We'd better get rid of these guns, in case we get stopped," I said. But Sonia remained silent, staring out the windshield.

At the first stream we crossed, I pulled into the left lane, stopped by the bridge rail, and tossed the silencer from my pistol into the water. I disassembled both pistols and dropped the pieces onto the floorboard by my feet. Then at the next stream I tossed out the trigger assemblies. This was barely done when another siren sounded in the distance. I turned east at the first highway I could find, figuring that the police would likely be looking for us on the main highway which ran north-south. I kept heading east around the north shore of Lake Mille Lacs, a body of water so big it could hold some of the smaller countries of the United Nations. I found two more streams where I dumped the rest of the gun parts except for the barrels, which were still lying between my feet. At the Interstate, I headed south toward the Cities, followed I-35W into Minneapolis, and pulled to a stop when I got to the middle of the bridge crossing the Mississippi. I opened the passenger window, leaned over Sonia, and tossed the remaining gun pieces and the melted video camera into the river.

During the entire time, Sonia didn't say a word. She continued staring out the windshield. I tried to get her talking. "Darling, I think we're finally safe."

But she did not respond.

It was mid-afternoon when we pulled up to her duplex in the Midway. She let herself out of the car, the first movement she'd made since I'd buckled her seat belt two hundred miles away. She walked toward the front porch, put her key into the slot, and pushed the door open. Before starting up the stairs, she turned to me and stunned me with what she said..

"Jake, I want you to pack your things and leave."

"Why?" I asked. "This nightmare is over."

"Just pack and go, Jake. You've changed. I can't keep living this way."

"But it's over. You don't have to live this way anymore."

She didn't respond. She went into Rodrigo's room and shut the door, leaving me alone to pack my stuff. I took off my muddy boots so I wouldn't drag any more incriminating mud onto her floor and dumped the boots plus my kevlar jacket and hunting clothes into two of her garbage bags. I put on a fresh set of clothes that had been stored in her closet, and stashed the rest of my stuff into a suitcase. Then I used her vacuum cleaner to suck up the dried mud we had tracked onto her carpet. This took an hour, an excruciating hour. I knocked on the door to Rodrigo's room and walked in. She was lying on the boy's bed, staring at the ceiling, still wearing the hunting clothes. Her eyes rolled over to watch me as I came through the door and sat down next to her. I put the palm of my hand on her cheek.

"No," she said. Her voice was cold.

"Please," I said. She was dry eyed, but I could feel my own eyes misting. "Can we talk about it?"

"No. It is too late."

"Why?"

"You've changed, and it's too late to change back. Bob did not have to be shot. He was already dropping his rifle. You've become a killer, Jake. Go!"

Needing to play for time, I said, "At least let me get rid of all that hunting gear you're wearing. The police are going to be coming around, and you don't want any evidence that you were up north."

I went to her kitchen, pulled out three garbage bags, and brought them back to her. "Put all those hunting clothes and the cell phone in here so I can throw them out."

She stood up and motioned for me to leave the room so she could undress in private.

"Do you want me to drive over to Dora's to get your credit card and your license?" I said loudly from outside the door.

"No."

"What's our story for the police?"

Her voice came back through the closed door. "We both had scrambled eggs, toast, and hash browns for breakfast. Coffee. No juice. We walked over the bridge to downtown Minneapolis and had a big fight because you got mad at me for spending too much time shopping. You dragged me back to your car and drove me here where I've been ever since, except for the hour I spent driving around to clear my mind."

She opened the door to hand me the garbage bags and said, "Now go!" She was wearing nothing but her beige underpants, bra, and the feega dangling from her neck. I gasped at the sight, and she closed the door.

As I started down the stairs, I took one last look back. My eyes paused on the dark wood archway between the living and dining rooms that was seared into my memory from the times I'd sat with her on her couch, beginning with that very first time when she'd started to strip in front of me. I swallowed hard.

I drove to the nearest car wash to clean the mud off my car. The white garbage bags I dropped into trash cans at various strip malls. I placed the prepaid cellphone under a front tire of my car, crushed it by driving over it, and tossed the pieces into separate trash bins. After all the evidence of our hunting trip was gone, I picked up a burger at a drive-in. Finally, there was nowhere else to go and I was forced to return to my condo.

Although I had lived alone in this condo for nearly five years, it had never seemed empty. Now it felt as barren as the moon. I collapsed on the sofa and flicked on the television. The only thing I remember is David Letterman doing a ten point countdown to something. I have no recollection what it was.

XXXVI

At eleven I went out and jogged two miles up the river and back, just to relieve the tension. It didn't do any good. I wanted in the worst way to keep jogging up to that sports bar in Highland Village, but I decided that Sonia would call any minute now with an apology for what she'd said. With that in mind, I returned to my unit and waited for the phone to ring. But it never did.

I set the alarm for six, but there was no need for that, because I didn't sleep the entire night. Every time I dozed off, my mind replayed the poof of the gunshot driving Moneybags back into the flames. Or the face of my old friend Bob splattering like a pumpkin when I had squeezed the trigger. Or the catatonic look on Sonia's face as she stared out the windshield the entire trip back. Or, worst of all, her words before I slunk out of her duplex, "You've become a killer." And she wasn't completely wrong. I had planned the whole thing, and Moneybags was finally out of our lives. For the first time since that banquet in October, everything had gone according to plan. Everything except for the propane tank exploding, Bob's face splattering like a pumpkin, and the empty feeling in my stomach.

When I finally crawled out of bed in the morning, I went

looking for a new set of tires for the BMW. Who knows whether
police investigators could trace the tire tracks I'd left in the mud
by the cabin? I had the installers put the old tires into my trunk,
and I drove to the Minneapolis side of the Mississippi, where I
pulled into a secluded parking spot, wheeled one of the tires to
the woods at the top of the embankment overlooking the water,
and tossed the tire as far as possible toward the river. Afterwards
I crossed over to the St. Paul side, parked across from the Catholic seminary, and did the same thing with a second tire. The
remaining two tires I disposed of in a similar fashion at the river
overlook by the Temple Aaron. There were probably ten thousand
tires sunk somewhere along the banks of the river, and four more
would not attract anyone's attention. I yanked Sonia's Saint Jude
medal from my neck in a fit of anger and flung it toward the
river. But it didn't go very far, and the last I saw, it was hanging
from a tree branch, swaying back and forth.

With that done, I picked up a late breakfast at the Day by
Day, bringing in a *Wall Street Journal* so Nancy the waitress
would think I was following my normal routine. Although the
paper was spread out on the table before me, I wasn't reading it. I
had it opened to a big display ad with a lot of white space where I
was jotting down further items that might need attention to cover
my tracks.

Li Vang shot me an anxious look when I came into the office.
She was becoming increasingly upset at my ignoring business
over the past few weeks. And I could hardly blame her, since her
goal of becoming a financial planner would suffer a big setback if
I let the business collapse. I worked hard to keep up with the
busy schedule she had lined up for me, and in fact I was grateful
to be kept occupied. Those were the only moments I didn't think
about Sonia or that fiery climax to our joint problem. I spent a
great deal of time helping Li prepare for her securities license
test. I showed her ways to prospect for clients and put her in
charge of an investment seminar presentation so she could gain

experience. Just before Thanksgiving, she passed her securities license test and I treated her to a celebration dinner with her family. We went to the Mai Village, a Vietnamese restaurant on University Avenue, a street that had been falling into oblivion until the Southeast Asians began immigrating a quarter century earlier. Today Asian names dot a string of restaurants, insurance agencies, auto shops, chiropractic clinics, dental offices, hair salons, fingernail stores, social service agencies, and other establishments that had rejuvenated the street. We sat at a long table near the indoor pond filled with exotic tropical fish, and it was a strange dinner. Everyone except Li and her brother spoke in Hmong, so most of the time I had no idea what anybody was saying.

By this time, I had stopped being mad at Sonia, and I was mad at myself. How could I have been so stupid as to have been sucked into her theories about Wellstone's death? Never had I made an investment decision on the basis of the flimsy evidence that we had about her theories. I had let myself be mesmerized by that woman.

The trouble was, she still mesmerized me, and she kept popping into my mind. I told myself that I was better off without her. That she was too blunt and opinionated and compulsively neat. She had not only insisted that we make the bed each morning before leaving her duplex, she'd even demanded that we do so the morning we'd left my condo with no intention of coming back.

But these were minor irritants. In truth, she'd been remarkably easy to live with. Instead of sniping at me with indirect messages when I tossed my clothes someplace she didn't like, she'd just come out and tell me to my face. When it came to planning something to do or someplace to eat, she would compromise at the drop of a hat. I missed that trace of perfume she'd bring into a room and that husky voice whispering in my ear.

I left several messages on her answering machine, but she never phoned back. I kept recalling the tender times between us. That mystical moment on her couch when she had started to strip just before Rodrigo burst in. The time we'd held hands by the lock and dam. And what I had told myself that time when I had woken up in the middle of the night at the Duluth hotel with her leg and arm draped over me; "This is all I really want out of life." I was getting insanely horny, and I got Jim Anderson to find me the phone numbers of some call girls, but I couldn't bring myself to phone them. Doing so would be to admit that Sonia was not coming back.

I missed Rodrigo. Listening to him correct his mother's English. Building the airplane out of Legos. His teasing "Oooh, Oooh, Oooh" when his mother had called me Amor. And the grin on his face when he had told me what "pehDAHsso de bosta" meant.

Since Moneybags' death had been so dramatic, it prompted a blitz of media attention that even made the inside pages of the *New York Times*. I received an envelope postmarked from Los Angeles containing a newspaper clipping of the murder scene. Just one phrase was written over it in a delicate woman's hand-writing, "Thanks for the tip." That brought a smile to my lips. I had grown to like Erika and was glad she'd gotten out while she could. I ripped up the note immediately.

The police were all over the place. Although my lawyer was able to keep them from confiscating my clients' records, they looked through all the file cabinets and left the records strewn on the floor. When they searched my condo, they confiscated my laptop computer, examined every piece of clothing, upended the furniture, and ripped the backs off the wall paintings just as Sonia had predicted. I spent hours being interrogated at police headquarters and I guess Sonia did as well. The waitress at the Nicollet Inn remembered seeing us on the morning of the killings and noted the foreign accent when the woman talked. The bill was duly charged to Sonia's credit card, and the little slash that Dora had put through the number seven made her handwriting look close enough to Sonia's that Officer Olson accepted it. Miraculously, we both stuck to the same story that we'd walked across the bridge to downtown Minneapolis after breakfast and then had a vicious argument.

When Sergeant Olson got to that point in the questioning, I asked. "You must be talking to her about the same thing. How'd she sound. Any chance she'd want to make up?"

"Do I look like Dear Abby?" he said sarcastically. Then he shook his head in bewilderment that to have asked such a dumb question I must be the most naive guy on earth. This, of course, was exactly the impression I wanted to leave.

Investigators also spent hours interrogating me about Lars' finances. But my own ignorance was a big help. My knowledge of his finances was almost entirely confined to his investments. I know very little about his laundromats, his consulting work with Radezewell, or even his income tax returns. My signature didn't appear on any suspicious papers. Even though Lars and Money-bags had obviously been laundering money, none of it could be traced to me. And the two culprits were now dead.

Somehow the police never found out about the two sources that clearly would have done me in if they'd been investigated, my father and Jim Anderson. Of course, the police would have to have been fairly lucky to have found out about them. There was no reason for them to think that the 911 call bouncing off of a cell phone tower in south Minneapolis had come from the Veterans' Home. After all, a rest home with its population of aging semi-invalids wasn't a very likely place to house murder suspects. As for Jim Anderson, the police also had no reason to connect him with the case, just so long as he didn't write any suspicious newspaper columns that would draw their attention. And, he wasn't likely to do that, unless he wanted to risk prosecution for his own role in all the things that had happened.

Eventually the news media went on to other things. You can't pull in readers or viewers with yesterday's violence. Even Fox TV lost interest. My name never appeared in relation to the incident, and the police began to regard me with less suspicion. I was starting to believe that I was home free.

At the end of the second week, I drove over to Loring Park to visit the art gallery. Sonia was wearing a splashy, multicolored, knit dress that curved smoothly over her body. When she saw me come through the door, her head jerked up in a startled look, but she agreed to have a coffee with me. I was still enchanted by the look of her and that husky voice. We walked across the bridge over the pond to a café on the other side of the park. The Walker Art Center loomed on one side in the backdrop and the big Episcopal cathedral on the other side. She stayed at least a foot away from me throughout the entire walk, as though she feared what her reaction would be if our shoulders should bump together. We brought each other up to date. Rodrigo was home and back in school and there had been no more threats to him or to her.

"Will you come back?"

"I don't think so, Jake." Think came out as theenk. I'd pay a fortune just to be able to hear that accent every day.

"Amor, I loved you more than anybody in my life. And I still do. I would do anything for you. Anything."

"Don't call me Amor. It's over, Jake."

"Why? We were like magic together. You know that."

"Jake, I cannot get that day out of my mind. I have nightmares about it."

"So do I. But why does that have to drive us apart."

"You killed them. I told you I didn't want a macho man. I told you that several times. Why did you have to be so macho?"

"It was self defense. They were going to cut off our fingers. You saw the pruning shears. And then they were going to kill us. We'd both be dead now if I hadn't shot them."

"I know that, Jake. I'm grateful to you for saving Rodrigo and me. But it's like being grateful to a hit man."

"That is a cheap shot." I bent forward, jutting my jaw out at her and staring her in the eye.

"I am sorry. I shouldn't have said that." She took her glance away from my eyes and looked down at the table for a moment.

"You are right, Jake. I did love you. I guess I still do. But too much has happened. I can't forget that you set up the whole thing. That you shot Bob even after he started to drop his rifle. And that you didn't even check to see if Chico was still alive."

Of course, if she had been all that concerned about Chico at the time, she could have checked him herself. But that wasn't going to be a winning argument, so I kept it to myself.

"Why did you have to be so macho? Why didn't you just give the camera and diary to the police and have them arrested instead of killing them?"

"And have you arrested and me arrested for breaking into Lars' house, stealing evidence, tampering with it, and lord knows what else? Lars' diary and the digital camera were stolen property, and the flash drive was tampered with. That evidence would have been tossed out of court. You know that. The IRS could have built a good case for income tax fraud. But that would take years, and in the meantime you and I would have been done away with. We were already fleeing from one hotel to another as it was. How long could we keep that up?"

"But you intended to kill them from the start."

"That is not true." I slapped my hand on the table, and she jumped as if she'd just touched a live wire. "I really thought they'd admit to pulling Wellstone's plane off course. And I really thought they'd lead us to hard evidence of Lars' murder that we could turn over to the police without implicating ourselves."

"Jake, maybe you didn't plan to kill them on a conscious level. But, remember that morning at Sergeant Preston's when we brain stormed our options for what to do with the photos. Every option we talked about had a bad outcome, especially for you. The only one that didn't was the one we failed to talk about, killing Moneybags. I believe you, Jake, that you didn't plan on a conscious level to kill them. But it was there on an unconscious level. There was no other way out."

I sat silent. If all this Freudian psycho-babble applied to me, then didn't it also apply to her? But there was no point in raising that question. She would come to it by herself in time.

"If it was all at the unconscious level, Jake, maybe I could live with it. But I can't forget Bob. At first I tried convincing myself that you had only shot him out of fear that he would raise that rifle and spray us with bullets. But as we sat in your car on that long ride back, I realized that you had another motive for killing him. You couldn't afford to leave him alive to become a witness against you. And I was a party to it."

Her eyes were sad and blank as she said that, and I was stunned by her accusation. I stammered in a voice that was barely audible, "That is not true."

"The bottom line, Jake, is this. There is a dark side to you that I never saw before, and it scares me."

"Sonia, everybody's got a dark side lurking under the surface. The stress we were under would have brought out anybody's dark side." Even your own, I thought, remembering the vehemence with which she had said she would shoot Pockface that night when we escaped from our kidnapers. But I didn't mention that.

"No, there is a dark side to you that I never saw before. You scared me that day, and you scared me now when you slapped the table. I remember that you were always so tender with me and so good to Rodrigo. But something in you has changed. Why did you have to turn macho? How can you ask Rodrigo and me to live with a man who frightens me?"

"Do I frighten Rodrigo?"

"Rodrigo misses you. He still asks about you. I had to buy

him a set of Legos, because he talked so much about the airplane you two had built with Legos at the mall. And he got mad at me when I threw away the photo that he had taken of you and me by the lock and dam."

She paused, and my stomach churned at the thought of her throwing out the only photo of us that she possessed. She went on in a voice that was dry and cold. "But Rodrigo didn't watch you kill your oldest friend."

I stared at her. I was so focused on her that it was like we were the only ones in the café, even though there were several other people present. I was mesmerized by the huskiness of her voice, the look of her eyes, and the scent of her perfume. I would have given anything for the right to reach out and cup my hand over one of those small breasts that were pressing against the knit dress. But they couldn't have been any more out of reach if they had been somewhere in Siberia.

"How do I get the money back to you?" The question brought me out of my reverie.

"What money?"

"The money we hid in my paintings."

"Keep it. You earned it."

"I can't keep it. It's blood money."

"Well, if you ever sued Radezewell Enterprises for the pain and anguish that Moneybags inflicted on you, any jury in the world would award you a lot more than what's stuffed behind those paintings."

"I told you. It's blood money. How do I get it back to you?"

"Keep it. Leave it in the paintings, just in case you or Rodrigo need it."

"I can't keep it."

"Then give it away."

She left shortly after that, stranding me at the table as I

watched her hips swing on her way out the door. I despaired at
the idea that I might never again see that sight.

But my mood lifted as I walked to the cashier to pay for our
coffees. When I'd asked her to come back, she'd hedged. She had-
n't say no. She'd said, "I don't think so." True, she jumped when I
slapped the table, but if she really thought that I'd murdered Bob
to keep him from talking, and if she were truly afraid of me, she
never would have walked alone with me across that park in the
first place. And she felt bad about not letting Rodrigo see me. She
was still in shock from the trauma we'd gone through. I probably
was, too. If I gave her some time and space, maybe she'd come
back.

The money, however, was another matter. Like it is to many
people raised in affluence, money was an afterthought to her.
She would give it away, just as I'd suggested, and if I wanted to
get her back, I would also have to get rid of my share. Otherwise,
she would never be able to rid herself of the suspicion that I had
killed Radezewell for the money. And if she did come back, I'd
never be able to get rid of a suspicion that it was the money she'd
come back for, not me. I had no choice. I had to dump the money.
I would hold back enough to cover the expenses that had been
caused by all this: my new tires, the security systems, my car re-
pairs, the hunting gear I'd bought, the motel bills at the various
places where we'd hid out, the money I'd paid Jim Anderson for
his help, anything at all I could remotely justify. But the rest of it
would have to go.

For a man who'd spent his entire adult life in the accumulation of assets, it was not easy tossing that much cash down the
drain. I changed my mind a dozen times. This was unreasonable.
No woman was worth $700,000. There must be millions of wo-
men who would give anything to land a man with that much
money. Probably thousands of such women just in Minnesota. On
the other hand, with the police and U.S. Treasury agents looking
over my shoulder, I couldn't just go on a spending spree.

Nevertheless, it was hard to give up this money in the hope that Sonia would come back, a hope that was looking more and more unlikely as each day passed. In this vein I placed a personals ad in *Street Scenes*. Professional SWM, 40s, seeks warmhearted companion who likes quiet walks by the river. This led me to dinner with a pleasant, blonde accountant who seemed to enjoy our conversation about the intricacies of financial planning and risk management. But there was no flirting or giggling fits or displays of passion, and neither of us bothered to phone back to the other.

I was only kidding myself. I'd spent the previous five years involved with various women and hadn't found a single one that I'd really wanted to live with. How many more years would pass before another Sonia crossed my path?

What finally pushed me to action was a realization that came as I was tying on my jogging shoes the day after my tepid dinner date with the blonde accountant. If I refused to give away the money now, I would regret it for the rest of my life. Even if it was all a pipe dream and Sonia still didn't come back, at least I could say that I had tried. I jogged up and down the river that afternoon brain storming every idea I could think of to give away $700,000.

XXXVII

If I had any doubt that Sonia would give away her share of the money, it was soon cleared up. The local TV stations covered a news conference held at The Mayo Clinic which announced that it had just received from an anonymous donor several of those red, white, and blue Post Office priority mail boxes that contained forty-five white envelopes, each holding $5,000 in cash, for a total donation of $225,000. All of it earmarked for conducting research on Williams syndrome. I wondered what Sonia had done with the other ten percent. There had been $250,000 in her envelopes. I could only hope that she hadn't wasted it buying any more contemporary art.

The fact that Sonia had actually given away her share of money increased the pressure in my mind that I had to give away mine. Being new to the business of philanthropy, I wasn't quite sure how to do it. Jim Anderson deserved something for all the work he'd done and for saving our lives. I used a pay phone to call him and make a lunch appointment at Figlios, the same Uptown restaurant we'd used before. I drove an extremely circuitous route to the restaurant, hoping to shake off any plainclothes cops who might be following me. And I wandered in and out of several book stores and shops, constantly turning my head in an effort to see if I was being watched.

"We're indebted to Chico," I said as we sat in the privacy of our booth amid a noisy crowd of drinkers and eaters. "I think his survivors deserve something." I pushed a large, sealed, manilla envelope across the table to him. "Put this on your lap and keep it inconspicuous. There are two packets inside. Keep one and send the other one to Chico's survivors."

"He didn't have any survivors," said Jim.

"No wife? No children? No siblings? I've never heard of a Mexican without siblings."

"No siblings," said Jim. "Nobody. This was the most alone guy in the world."

"Jesus," I said. "Then keep both packets."

"Why?"

"You earned it. Just spend it slowly so you don't draw any attention to yourself."

With the cops investigating my activities, we agreed that it would be a good idea to keep a distance from one another for a long time.

Subtracting the ten envelopes I'd left for Jim and Chico, my balance was down to one hundred forty envelopes that I needed to get rid of. The most reasonable thing seemed to be to spread it around to people who could really use it. I put $1,000 into a number ten envelope and wrote a note.

> To whoever finds this envelope:
> This money is to be used to advance your education. Spend it on tuition, school costs, books, or anything that will help you advance your marketable skills. Do not make any noise or draw attention to yourself. Just take this money and quietly go home.
> Santa

From the phone book, I xeroxed the addresses of every public library within the city limits of Minneapolis and St. Paul, drove to the branch library nearest my the Highland Park condo, pulled a science book from the shelves, and slipped the $1,000 envelope between the pages. Anybody checking out a science book was likely to be a serious person who would make good use of the money. Then I did the same at every branch library on my list. Since there were two dozen of them, the task took me an entire day.

I must have greatly overestimated the readership of science texts, because two weeks passed without any feedback. I even visited the Highland Park Library to check if the money had been taken yet. It hadn't.

Finally, the television news reported a near riot at the Lake Street Branch in Minneapolis, when a high school student found the envelope. The envelope was torn from her hand and the bills scattered on the floor. Several people dived for them, cracking heads together and overturning a table in the process. Four teenage boys and one girl ran out of the library, shouting happily as they passed through the door. Maybe it was a mistake to put the money in a poor neighborhood. But the next day a similar thing happened at the St. Anthony Park branch library, which is located in an affluent and highly-educated neighborhood. The rich didn't behave any better than did the poor. I don't know why I thought they would.

By the third day, several libraries reported hordes of people ripping pages out of books, throwing stuff indiscriminately on the floor, disrupting the work of the regular patrons, and sometimes cursing in frustration when they couldn't find any money. Even some suburban libraries were attacked, despite fact that I had not yet planted a single envelope in the suburbs.

By day five, the hordes of people trashing the libraries got so bad that both Minneapolis and St. Paul made a joint decision to close their libraries for a week to conduct their own searches for the envelopes and put things back in order. They would use any money they found to repay themselves for the cost of cleaning up. The Minneapolis police estimated that their costs for restoring order in the libraries added up to $5,000, and they sent a bill for that amount to the Library Board. Sixty-seven people had been arrested. A dozen were treated for minor injuries at local emergency rooms. One elderly man had a heart attack when he found the envelope, only to have it ripped from his hands by an unruly teen-ager. An old lady became the subject of several human-interest stories on TV when, during one of the melees, she accidentally pushed the print button on the library computer she was using, and several pornographic pictures were printed and picked up by schoolchildren on a field trip.

The *Minneapolis Star Tribune* called on Santa to stop freelancing and just give the money to charity. The heads of Catholic Charities, United Way, United Jewish Appeal, and the United Negro College Fund wrote letters to the editor asking Santa to give them the money. One radio disk jockey accused Santa of being a communist. If Santa were a true American, he would give the money for boys' athletic programs to counteract the corrosive effects of Title Nine, which was giving unfair advantages to female athletes. Normally, I would have endorsed any attack on Title Nine, but I bristled at being called a communist. So I ignored the plea.

At this point I decided to get out of the philanthropy business and just give the money to organizations that could make good use of it. But which ones? In some respects, this whole problem was a result of Wellstone. If Moneybags had just not insulted him at that banquet and if Sonia had just kept her big mouth shut, the whole sequence of events since then might never have taken place. What better way to get rid of the money than to give it to causes favored by Wellstone? I don't know if that's what Paul would have wanted, but he would hardly object.

The next time I went jogging, I headed toward one of the

bookstores in the Highland Village shopping area and bought a copy of Wellstone's *Conscience of a Liberal*. I underlined every charitable group mentioned in his book, taking special care to exclude the political ones that I could not support, and I ended up with a list of mostly mental health and environmental groups. I printed address labels for each group, pasted them on envelopes, and divided up the remaining money evenly among all these envelopes.

Of course, distributing all this money at the same time in the Twin Cities would draw a lot of attention and spark a campaign to discover Santa's identity. So I got into the BMW and headed toward Chicago. I dumped several packages into mail boxes when I stopped for lunch in Madison, and I dropped off the rest at mail boxes in the Chicago suburbs. Then I turned around and headed home. By the time I got back to my condo, it was midnight.

You're supposed to feel uplifted when you do a good deed. The only thing I felt was numbness.

XXXVIII

Sonia's art show opened on the first Friday in December. She had told me to stay away. But it's a free country, so I came nonetheless. With bright lights shining down on the paintings, chic women in fancy dresses, well-heeled men in Armani suits, and white-clad waiters toting trays of wine, the gallery sparkled with excitement. The dark, enchanting presence of Loring Park across the street made the brightly-lit gallery stand out like a star in the night.

She was playing a role I'd never seen before, but she was perfect for it. Looking regal in her black velvet gown, she circulated among her guests, the elite of the Minneapolis art world. I, by contrast, could relate to these people only if the topic was money. I comforted myself with the hope that there might be a client to be picked up if I could just steer a conversation in the right direction. I admired Sonia for the smoothness with which she mingled, especially among the men. She would touch someone on the arm, or flash that ear-to-ear smile, or nod knowingly at the one she was talking to, and he would visibly relax his shoulders. Most people would pay thousands of dollars to learn how to do what to her was second nature. It gave me great happiness to watch her in action.

I picked up a glass of cola in order to have something to do with at least one of my hands as I walked around the room. Not knowing anyone, I browsed the art, waiting for the opportunity to tell someone how I could make him another million dollars. I was studying one piece intently when I heard her husky voice behind me.

"Hello, Jake," she said, pronouncing my name Zhaak as she does.

I turned. She didn't touch my arm, or flash the ear-to-ear smile, or nod knowingly at anything I said, or use any of the other gestures she'd been using all night to put people at ease. But she didn't tell me to go way. I viewed that as a sign of welcome.

"You look ravishing."

She didn't smile or say thank you or compliment the new silver-tinged linen suit I was wearing without a necktie so I could look a little more playful as she'd suggested that day at the conservatory. But she also didn't remind me that she still regarded me as a killer. So I figured things were getting better between us. Of course, if I hadn't killed those goons a month ago, she herself would be dead now, instead of standing here in front of me with a trace of perfume, the polished Afro-Brazilian feega dangling from the silver chain around her neck, a hint of her breasts showing over the top edge of that luxurious velvet gown, and her black hair swept up into an elegant pile on top of her head. She must have spent half the day at a hairdresser.

"Jake, you have no interest in art. Why are you here?"

"I've watched you plan this show for two months. I wanted to see it."

She didn't react.

"You have a good turnout, and it looks like a great success. I love the way people are responding to you. Congratulations."

She smiled for the first time. She had to know that I'd meant what I'd said. And this had to have pleased her, even if she did regard me as a killer.

"You still like garden scenes, I see." She gave a warm smile as she nodded toward the painting I had been studying.

"There's something about it that grabs me. The old man and the little boy remind me of Don Corleone and his grandson in the first Godfather movie." I bit my lip the moment the words were out of my mouth. Since she mistrusted my dark side, I was nuts to tell her I had fond reminisces of a mafia movie.

"I'm not familiar with that movie. But I have something that might convey the same sentiment and suit you better."

She led me diagonally across the room through the people to a small painting of children fishing in the Mississippi. Clearly identifiable in the background was the lock and dam by the Veterans' Home.

"This is a better picture than the other one?"

"These are not pictures, Jake. They are paintings."

"This one is better?"

"I can't say it's better. It is a sort of primitive art. It has some flaws that tell you it is a new artist who hasn't yet mastered his craft. But there is a poignancy in the children that does not show up in the other painting. I think that a small painting of a Mississippi scene would fit into that blank space you have on the wall across from your couch. It would be a visual complement to the marvelous vista you have. And if you ever moved, the painting would always be a warm remembrance of what you had."

"Especially," I said, pointing at the top of the painting, "the lock and dam in the background."

Her mouth dropped open, and her eyes bugged out. She looked like she'd been punched in the stomach. And I knew, as sure as I knew that the Minnesota Vikings would blow their next shot at the Superbowl, that she had not up to this moment made a connection between this painting and the magical moment she had once shared with me by the lock and dam, telling me "Ti amo," and reminiscing about how she'd gotten started in art history as a teen-ager in Sao Paulo. If she had seen that connection a week earlier, this painting would not be on exhibit. That artist didn't know how lucky he was. It took her a few seconds to respond.

"Oh, Jake. I am so sorry. I didn't see that before. I tell you I did not see that. It's over between us, Jake. It's over. I just did not see that." She was starting to talk faster, as she does when she's upset, and she drew her hands up to her cheeks.

The last thing I wanted was to embarrass her, so I asked, "Would it be better if I left."

"Yes. Please go." She didn't look at me. She just kept staring at the lock and dam in the background of the painting. Then, with a great deal of poise, considering the shock she'd just had, she stepped into the restroom where she could take a moment to regain her composure.

A light snow was falling when I stepped out of the gallery, but it was melting as fast as it hit the pavement, and my heels clicked on the wet sidewalk as I walked toward my car. I began humming, "The Girl from Ipanema." Her brain might think it was over between us, but her gut hadn't got the message yet.

XXXIX

Whatever her gut was telling her, however, it didn't get her charging in my direction. Two weeks passed without a word from her, not even a Christmas card. And that, oddly enough, helped me realize that I needed to get on with my life and stop moping about her. I tossed out the picture that Rodrigo had snapped of us by the lock and dam, put another personals ad in the newspaper, and joined my father for Christmas dinner at the Veterans' Home.

"I'm going to miss those two," he said. "I told you to treat her good."

"I did treat her good. It's just that everything fell apart at the end. I have a dark side, she said. She hated all the violence that happened, and to tell the truth, I don't like it all that much myself. I wish there had been another way. But there wasn't."

"Don't tell me another word," he warned. "Parents don't have immunity from testifying against their children."

"Anyway, I've got to move on with my life." I shrugged. "And as nice as she was, moping over her won't help me do that."

He nodded his agreement, but his face had a strange look, as though he was biting his tongue to keep from speaking his mind.

On Friday after Christmas a blizzard blew into town. Outside my condo, twelve stories down, everything on the ground was covered in white. Tree branches sagged from their heavy coating of snow, and the weather forecasters predicted another foot before the storm was over. Travel would be impossible by morning. The snow made my condo seem all the more barren and isolated. On my desk, next to the telephone, was the list of call girls that Jim Anderson had given me. I had pulled it out earlier that afternoon, and it was still sitting there at nine o'clock that night as I slouched on my couch and watched the TV explain how bad the blizzard was going to be.

I was surfing channels when the buzzer rang from the building lobby. "Hello?" I said into the intercom.

"Zhaak, may I talk with you?"

Her voice was unmistakable, and my pulse rate jumped, but I didn't say anything. Having started the process of putting her out of my mind, I wasn't eager to start digging through the ashes of our relationship. Nevertheless, I punched the button so she could come through the security door.

While she came up on the elevator, I grabbed the newspapers strewn on the floor, my jacket tossed in a corner, and a TV tray, and stuffed them in the entry closet. I hid the list of call girls in my pocket, ran to the bedroom, and kicked some dirty clothes into the bedroom closet. I was wiping a dirty tee shirt through the dust on the coffee table when she knocked on the door.

She stepped out of her snowy boots and handed me her coat. As I put it in the closet, she gave an awkward glance at the trash I'd piled there.

"Where's Rodrigo?"

"He's with his father for the weekend."

I led her to the living room to sit down, but she walked toward the picture window, stopped several feet short of it, and looked out for a moment at the snow falling, her back to me. Beyond her was the Minneapolis skyline, even a portion of the old

Stone Arch Bridge that was lit up. She was standing in her stocking feet, wearing the same blue skirt and white blouse she'd worn the day she'd invited me over for dinner. She turned toward me and said, "Jake, can we start over?"

Sometimes I talk too much. All I had to do was say yes, but instead I asked, "You're no longer frightened by my dark side?"

"I can't change the fact that you killed those people, or that I helped you do it. Or that I should have known it was in the back of your mind all along. At first I thought that if I came back to you I would be like the wife of Al Pacino in *The Godfather*, accepting the profits of crime. It would be the same as having kept that money in my paintings. It was blood money. I couldn't live that way, Jake."

"You told me you hadn't seen *The Godfather*."

"I rented it after you mentioned it to me. As I thought about it, I came to see that there was a big difference between the Godfather and us. We did a terrible thing in setting up those killings, and your shooting Bob was inexcusable, but we really were in a desperate situation, and we do not kill people for a living like the Godfather did. You are never going to kill anybody again, Jake. And I am never again going to be an accomplice to a killing."

"So you forgive me for killing Bob?"

"It's not up to me to do that. I can only ask God to forgive me for what I did. How you get forgiveness is up to you."

"But I'm not too macho?"

"I hope not. I want to put it behind me. I know it will not be exotic like it was before, but I am so lonely, Jake. I want to start over. Can we start over?"

"I still can't promise you more than one day at a time."

"I know that."

I put my arms around her and we hugged for two or three minutes without saying anything. Then she put her hands on my chest and pushed me back.

"Sit down, Jake."

I sat on the couch. She backed off until she was about ten feet from me.

"I did not get to finish this for you the other time."

She lifted her hands to the neckline of her blouse and began undoing the buttons.

XL

I'll never understand why she saves so many of her serious conversations until I'm half asleep, but there I was starting to nod off when she rolled onto her side and propped her head up on her hand. She jabbed me in the ribs, "Wake up, Jake, it is barely ten o'clock."

"Don't you ever get sleepy afterwards?" I asked, hoping.

"Sometimes," she said. But this wasn't going to be one of those times. So what was I to do? After a woman has come back to your life and given you a glimpse of heaven, you can hardly tell her to shut up and go to sleep. I rolled on my side to face her as she lay there with the St. Jude medal dangling from her neck. I slid my hand over the narrow curve of her waist and cupped it over one of the breasts. She didn't stop me. She just smiled. But she waited until I withdrew my hand before she said anything.

"I'm hungry, Jake. Do you have anything we could eat?"

"Popcorn," I said. I pulled on my robe and tossed my extra one to her. I took my popcorn popper from under the kitchen cabinet.

"You don't just nuke it?" she asked.

"It tastes better this way."

We sank into my couch, with the popcorn bowl between us,

a can of cola on my end table, a cup of tea on hers, and our feet resting on the coffee table. Her black hair streamed on the back of the couch where she rested her head. Outside, the snow was still falling and everything twelve floors down was covered, except for the dark waters of the Mississippi flowing through the white blanket. The condo felt like a warm cocoon.

"I think I was wrong," she said.

"About what?"

"About Paul's death. Maybe he was in fact murdered, but I just don't know anymore. He certainly wasn't killed by Money-bags and probably not by the CIA. And I don't know who else might have done it. Maybe you were right all along."

"It was just an accident?"

"Maybe. But I will tell you this." She paused and turned her head to give me a serious look. "Once he was dead, somebody did their best to kill what he stood for. After Rick Kahn gave his im-passioned eulogy at the memorial service, it was like the whole right-wing propaganda machine rolled over him. It rolls over ev-eryone."

She grimaced and tensed and leaned forward on the couch, clenching her hands.

"And that was just the start, Jake. Think of all the things Paul stood for that are going down the drain now. A better envi-ronment, better health coverage, a fairer tax burden, and a less warlike foreign policy."

"You sound like a Democratic politician."

"I don't care what I sound like. I am telling you what I feel. He had ideals, Jake. And that is what they killed."

"No they didn't," I said. "It's like that bumper sticker on your car: Wellstone lives. His spirit lives as long as you live up to his ideals. He passes something on to you and you pass it on to some-one else. That's the way life is."

She gave me stern look, which slowly morphed into a smile. "Amor, you have become a philosopher."

"Not me. I'm just a conservative businessmen trying to make an honest buck. I didn't even agree with half the things he said. But I do agree with those ideals you mentioned. And when you gave away all that money, you lived up to those ideals. That is something I have to admire."

"Jake, you did the same thing. All those envelopes stuffed with cash that you gave away. That had to be you. It was all over the news. You lived up to your ideals, too." She gave me her big ear-to-ear grin, flashing those white teeth, looking pleased.

"No, it wasn't idealistic. I just wanted to get you back. And that would never happen as long as I kept the money."

"The fact is, you gave it away. And I was so proud of you when I heard about it." She took my hand and we leaned back on the couch watching the snow come down.

"What happens now?" I asked.

"With us?"

"Yes."

She gave me a warm smile. Not the uninhibited ear-to-ear smile this time. But a warm smile, nevertheless. "I go on selling art. You go on selling investments. I look after Rodrigo. We pick up our journey."

"Can I move in with you?"

She waited a long moment before responding.

"Rodrigo can be difficult. You'd have to have a lot of patience with him, and you'd have to be very careful not to look like you were taking over for his father. He would resent that. He might resent you for awhile anyway. Can you handle that?"

"I'll try."

She gave me a slightly anxious look, like she had something touchy to add. "I know you live one day at a time, but I cannot accept you moving in today and then moving out tomorrow the first time something goes wrong. I won't do that to Rodrigo. Your intent has to be for a long journey. And you have to decide before you move in. If you want to move in, Amor, marriage has to be in the deck."

I smiled warmly at her mangling "it's in the cards." But all I said was "It's in the deck."

She grinned, reached her hands behind her neck and undid the clasp of the silver chain holding her St. Jude medal, just as she had done that one day so long ago. Then she draped the chain over my neck and rehooked it.

The End